Cherub's Play

by

Katie Grant

Cherub's Play

Contact Information: info@thewildrosepress.com

Cover Art by *Kristian Norris*

The Wild Rose Press, Inc.
PO Box 708
Adams Basin, NY 14410-0708
Visit us at www.thewildrosepress.com

Publishing History
First Fantasy Rose Edition, 2018
Print ISBN 978-1-5092-2225-4
Digital ISBN 978-1-5092-2226-1

Published in the United States of America

They all heard a soft, "Ga, Ta, Bupapa, Saah," float in from the next room.

"Ah," Austin said. "That would be Little Jeffrey?" He started to get up when the blanket slipped from his waist. Sandra stifled a gasp. Realizing he was naked beneath the blanket, Austin sat back down and clutched the blanket to his lap. Sandra glanced out the window in embarrassment.

"Okay," she said. "Maybe we do have a baby here, but I'm sure he's not yours."

"I would have said that myself a couple of days ago."

"We have a real special baby here, mister," Jake said. "He come swooping down out of the sky, delivered by the Great Stork himself."

"Jake." Sandra crossed her arms. "A man your age ought to know that storks do not deliver babies." She didn't want to have that argument all over again. How in the world had Jake and the other men gotten it into their heads that the Great Stork brought the baby to Misha Ranch?

Dedication

Cherub's Play is dedicated to the dreams, dedication, and perseverance of fiction writers everywhere, published and unpublished. Keep up the good work.

Chapter 1

Geoffrey Almaric always found it unsettling to leave heaven for a mission to earth. Heaven was so...perfect, while things on earth seemed to get messier every time he paid it a visit. In heaven Geoffrey *was* somebody. The Archangel Geoffrey Almaric Behir de Giverny, to be precise. Nicknamed "Geoffrey the Avenger" after the Battle of Jericho. In heaven, his credentials were impeccable. On earth, nobody knew him from Adam.

On his most recent missions to earth, Geoffrey had to sneak around like a thief in the night. Gone were the good old days when he could plunk down in front of a family on the road to Damascus and announce that he was Geoffrey the Avenger, an angel from heaven. People had gotten way too sophisticated for that. Geoffrey knew from bitter experience that people might actually laugh at him. Worse, he might be arrested and spend the night in what was euphemistically called a dormitory, with unpleasant tattooed men who referred to him as Princess Peach. Why, he had no idea.

Modern times called for more subtle and "mysterious ways" of getting the Word out. On a good day he could appear to some wide-eyed school children as a glowing light from atop an oak tree. On a bad day he could do nothing more than roast the heavenly image into a flour tortilla and hope for the best.

On his last mission, he appeared to a disbelieving New Yorker through the flames of a potted geranium, burning in the window of his forty-second-floor apartment. He would have much preferred some long-stemmed irises or a spray of blood red roses, but one had to work with the tools one was given. It wasn't the best of circumstances, but Geoffrey took much pride in his work. After all, the owner of the geranium did get the message. He had three weeks to think about it in his private room at the Bellview Hospital, with the help of some generous medication.

But now something new was amiss. How could he, one of heaven's most senior angels, have gotten himself into such an odd and embarrassing situation? He waved his, or someone's, short, plump arms and chubby, little hands in the air. Nothing looked familiar. His lips parted and he tried to speak, but all he could manage was a soft, "Goo Goo Gaa Paa." Unbidden, a small stream of drool spilled from the corner of his tiny, tender mouth. Then, most embarrassing, he promptly filled the red bandana that served as his diaper.

****

"Ooo-wee, he's done it again," Jake Johnson said. The lanky old cowboy held the infant at arms' length and set him back in the makeshift crib made of pine two-by-fours he and the other ranch hands had hammered together.

Sandra Coulton came in from the kitchen, finished wiping her hands, and flung the dish towel on top of the ranch's HAM radio.

"Jake," she asked with mock sweetness. "How would you like to learn the delicate art of changing a diaper?"

2

"Right now?"

"Now's as good a time as any."

"Ah, I don't think so." He grinned, showing his one gold incisor. "You know you cain't teach an old dog new tricks." He snatched the sweat-stained Stetson off his head and backed away from her like she'd asked him to lie on the kitchen table and donate a kidney.

"There are seven men on this ranch and none of them can do a simple task like changing a baby's diaper."

"No, ma'am," Jake agreed.

"Maybe I should hold a class tonight after supper and give you all a demonstration."

"If you think so, ma'am," Jake said without conviction. "Right now, I'd better feed the horses, don't you think?" He wiggled his fingers at the baby. "So long there, little fella."

Sandra shook her head slowly as Jake beat a bow-legged retreat, spurs jingling on the hardwood floor. At the doorway he stopped and looked back at her.

"You give that boy a name yet?"

"No. I can't do that until I know whether he already has one."

"Well, meantime, me and the boys was thinking the name Jeff might work just fine.

"Jeff?"

"Yep. Little Jeffrey Coulton. It's got a ring to it. Don't you think?"

She laughed. "I'll keep it in mind." She waved him away and turned her attention to the messy child.

****

Jeff. No, Geoffrey. The name spun in front of the baby's consciousness like a colorful mobile, dangling in space, calling to him through his foggy confusion. Yes, his name was Geoffrey. But how did he get so small? And why was this mortal woman, cute as she might be, taking off his pants? A wave of embarrassment flooded through him as he felt cool air wafting over his exposed private parts, parts he normally didn't even have.

"Please unhand me, madam."

"Goo Gah Wah Pah," was all Sandra heard. She cooed back at him and lightly tickled his round plump tummy.

Geoffrey smiled in spite of himself, and a little more drool dribbled from the side of his mouth.

"Very charming, Geoffrey Almaric," a familiar voice said.

Geoffrey rolled his head to the side. His pale blue eyes focused on a white-robed angel, complete with tall, feathered wings, standing in backlit radiance next to Sandra Coulton. She continued to change his diaper, packing a small towel under the new bandana. She paid no attention to the heavenly visitor.

"Gabriel!" Geoffrey said. "What are you doing here? I mean, what am I doing here? And where are we?"

"My, you're a talkative little man," Sandra said.

Gabriel's smile held no warmth. "I dropped in to see how things were going, 'little man.' Made any progress?"

"Progress? Of course. Progress at what?" Geoffrey squinted, trying hard to put the pieces together. The appearance of his rival, Gabriel, was almost as confusing as waking up as a baby. He reached for his fellow Archangel, intending to clutch his robe. Instead, Sandra took his arm between her thumb and forefinger and played with it back and forth.

"Gabriel, what's going on?"

"Can't we remember? I suppose you can blame me for that." He closely inspected the tips of his wing feathers as he spoke. "I took the liberty of giving you a tiny bump on the head once you had taken on your corporeal form. Not a nice thing to do to a baby, I suppose, but we all thought it might make our wager a little more even this time."

"Wager? I'm here on a bet? What am I supposed to do?"

"Nothing, as far as I'm concerned." Gabriel brushed at his wing feathers. "You're the one who thinks he can do it all." The heavenly apparition flicked away a piece of lint from his wing. It sparkled and disappeared into thin air. "Mind you, you still have your standard angel powers. All, except one. *He* wouldn't let me take away any more than one. Even so, at the last minute I decided you could use another small handicap. So, I gave you one."

"How am I supposed to do something if I can't remember what it is?"

"There are clues. You just have to find them."

"Damn you, Gabe." A clap of thunder exploded outside. Just outside. Geoffrey sighed. The Boss was listening. "Okay," he said. "Just tell me this—"

"Gotta go," Gabriel said. "And remember, the clock is ticking."

"No. Wait!"

"Ta-ta, little man." He wiggled his fingers goodbye, just like Jake had. The beatific glow faded until Gabriel's image disappeared completely.

****

5

Standing at a small table, Sandra pressed a final length of duct tape onto the fresh diaper, put her hands on her hips, and admired her work. Not bad for a twenty-seven-year-old who didn't have any kids of her own. She crooked a finger under her lower lip. Jeffrey Coulton. The name did have a ring to it.

She shuddered to think what might have happened if the cowboys hadn't spotted the baby sitting on the ranch house roof, laughing and waving at them from his perch. How on earth had the boy gotten there, and where had he come from?

One of the ranch hands stuck his head in the door. "The float plane's a comin'," he said.

That would be their supply delivery. Isolated as it was in a remote bay on Alaska's Beaufort Peninsula, Misha Ranch depended on weekly flights from Prudhomme Bay to deliver food, mail, and other necessities. That week, Sandra was expecting the airplane to deliver a rifle she had ordered, one that fired a tranquilizer dart big enough to bring down even the largest grizzly. She wanted the gun for her research on bears, which sometimes required her to fit the temperamental beasts with electronic collars so she could track them by radio telemetry.

The small Cessna float-plane droned in a circle over the ranch house, signaling its arrival. Sandra started for the front door but paused when the airplane's radial engine sputtered and coughed. It caught for an instant and sounded okay. Then it quit completely and there was nothing but silence. Sandra set the baby down gently in his crib. Then she ran for the door. The pilot, Doc Murray, had to be in trouble. She burst outside and saw the ranch hands standing here and there in the yard looking up into the sky, shielding their eyes from the bright Alaskan sun.

"Where'd he go?" she heard Jake ask.

"Must have landed over in the river," someone else said.

Sandra knew the airplane couldn't land safely in the shallow Deadhorse Creek, and she feared the worst. Everyone's head turned when the airplane's engine let out another muffled cough, somewhere behind them. A few whispers from the exhaust followed. The pilot was cranking over the starter without success. The aircraft wafted drunkenly up and over the top of the ranch hands' bunk house, its wings dipping from side to side. It dropped down and whooshed by Sandra, not more than fifty feet in front of her, passing low enough to snag one of its pontoons on a clothesline of fresh laundry, trailing it like an advertising banner out into the bay.

Skimming the surface of the water, the aircraft almost landed safely. Almost, but not quite.

At the last second, the airplane lurched forward, its nose diving softly into the water. The bright yellow tail fin shot skyward as the plane flipped over onto its top. Upside down, the fuselage quickly sank beneath the dark surface of the bay until the water level reached the top of airplane's floats. Fearing for Doc Murray's life, some of the cowboys ran to the water's edge and dove in. Others danced on the shoreline, trying to remove their boots. Jake reached the airplane first, took a deep breath and executed a perfect jackknife dive.

"Wait!" Sandra called.

Too late. Jake's descent stopped suddenly and his red socks wiggled in mid-air. He had just driven himself head first into the muddy bottom of the bay, which was only five or six feet deep near the shore.

He splashed to the surface, black-faced and muttering a curse. Then he spat water and dipped down again, this time feet first. Moments later he surfaced with the limp body of the pilot flopped over his shoulders like a sack of grain.

Dead weight.

"Help me, boys," he said. "I think he's swallered most of the bay!"

A line of cowboys passed the pilot along, hefting him from man to man, until they could stretch him out on dry land. Sandra was relieved to see that it wasn't Doc Murray lying on her beach, but when she looked more closely she did a double-take. No, it certainly wasn't Doc Murray. This man was much younger and in much better physical condition, assuming he was still alive at all.

****

Inside the ranch house, Geoffrey raised his baby head as much as he could to see through a window, but his young muscles were not yet up to the task. "Goo Wa Po Tah," he said to no one in particular. *Of course he's still alive. I haven't completely lost my touch. But you'd better do something quickly. It would be just like the Boss to call a man home right after I've performed a miracle to save his life. He doesn't like being second guessed.*

Geoffrey was pleased to learn he could still manipulate physical objects, to some extent at least, and he checked that power off the list of those Gabriel might have taken away from him to win their bet.

****

Sandra searched for a pulse and breathed a sigh of relief when she found a weak one beneath the warm skin of the pilot's neck. Then she inspected the rest of him for injuries. The man's thick, shaggy black, shoulder-length hair was matted down on his forehead. Water dripped across a two-inch scar along the line of his squared jaw, on the right side. Since it wasn't bleeding, she assumed the mark was a remnant of some earlier misadventure.

Except for the scar, the man's smooth skin was a light shade of reddish brown, as if he had gotten the perfect tan on some sun-drenched Caribbean island. He had what her mother would describe as a Roman nose, strong and narrow, but not too big for his rugged face. His eyes were closed, but his bushy brows and long dark lashes hinted to Sandra that the man's eyes would be large and probably quite appealing.

An enormous knife was sheathed to the man's blue jeans, just above his right boot. But even without the knife, the man's scar and rugged features made him look dangerous.

If she had to, Sandra would bet the stranger was a drifter with no permanent home or real occupation, at least no legal one. Certainly no family. All-in-all, he was the kind of man she would avoid on a lonely city street, but not without looking him over once or twice—he was that much of a hunk. Hunk? She hadn't used that word since she was in high school. She shook her head lightly, hoping to dislodge the word from her vocabulary.

Then she noticed the man's almond-skinned cheeks and full lips were starting to turn blue.

"He don't look like he's breathing," someone said.

"What are we gonna do?" someone else whispered.

"He probably has water in his lungs." Sandra stood up, placed one of her boots on an empty wooden rain barrel and kicked it onto its side. "Throw him over this."

She had seen the technique in old movies, and she didn't know what else to do. Two of the men wrestled the pilot's six foot plus frame onto his stomach over the barrel. They rolled him back and forth until he coughed and sputtered, sounding a lot like the dying airplane engine.

"That's enough," she said.

The cowboys gently lowered the man back to the ground. Sandra bent over and tore open his plaid shirt, thinking she should check for a heartbeat, or other injuries. But she stopped short, struck shy when she saw the man's sculptured pectoral muscles and washboard stomach. That and the act of opening a man's shirt so abruptly reminded her of a more intimate kind of urgency. She glanced up at the cowboys out of the corner of her eye. Could they sense her embarrassment?

"Wow," one of the hands said. "I didn't know flying an airplane was such good exercise." Somebody else punched the cowboy hard in the shoulder.

"A lot of guys get that way in prison," another man said. "They got time on their hands, and there's nothin' else to do there but lift weights."

Sandra realized she hadn't heard the pilot breathe. She dropped to her knees and nuzzled her ear next to his breast bone. Thankfully, the cowboys hushed. As if responding to her touch, the man took one deep, ragged breath, coughed, and started to breathe regularly. He would probably live to crash another airplane.

They carried him, still semi-conscious, up to the ranch house and laid him out on a couch in the living room. One of the cowboys took off the man's soggy boots, and carefully removed the knife. Sandra got a blanket out of the closet while someone else stripped him naked. To no one's surprise, the stranger's legs and the rest of his anatomy were as finely sculptured as his chest and arms.

The men covered the pilot with a blanket up to his armpits, leaving his arms exposed. Sandra averted her gaze, embarrassed to be caught staring at the body of a man who could make a fortune modeling men's underwear. The whole company stood around the couch and looked down at the stranger. Some of them had removed their hats, either because they were inside and thought it polite, or perhaps they expected the pilot to die. They all marveled at the quality of the red and black fire-breathing dragon tattooed on the man's left bicep. These just confirmed Sandra's initial impression of the stranger, that she could see him frequenting dark alleys and smoky pool halls of any big city. But this fellow hadn't been content with one tattoo. On his right forearm, a thin, tastefully rendered arrow, complete with chiseled stone tip and multicolored feathers, ran from his elbow to the back of his wrist.

"You think he's some kind of foreigner?" a hand named Leonard asked.

"Could be an Inuit," Jake said.

"What country do they come from?"

"They're Eskeemos, dang it. They come from up north."

"Oh."

11

Sandra considered the molten richness of the man's skin. She decided that his children, if he had any, were probably quite beautiful. Then she glanced at the lethal looking knife lying on a table and realized that men like this were probably better off without children. She shook her head again to clear it of such stray thoughts.

"You sure you want to leave him here?" Leonard asked.

"Why not?" Sandra asked.

"Well," Leonard said slowly, "we don't know nothing about him. Could be he's done something to old Doc Murray."

"He ain't much of a pilot, neither," Jake added. "And for all we know, he might of robbed the bank in Prudhomme Bay and stolen Doc's airplane for the get-a-way."

"Oh, stop it," Sandra said. "There *is* no bank in Prudhomme Bay."

"Could be he throwed Doc out of the plane somewhere over the ocean," Leonard said, looking to Jake for confirmation. He and the other men nodded their heads and mumbled agreement with their suspicions. Sandra rolled her eyes. That made about as much sense as…as finding a baby on the ranch house roof. What would happen next?

"I'm sure there's a perfectly logical reason for his being here." She knew there had to be, but even she felt a twinge of trepidation about the handsome stranger's sudden appearance. He looked like the kind of man who lived outside the normal channels of civilization, and something about that idea excited Sandra and struck fear in her, all at the same time. Life could get a little boring after a few weeks in the back-country, but she didn't need anyone disrupting her otherwise orderly research.

"He'll tell us all about it when he regains consciousness," she said.

"Hey," Jake said. "It looks like he's coming to."

Sandra caught her breath. The pilot's dark eyes fluttered open and focused on her.

"Should we get him some water?" Everyone scowled at the cowboy who made the suggestion.

"Look, he's trying to say something," Leonard said, pointing at the man's mouth.

The pilot's lips stirred under what must have been three days' worth of beard.

"How..." he whispered.

"He wants to know how he got here," Leonard said.

The pilot shook his head slowly.

"How..." he repeated but seemed to run out of breath. Sandra bent forward and placed her hand softly over his.

"Take your time," Sandra said. "You've just had an accident."

"I think he wants to know where he is," said Leonard.

"Leonard," Sandra said. "Why don't we let *him* tell us what he wants to know?"

They all watched the pilot closely. Nobody wanted to miss the stranger's first words.

Sandra shivered when his eyes, dark as a starless sky, fixed on hers again.

"How?" he asked. "How did...your hair...get... that awesome color?" Then his head lolled to the side and he passed out.

Sandra stared at him, slack-jawed. Well, what had she expected? Men had been fascinated by her hair ever since she was twenty-three years old. If she hadn't been allergic to hair dye, she'd have changed it long ago. After all, she didn't need a constant reminder of that awful experience, four years earlier. A lot of things had changed that day—not just her hair color—and she hadn't stepped foot inside a church ever since. The doctors were unable to explain the transformation in her hair medically, but she knew what had caused it. It was emotional trauma, pure and simple.

She would give anything to be a brunette again. Instead, after that one miserable day, her hair had lightened to a medium auburn almost overnight, all on its own. Most of it, anyway. Some of it went further, sliding all the way to red, as if to accent her new look. Finally, adding insult to injury, a number of rebellious strands faded prematurely to silver.

In the end it turned an unusual but pleasing mix of colors. But Sandra wasn't ready for the changes, either in her hair or in her life, and she had hidden in her apartment from her fiancé for two full weeks. The fiancé didn't understand, but Sandra called off the wedding, and that was the end of that. Except for her hair. After she received enough compliments from people she didn't suspect were patronizing her, she took a long look at herself in the mirror. What she saw was unique. Her gently curling locks had settled into a rather dramatic, reddish-marbled hue. It looked like Vidal Sassoon had transformed some punk hair color into a classic styling.

When she became a wildlife biologist, she kept her hair short, as much for professional reasons as to staunch the flow of questions from curious men. But in Alaska she had no reason to keep her hair a "professional" length. There were few eligible men around, not to mention hair salons, so eventually it grew to her shoulders, and she kept it corralled in a loose ponytail.

She sighed. The first stranger to come around in ages, and all he noticed was her hair, not her eyes, not even her breasts, thank you, which she had every reason to be proud of. Nothing had changed.

"He doesn't seem very dangerous," she said. "Let's let him rest awhile. I'll radio Prudhomme Bay and see if I can find out who he is."

"Good idea," Jake said. "They can tell us whether this guy's on a jail break, or something."

She laughed. "I'll let you know if we need to lock him in the smokehouse."

"You just yell if this jasper gives you any trouble," Leonard said, "and we'll come a running."

The other men nodded like they were ready for a good fight.

"Thanks. He won't give me much trouble in his present condition." Then, glancing at the man's extraordinary physique one more time, Sandra doubted her own words. But she had had enough excitement for one day. "Why don't we try to get things back to some semblance of normalcy around here, okay?" She tried to sound brave.

She shooed the men out of the house to attend to their various chores. "And don't forget to bring in that laundry," she called after them. "Before it floats away."

She snatched the towel off the radio, where she had thrown it earlier, and looked into the next room at the crib. "Who said it would get lonely in Alaska?" she said to the nameless baby.

Then she did a double take. For a moment it looked like the baby's eyes were following her every move.

****

Criminy, Geoffrey thought. *Why did they have to make me a baby on this assignment?* Most of the time he couldn't see Sandra from his crib, and he had to use his angel senses to find out what she was doing. At that moment she was headed for the radio.

The radio. Should I let her use it? How am I supposed to know with amnesia, for God's—uh, for cripes sake? Damn that Gabriel, anyway. Another peal of thunder sounded, this one a little farther away. *Okay, okay. But I've got a bad feeling about the radio. I'm not sure I want her talking to the outside world until I figure out what's going on here.* He thought hard, trying to remember his mission. The more he thought, the more he worried.

Sandra tuned the radio to the frequency of Prudhomme Bay, which would have been the next lonely spot of civilization down the road, if there had been a road. Transportation to and from the small stations and settlements on the Beaufort Peninsula was strictly by boat or seaplane, and a boat might take two days to reach a port of any real significance.

Geoffrey listened to Sandra and the crackling radio speaker.

"Prudhomme Bay, Prudhomme Bay," she said. "This is Misha Ranch. Come in please. Prudhomme Bay…"

Misha, thought Geoffrey. *That's a nice name. It's Russian. A term of endearment for…a bear.* Linguistics was one of Geoffrey's specialties. *I wonder if bears have something to do with my mission.*

He let his mind conduct a mental search, kind of a feeler, sensing the wildlife in the wooded areas surrounding the ranch. *Ah, there it is. Ursus arctos horribilis. A Grizzly Bear.* Geoffrey marveled at the bruin's sharp teeth and ferocious claws. *Appropriately named,* he thought. In his mind he could see the giant animal lumbering through the woods, not all that far from the ranch, he noticed. He mentally smoothed the beast's golden-brown coat. It stopped and sniffed the air, as if it had smelled food. Then it started shuffling in the general direction of the ranch.

Oh, my goodness. A shiver raced down Geoffrey's tiny spine and he quickly withdrew his angel consciousness from the bear. He didn't want to get too close to one of those, not while he was still a snack-size baby, anyway.

A new voice on the radio got his attention.

"Misha Ranch, this is Prudhomme Bay. Hello Sandra, this is Bernie, over."

"Hi, Bernie," Sandra said, "We've got another guest at the ranch today."

"Doc Murray pay you a visit?"

"Well, his airplane did anyway—"

Geoffrey sensed trouble and mentally snapped his fingers. Everything in the room stopped. Sandra stood at the radio, seemingly frozen, mouth open in mid-syllable, ready to explain about the crash, and that Doc Murray hadn't been flying the airplane.

"Okay," Geoffrey said. *"I still have the power to suspend local time. I can cross that power off the list."*

****

Standing just outside, under the window, Jake Johnson was busy chopping wood when he heard Sandra calling Prudhomme Bay. Since he didn't get much news from the outside world, he quit chopping and set down his axe to listen in on the conversation. He had just lit up a hand-rolled cigarette when he realized Sandra wasn't talking. He looked up at the window and saw her, microphone held at her open mouth, standing in silence.

"Humpf. Scientists," he muttered. "Can't have a normal conversation. Always got to know exactly what they're going to say before they say it." He decided whatever Sandra was going to talk about wouldn't be all that interesting, and he went back to chopping wood.

Back inside, Geoffrey mulled over the situation. There was something important about this interloping pilot, something he couldn't put his finger on. Not that he could put his chubby little fingers on anything at that moment, including his own naval, but he had the distinct feeling Sandra shouldn't resolve the question of the pilot too soon. What could he do? He decided to end the radio call and give himself more time to think.

****

Sandra stopped talking in mid-sentence when a burst of static cut her off. "Prudhomme Bay, Prudhomme Bay. Bernie, are you still there?" More static. She sent out the call a few more times and got nothing out of the radio except white noise. She clicked the set onto standby mode and looked over at a long computer printout hanging on the wall. Finding the day's date on the table, she ran her finger along a horizontal line until she read the number in a small box.

"That's odd," she said to herself. High sunspot

days usually came in fall or winter, but what could she do? Any communication with the outside world might be difficult. As close to the North Pole as she was, solar radiation often disrupted her radio signals. No matter. She would try again later.

That's better, Geoffrey thought. He decided to keep everything just the way it was, if he could, until he figured out what he was doing at this lonely outpost. Unfortunately, for the moment he could do little more than wait and watch the events unfold.

Sandra came back to the crib and looked down at the baby, fingering his diaper to check its snugness.

"What am I doing here?" Geoffrey asked her, but it came out, "Goo Waa Saaa."

"What are you doing here, you poor thing?" Sandra asked him absent-mindedly. She adjusted the duct tape holding the bandana diaper together. "I wish I knew."

"Where am I?" Sandra heard the pilot's groggy voice coming from the couch and she walked back into the living room. The man had barely regained consciousness and sounded like he was waking up with a bad hangover. Probably not an unusual feeling for a character like him, she thought.

"You're still on Planet Earth," she said.

"I suppose that's something to be grateful for," he said.

Sandra had a view of the top of his head and realized he couldn't see her. She walked toward the front of the couch as they spoke.

"Your wet clothes are hanging on what's left of our clothesline outside."

"Huh? Outside? The last thing I remember, I was outside, but I was coming down to Planet Earth pretty fast. And then I saw this angel…" His voice trailed off at the wonder of the memory.

Sandra stood in front of him with her arms folded.

"It was you," he said.

"No, that was me." Geoffrey pouted from his crib. *"How quickly they forget."*

Sandra appreciated the man's come-on, even though she knew his type. He was a scarred-up stunt pilot with more muscles than any two ordinary men, and he probably had just as many muscles between his ears. No, this man had the look of a scoundrel and was probably up to no good. The fact that his first comment was about her hair hadn't helped.

"I'm not an angel today," she said. "Just a woman. And who exactly are you?"

She practically felt his gaze roam the length of her body. "If you're just a woman, I hope I *am* still alive."

He lowered his feet to the floor, sat up, and rubbed his eyes.

Sandra meant to say something like, "Take it easy, you've had a bad accident," but the blanket fell off the man's broad shoulders, and the words stuck in her throat. She had only seen a chest that well-muscled on Chippendale dancers a friend once hired for a bachelorette party. She glanced away. As the heat rose in her cheeks, she looked around for some air conditioning, then remembered the ranch house didn't have any. No matter. She would cope.

"Let's start over," she said. She pulled a straight-backed chair in front of the couch. "My name is Coulton, Doctor Sandra Coulton. I'm a biologist, and unfortunately you're a guest here at Misha Ranch."

He gave her another look. "How unfortunate could

that be?"

"Quite. Your airplane—Doc Murray's airplane—is upside down in the bay." She hooked her thumb in that direction.

He looked startled by this news and worried, as if he'd forgotten all about the accident. Sandra's eyes momentarily lost focus. She couldn't make up her mind whether to comfort the man with a hug, trace the outlines of his biceps lightly with her fingers, or flee from the house altogether. All of these seemed like potential options.

Instead, she looked at the back of her hands. "You were lucky to escape with your life."

"I guess I have you to thank for that." He raked his hand through his still damp hair.

"I had a lot of help." She picked up a copy of the American Journal of Cytology from an end table and fanned herself with it.

"I don't mean to sound ungrateful," he said, "but it's been a bad couple of days."

Just a couple of bad days? Sandra's suspicions went on alert, and she wondered what a good day looked like for such a rough character.

"I'm sorry," she said. "And I don't want to sound unsympathetic, but I…and the men outside—there's seven of them you see—we all want to know exactly what you were doing with Doc Murray's airplane."

"Seven of them, eh? Are they dwarfs?"

"No. And I'm not Snow White." She tried to sound strong, just in case this man really was up to no good. "Don't you think it's time you told me who you are and what you're doing here?"

He glanced up at her, as if he were really seeing

her for the first time. "Yeah, I suppose you've got a right to know that."

Sandra leaned back in her chair, her arms folded, waiting. This would be good.

"My name is Smith," he said. "Austin Smith. And I'm looking for a baby."

Chapter 2

Sandra clutched the bottom of her chair to keep from falling over.

"You're looking for what?"

"A baby."

She fought the urge to jump up and run to the baby's crib, to protect the child from this stranger at all costs. But Mr. Smith didn't know she had a baby, yet, so she stayed in her seat.

Austin rubbed his eyes. "I heard this radio call, you see, when I was in Prudhomme Bay, saying you had found him. I came as soon as I could."

"Just like that?"

"He's supposed to be my son."

"Supposed to be?" Sandra put her hands on her hips. "Says who?"

"So, you *do* have a baby here."

"I'm not saying we do or we don't." She simply couldn't believe this man had anything to do with the baby in the next room. She watched closely as Austin, still trying to wake up, absent-mindedly brushed the sparse hair on his chest. Then Jake came through the doorway, and Sandra gaped at him like he was her father, and he had just caught her kissing Austin on the couch.

"Miss Sandra," Jake said. "With all the excitement, did we forget to give Little Jeffrey his noon-time feed?"

"I don't know what you're talking about," she said. That sounded foolish, even to her.

"Please," Geoffrey said from his crib. *"No more warm milk. I can hardly control my bladder as it is. Haven't you got some pasta? A nice croissant, perhaps?"*

They all heard a soft, "Ga, Ta, Bupapa, Saah," float in from the next room.

"Ah," Austin said. *"That* would be Little Jeffrey?" He started to get up when the blanket slipped from his waist. Sandra stifled a gasp. Realizing he was naked beneath the blanket, Austin sat back down and clutched the blanket to his lap. Sandra glanced out the window in embarrassment.

"Okay," she said. "Maybe we *do* have *a* baby here, but I'm sure he's not yours."

"I would have said that myself a couple of days ago."

"We have a real special baby here, mister," Jake said. "He come swooping down out of the sky, delivered by the Great Stork himself."

"Jake." Sandra crossed her arms. "A man your age ought to know that storks do not deliver babies." She didn't want to have that argument all over again. How in the world had Jake and the other men gotten it into their heads that the Great Stork brought the baby to Misha Ranch? Their insistence on the story grated on every fiber of her scientific training. Not to mention common sense.

"Maybe yesterday I didn't believe in the stork," Jake said to Austin. "But Little Jeffrey sure was born different. We all saw it." He spread his arms out, imitating a soaring bird. "This here big ol' bird, with a long, skinny beak, glided down outta the clouds and set that boy right smack on the roof. Pretty as you please."

"That would have been Gabriel," Geoffrey said from his crib. *"He's always been sensitive about the size of his nose. With good reason, I might add."*

"On the roof?" Austin asked.

"Jake, please." Sandra felt like she was losing control over the situation.

"Well now, how do *you* think he got up there, Miss Doctor who's really only a biologist?" Jake said.

He stumped her with that one. "I'm sure there's a logical explanation," she said, "even if we can't think of it right now."

"Maybe. But there's one thing I can't understand about the delivery," Jake said, putting his fist to his chin. "It's the strangest thing. Right after the stork set the baby down next to the chimney, he gave the tyke a little rap on the melon."

"Jake. Thank you for reminding me to feed Little Jeffrey." Sandra realized she was calling the baby by the name Jake and cowboys had given him. She got up from the chair and guided the old calf-roper toward the front door. "I think I can handle Mr. Smith. Tell the boys outside everything's okay." Then, in a whisper, she said, "This Austin fellow might try to take the baby away from us. Stay close by."

Jake winked and nodded as though he were acting in a play and trying to be seen in the back row of Carnegie Hall. He high-stepped out the door whistling "Zip-a-Dee-Doo-Dah" a little too loudly to himself.

Sandra watched him go, shaking her head. She turned back to Austin and was shocked to see him through the doorway in the next room. He had wrapped the blanket around his waist and was standing over the baby's crib.

She ran to Austin's side, ready to snatch the baby from his arms, but he hadn't picked the infant up. Instead, he had extended his index finger to the child, who grasped it in his small fist.

"I might as well do some bonding for the baby whose body I'm borrowing," Geoffrey said.

"With a grip like that, he really could be my son," Austin said.

"You don't know for sure?"

"They all kind of look alike, don't you think?"

That wasn't an answer to her question.

"Shouldn't you be able to recognize your own child?" She felt helpless at the sound of the question. All he had to say was "yes" and there might be little if anything she could do to stop him from taking the baby away.

"You'd think I would recognize him, wouldn't you?"

What did he mean by that? What kind of father wouldn't recognize his own son, even if he were only a few months old? She stood there for a moment, her head next to Austin's bare shoulder, looking back and forth between the baby and the man, trying to see any kind of resemblance. There wasn't much, but her gaze lingered a bit longer on Austin's dark eyes than she had intended.

No matter. She had made up her mind. No way would she let Austin take the baby away, just because he said it *might* be his. He would have to prove it, somehow. Even if he did, she might not let someone as questionably qualified for parenting as this Austin

Smith character take custody of a helpless baby. After all, it was her roof they had found Little Jeffrey on, and she had gotten used to taking care of the child. She and the child had...had bonded. Well, at least she had bonded, even if the child hadn't. She realized now that the baby's appearance had triggered mothering instincts in her she didn't know she had.

The more she thought about it, the more her temper flared. She clenched her fists. She would fight him all the way to the Supreme Court if she had to. She had a momentary vision of herself in a dark blue suit, standing before the court bench, arguing for custody of Little Jeffrey. A withered, old justice in a black robe and powdered wig pointed a bony finger down at her, his eyebrow arched. "And how did *you* come by the child, Doctor Coulton?" he asked.

"I found him on my roof, by the chimney your honor. In the woods...in Alaska..." Her voice trailed off.

"Rejected!" Her vision vanished with a bang of the gavel and she focused on Austin.

"Look," she said. "If you don't recognize your own son, I'm certainly not going to let you take this baby away from me, er, here."

"His name's Little Jeffrey?"

"That's what all the dwarfs—I mean the men—call him."

"Jeffrey Smith. It has a certain ring to it. It sounds to me like you've gotten attached to him, too."

She heard a note of sadness in his voice, and she thought for moment that Austin might be weakening.

"If you don't recognize him," she asked, "what exactly makes you think he's your son?"

"He was given to me."

"Given to you? Like a present? Like a box of chocolates?"

Austin let go of the baby's hand and faced her.

"Not exactly." He grasped both her shoulders. "It was fate, in a way, his coming into my life. Kind of like you, for that matter." He started to say something else but stopped and let go of her when the blanket began to slip below his hips. He held the blanket up with one hand and waved her away with the other as he strode into the kitchen. "Never mind," he said over his shoulder. "You wouldn't like the explanation. Do you have any coffee?"

Sandra rolled her eyes and followed him. In the kitchen she watched him pour a cup of coal-black tar from a pot the cowboys had kept warm since four o'clock that morning. He sat down at the kitchen table and took a sip. He looked at the cup. "Not bad," he muttered, and took another. Then he rubbed his eyes.

As she sat down opposite him, she saw three of the cowboys peeking in the window behind Austin and silently shooed them away with a wave of her hand.

"So," she said, when it looked like Austin wasn't going on with his story. "Do you want to tell me about it?"

He considered her for moment. "How *do* you get your hair that color?"

"Auugh!" She threw up her hands. "Look. If I tell you how my hair got this color, will you tell me who you are and what's going on here?"

"Sure."

"It's natural. It's my real hair color. It's been this way since I was twenty-three. There. Now you know.

What about you?"

"It's lovely," he said quietly. "Like the rest of you." A wan, sincere smile spread over his face, a smile that melted Sandra's anger and frustration like snowflakes on the wood stove. It made her suddenly feel defenseless. And she hated that.

She sighed. Every Alaskan ranch needed a charming rogue, didn't it?

"Mr. Smith…" she prompted.

"Yes, and now you want to know what I'm doing here." He rubbed the back of his neck with one hand, clearly uncomfortable with what he was about to say. "I guess it's this way, Sandy."

"Sandra."

"Right."

His look of disappointment gave her a pang of her own. What was wrong with 'Sandra,' anyway? It was a better fit for a PhD research scientist. Sandy sounded more like a television news weather girl.

"Sandra," he continued. "As you might have guessed, I don't actually know for sure whether Little Jeffrey is my son or not."

"I thought so."

"But, I believe he is, especially because of how you found him. A few days ago, I stopped in Prudhomme Bay, on my way back to the States from Burma. I was hitching a ride on a Flying Tiger out of Jakarta. I had been running, uh, cargo between Indonesia and Burma for about a year but, well, let's say things didn't work out the way I'd hoped they would."

"Uh, huh." Just like the rest of his life, Sandra figured.

"Anyway, I'd had a pretty good time in

29

Prudhomme Bay the first time I came through, so I stopped over again on my way back. I hadn't been there more than twenty-four hours when this, this…woman comes up to me in the Wet Whistle Saloon and sets Little Jeffrey, over there,"—he pointed in the direction of the crib—"right in my lap." He gestured at his lap with both hands, like Jeffrey was going to appear there out of thin air.

"Sounds like your first visit to Prudhomme Bay was something more than a 'pretty good time.'"

"It does, doesn't it? In fact, the woman said to me, 'It's time to reap what ye have sown.' But I swear to you, as God is my witness, I'd never seen the woman before in my life."

"Then why did she pick you?"

"I didn't get a chance to find out. She just said, 'It's your turn now, dad,' handed me the baby and disappeared. I tried to find her for two days, but no luck."

"And you have no recollection of the woman at all—I mean from your first visit to Prudhomme Bay?"

"None whatsoever."

A likely story, Sandra thought. She looked again at Austin's scars and tattoos and decided he may have been too inebriated at the time to remember his original dalliance. The only thing that redeemed him in her eyes was the fact that he hadn't immediately abandoned the baby at the first opportunity.

"What a sad story," Geoffrey said to no one in particular. He turned his head as far as he could, but he couldn't see them talking in the next room. He settled for inspecting the man's aura, which he found quite colorful and pleasing. Yes, he rather liked this Austin

Smith, who seemed to have a *joie de vivre* much like his own. Perhaps he could do something to help the fellow, and the woman too. It would give him something to work on until he found out what he was really doing in Alaska. It would keep his intervention skills sharp, and it might be fun. More importantly, it might help him find out which of his angel powers was missing.

"Your story doesn't explain how the baby got to the ranch, now does it?" Sandra said.

"No. That part's a little strange."

Sandra wanted to hear Austin's explanation, something logical she could tell the cowboys, to debunk their story about the Great Stork. On the other hand, if Austin couldn't come up with a plausible explanation for how the child got onto her roof, it would be hard for him to claim fatherhood. That thought gave her some comfort.

"Go on," she said, smiling in anticipation.

"Well…after a couple of days, I gave up searching for the young lady, uh, mother, and I was going to the sheriff's office, since there isn't much in the way of social services in town. On the way, I sat Little Jeffrey down on a bench and bent over to tighten my boot lace."

Sandra noticed that even Austin had started calling the child Little Jeffrey. The fact that he had been with the baby for two days without giving him a name of his own only heightened her suspicions. How good a father could he be?

He scrunched up his face and held up his index finger. "I had my back turned for only a second. Just a second, mind you, when I felt a gust of wind." He made a scooping motion with his arms for emphasis. "You know, a great big gust of wind."

"Yes, yes. Then what happened?"

"So, I turned around to grab the baby, but he was gone."

"Just like that? Blown away?"

"Just like that. I was frantic. I looked under the bench, everywhere, but nothing. Then I looked up. And way up there," he said, pointing, "high in the sky, I saw a small black spot, getting farther and farther away. The only thing I could think was that a great bald eagle, or maybe a…a—"

"A stork?"

"Yeah, like a stork or something had carried him off."

Good God, it was true. The Great Stork had delivered the baby to her rooftop, and it looked like the child belonged to this derelict drifter.

Confusion, dismay, and jealousy shot through Sandra, all at the same time. She didn't know whether to laugh or cry. Little Jeffrey was going to be taken away by a stranger who had allowed his child to be stolen by a bird. She took a deep breath and tried to get control of her emotions.

"I was horrified," Austin said. "I didn't know what to do."

"And you expect me to believe that?" she said, hoping she sounded like she didn't believe him.

"You said you found him on your roof, didn't you? How else do you suppose he got there? Anyway, when I overheard your radio call to the sheriff, I found out where you were, and took—borrowed—the first airplane I could find and flew right over."

"So, Doc Murray didn't loan you the airplane, did he?"

"There wasn't time to ask."

"And you didn't rob a bank in Prudhomme Bay?"

"What?"

"Nothing. I just wanted to make sure." She got up from her chair and poured herself a cup of coffee. She took one look at the murky black sludge and set the cup down on the counter without taking a sip.

"You can't have him," she said.

"Why don't you both keep me?" Geoffrey said. *"You seem like nice people, and you obviously like each other, in spite of your differences."*

Austin's eyes flashed black lightning. "I'm not sure *you* can decide whether I keep my own son."

"It's my decision for now. The baby's in my custody. If you can get to what passes for a hospital in Prudhomme Bay and establish that you're the father with a DNA test, well, then maybe we'll talk about it."

"But even that might not be good enough for you, huh?"

"Let's say I have a hard time believing you'll make it to any PTA meetings on a regular basis, okay?"

His shoulders slumped, and she almost felt sorry for him. Almost. She could only imagine what kind of "cargo" he had been running in Burma. Whatever it was, she knew the business wasn't something to which a young boy should be exposed. What school would he attend? Who would be his mother? It was a shame that a man as good-looking as Austin had never settled down, and probably never would.

But, in the dim recesses of her mind, it dawned on her that she might be guilty of the same character flaws.

A few years earlier she had given up her own chance to get married, to raise a family and lead a "normal" life. Now she was studying bears in Alaska. It seemed like the thing to do at the time, but she hadn't appreciated how isolated she would be during her field work.

"Look," Austin said. "How can you judge someone you've only just met?"

"I think I know quite a bit about you already. First, you've been engaged in some questionable enterprise on the other side of the world for the last year. Second, when you're passing through this part of Alaska like a hobo, you have such a good time partying you can't remember the women you meet, and with whom you evidently—"

"Now wait a minute."

"And finally, it looks like you let your own baby, or somebody's baby anyway, get blown away in a gust of wind when you weren't looking."

He ran his fingers through his drying, shoulder-length hair. "I know it looks bad, but I had no idea something like that could happen. I don't have much experience with kids, but I'm a quick study. If I had a little more time…"

"It's not that easy," she said. "Psychological studies have shown that people seldom change their basic behavior, even when they want to."

"No one's ever done a psychological study on me."

"That could be arranged."

"You put a lot of stock in testing, don't you?"

"I'm a scientist. I—" A voice crackling over the radio interrupted her.

"Misha Ranch, Misha Ranch, come in please. This is Murray Flightlines."

Geoffrey's angel senses snapped to attention. He almost intervened, but he hesitated. Now that he'd met Austin, it didn't seem like a radio call would be such a problem. But...

"That's Doc Murray," Sandra said with a cheerless smile. "Now you can tell him that you 'borrowed' his airplane. And what you've done with it."

Sandra was grateful that someone from the outside world had been able to get through in spite of the sunspots. On the other hand, Doc Murray might confirm Mr. Smith's claim that he was Little Jeffrey's father. Sooner or later, for better or worse, the mystery had to be solved. She walked to the radio, picked up the microphone, and pressed the talk button with her thumb.

"Hi, Doc. This is Sandra. I've got someone here who'd like to talk to you."

"It's not Sarah Mockingbird, is it?" he asked. "She didn't show up for work this morning."

"No, Doc. I'm pretty sure this guy didn't show up for work either, but he has a confession to make."

She waved Austin over to the radio. He adjusted the blanket draped around his waist, got up, and walked over to her.

"Even a pilot of your limited skills should know how to work one of these." She held out the microphone to him. As he took it from her, his strong hand momentarily cupped hers. During that fraction of a second, Sandra felt like they were holding hands. It was a startling and intimate sensation. Her eyes opened wide and she pulled her fingers away slowly.

Austin watched her as he spoke. "Hello, Doc. This is Austin Smith. How's the weather in Prudhomme

Bay?"

"Got a front moving in, Austin," came the reply through the speaker.

Sandra's jaw dropped. Austin had known Doc Murray all along.

"Did you have any trouble getting to the ranch?" Murray asked.

"Just a bit, Doc."

"I'm not surprised. You took the wrong plane. The one you borrowed was way overdue for service—"

A burst of static shot out of the speaker.

"What's that, Doc?"

They heard nothing but white noise.

"This is getting fun." Geoffrey pulled in another fistful of highly charged ions from the upper atmosphere and pummeled the radio signal into oblivion.

Sandra tried several more times to raise Doc Murray, but with no luck. She sighed. Now everyone back in Prudhomme Bay would think things at the ranch were just fine. Never mind that she had an airplane upside down in the bay, just offshore. And never mind that a globetrotting bush pilot had shown up to take Little Jeffrey away. But with communications down and the plane out of action, she wasn't able to do anything about Mr. Smith right away.

She sighed and collected herself mentally, then turned to face Austin, but he had disappeared. By the time she found him in the kitchen, he had pulled an electrical extension cord from one of the drawers and tied his blanket firmly around his shoulders and waist like a Roman toga.

"Who's Sarah Mockingbird?" he asked. He started

humming quietly to himself as he pulled things out of the cupboard, starting with a bottle of Sandra's homemade baby formula.

"Sarah?" Sandra said. "She's a local character in Prudhomme Bay. Nice woman, but a character. Like you."

Austin set a large bottle of Homer's Hot Springs whiskey on the counter next to the baby formula. Then a jar of peanut butter.

Sandra stepped forward and snatched up the whiskey. Then she looked at the baby formula and grabbed that as well. She put the whiskey under the sink and the formula at the far end of the counter. "Look, Mr. Smith."

"Call me Austin." His voice was muffled, since he had poked his head inside the cupboard.

"Mr. Smith. Regardless of whether you are Little Jeffrey's father or not, he is in my custody for the time being, and I can take good care of him without your help."

Austin pulled his head out of the cupboard and looked at her. "Do you have any bread?"

"It's in the bread box," she said, pointing to it on the counter. Then she stamped her foot lightly. "Please. *Listen* to me, Mr. Smith."

Austin stopped, loaf of bread held in mid-air. "Yes?"

She took the bread out his hands and set it on the counter to keep his attention.

"I have work to do, and I've got to leave. I'll feed the baby and put him down for a nap before I go. He may not need changing for a while, hopefully not until I get back."

"Where are you going?"

"I have to check on the bears I'm studying."

"Can I go?"

"No."

"Why not?"

"Because the fewer people I have tramping about in the woods the more likely I'll be able to find and study the poor beasts without scaring them off."

A look of worry crossed his face. "Wait a minute. You're going into the forest to *look* for bears? Alone?"

She understood his concern. After all, her own father had been killed by a bear, and more than once she suspected she had chosen to study bears to overcome her lifelong fear of the animals.

"It's my job," she said. "Among other things, I'm taking a census."

"Aren't there better ways to do that? I mean, in this day and age, don't you have satellites or electronic equipment or something?"

"As a matter of fact, I have some GIS homing collars, but I doubt if the bears will bend down and let me put them around their necks. If I had my rifle, I could tranquilize them first. But I don't. Right now, it could be rusting inside the airplane you dropped into the bay."

"Sorry." Austin opened the bread bag and took out two slices. "So, how have you been keeping track of the bears?"

"I've been using physical characteristics unique to each animal to identify them. I try to keep track of them visually, with binoculars, but it's not easy."

"How far does a bear roam?" He unscrewed the lid from the peanut butter jar, dipped two fingers in and started spreading the mass out on a slice of bread with his hand. She stared at him in mild disgust as she spoke.

"Actually, once they find food and a warm place to sleep, the big lugs settle right in." The potential irony of her words wasn't lost on her. As Austin ate, she picked up the jar of peanut butter and looked inside at the tracks his fingers had made. She considered throwing the jar away but shook her head and set it back down on the counter.

"That's why I'm doing my study," she said. "To find out how many bears there are in this section of the forest and why they live where they live."

"Who wants to know?"

"What?"

"Who wants to know how many bears are out there? Does it matter?"

"Of course it matters."

She had never questioned that. She knew that a bear census—and knowing how the bears lived—was a valid study objective in its own right.

"It's primary research," she said. "Other scientists will interpret my information for a variety of purposes."

"Humph," Austin said, his mouth full of peanut butter sandwich.

With his free hand he picked up at a small framed photograph resting on the kitchen table. "Who's this guy?"

"That's my father." She gently but firmly took the picture from Austin's hands and inspected the frame for peanut butter smudges. The photo showed her father crouching next to an unconscious, tranquilized bear. He was ready to fit a radio collar on the bear's neck.

"He studies bears, too?" Austin asked.

"Yes." Sandra set the frame down and looked at it with her arms crossed. "You might say he was—is—my inspiration."

"Good looking guy. I think you have his eyes."

"Thanks," she said. Okay, Austin had just made a couple of easy points with her, but she didn't need him poking through everything at the ranch.

"What's your father doing these days?" Austin asked, looking over her shoulder. "Is he here somewhere?"

"I wish he were," she said. "He's…deceased."

"Really? I'm sorry. He doesn't…I mean—"

She knew what Austin was trying to say. "You mean he doesn't look that old in the photograph?"

"Yeah."

"He wasn't. He was killed by a bear when I was just twelve years old."

"Oh."

He gave her a questioning look, but there was more to it than that. His eyes and crooked smile were a mix of confusion, sadness, and possible admiration. She had answered all these questions before, so she knew what he was thinking.

"Yes, I decided to study bears, too. Aside from my own interest in zoology, working with bears keeps me connected with my father, in a way. When I'm out in my research blind and I see the bears in their habitat, I know my father must have had the same sense of wonder and curiosity."

"I guess you miss him a lot."

She felt the sting of tears welling in her eyes. "I miss him all the time," she said quietly. She hadn't spoken to anyone about her father in years, least of all her mother, and it surprised her how strongly she still felt the loss. It also surprised her that Austin had so easily tapped into her feelings about her father. For a second she thought he was going to reach out and take her into his arms for a hug. She probably would have buried her face in his chest and sobbed, but apparently, he didn't realize how much his comment had affected her.

"I'm sorry," he said. "I mean that he's gone, not that you feel close to him when you're out in the woods."

"I know what you meant," she said. "Thanks."

He put his hands on his hips, a gesture that struck Sandra as very much like a man. Not manly, necessarily, but man-like. Like a man who, after correctly identifying how sorry everyone felt about Sandra losing her father, was ready to move on. No more discussion needed. No dwelling on emotional subjects. It was so utterly different from the sensitive, caring look he had given her moments earlier. Her heart had hit a small speed bump.

Bump up. Bump down. Now she had to drive on like nothing had happened.

She wiped a bit of a tear from the corner of her eye.

"Anyway," she said. "Since you're apparently some kind of guest here, at least until we can contact the outside world again, please try not to cause any trouble. I'm going to feed Little Jeffrey and take off. I'll be gone for four or five hours. I'm sure you can borrow some clothing from one of the cowboys. In return, you might help them with their chores. That way they can look in on the baby."

"Wait a minute." Another look of concern knitted

Austin's trim, dark eyebrows. "You have men here and they're not going with you?"

"No, they have their own responsibilities. My research grant keeps this place going as a working ranch. There are several hundred head of cattle in nearby pastures. Tending them is hard work." Hard work—the man certainly had the muscles for it. "It's something you might enjoy, once you get used to it."

Unable to speak with his mouth full, Austin simply raised a questioning eyebrow as Sandra turned and left.

****

From his crib, Geoffrey had watched the colors of Sandra and Austin's auras as they talked to each other. Bright sparkling patterns swirled around them, mingling and creating an interesting subtext that had little to do with the words they spoke out loud. Yes, Austin was genuinely fearful for Sandra, as perhaps he should be, since his other feelings for the woman appeared to be very strong and sincere.

And, whether he knew it or not, Austin's sympathy for the loss of Sandra's father struck a chord deep inside the woman. Geoffrey also saw the ever-so-gentle tingle of anxiety that Austin stirred in the shuttered rooms of Sandra's heart. In a small but growing way, she was touched that Austin, as dangerous as he looked, might be afraid for her safety. Studying bears in their natural habitat could be risky, if it wasn't done correctly, and even then, there might be surprises. After all, Sandra's father had died doing this kind of research.

But Austin's concern for Sandra wasn't the only cause of the complex changes Geoffrey saw flickering in the woman's vibrant aura. Consciously, Sandra distrusted Austin because of his unruly looks and questionable past. Geoffrey understood that. Mortal men and women were always obsessing about their superficial differences, but there was something more going on here.

Geoffrey studied the shifting, pulsing shades of Sandra's true feelings, knowing she couldn't. She was almost completely cut off from them. Archangels weren't experts on the subject of human emotions, but what he saw fascinated him. Sandra wasn't afraid for her own safety, and she wasn't really afraid of Austin. A different kind of fear lurked within her so deeply that even Geoffrey had trouble seeing it clearly. Something was going on, something serious, and something to which Sandra was still completely oblivious.

From what Geoffrey could gather, Sandra was afraid that Austin might fall in love with her. She might welcome that love, if she would only let herself. But Sandra was also afraid that, if Austin or any man came into her life, he might leave and break her heart. That wasn't an uncommon fear among mortals, but Sandra and Austin had just met each other. They were perfect strangers, and Sandra couldn't imagine that she and Austin might have a life together. So what made her so fearful he might leave?

Whatever the cause, Sandra was already pushing Austin away. Geoffrey pitied her, and he pitied poor Austin. If Sandra didn't understand her own fears and feelings, how could Austin? Austin Smith was going down a familiar path, falling in love, and he would likely find nothing but heartbreak at the end of that road.

Chapter 3

As it happened, Austin and a lumbering cowboy named Raymond wore the same inseam and sleeve length. Raymond agreed to lend Austin a pair of blue jeans and a flannel shirt. To top it off, he gave Austin a broken in, sweat-stained Stetson to keep the sun off his face. In return, Austin promised to check on some calves and their mothers grazing in a pasture in the neighboring national forest.

While Raymond kept an eye on Little Jeffrey, Austin went to the barn, picked out a good-looking bay and a serviceable saddle. He worked under Jake's watchful eye. Jake seemed to be the foreman, but, at six-foot-three, he was certainly no dwarf. Jake had been reluctant to let Austin take the horse and tack until Sandra said it was okay. He seemed amused by the idea that a pilot would be helping them out for a few days. Then he watched Austin saddle the horse.

"You cinched up that old terrapin right smartly, Mr. Smith. Looks to me like you've done this before."

"Yeah," Austin said, adjusting the bridle. "Once or twice." Jake's old-timer terminology reminded Austin of his childhood. He had practically grown up on a horse, but lately the opportunities to ride had been few.

"I guess you'll do fine," Jake said. "Take good care of Clover now and bring her back before dark. She gets a might grumpy if she doesn't get her bag of oats around six o'clock."

Austin nodded. "What's the deal with Sandy?" he asked casually, as he stroked the horse's neck. "You always let her go off into the woods by herself like that?"

"Don't you worry about that little gal. She knows what she's doing out there."

"What is she doing out there, anyway?"

"Talking to the bears, I guess." Jake smiled at him.

"What if she ever got into trouble? How would you find her?"

"Oh, we'd find her." Jake waved him off as he walked away. "She's got a research blind out by the lake, a couple of miles up the river. That's where she'd be."

Austin smiled. He hoped he'd made a friend of Jake, but he knew the old man, like Sandra, probably thought he was a scoundrel. Oh, well. One day at a time. He stashed another peanut butter sandwich and a bottle of water in a small backpack, mounted up, and rode away from the ranch.

He was relieved to find that the hours he'd spent in the cockpit of an airplane hadn't dulled his skills as a horseman. In forty-five minutes, he found the small herd of cattle grazing peacefully. Everything was in order, and he could return to Misha Ranch, if he wanted. But the sun warmed his face, and it was too nice a day to ride straight back. Besides, the cowboys would probably put him to work on something else, so he let Clover have a little rein. The horse trotted happily away from the pasture and into the woods, letting Austin discover tall stands of blue spruce and flower-strewn meadows that flooded him with memories of his childhood on the reservation in Montana. He thought about where life had taken him, from his days as a scrawny Indian kid with a chip on his shoulder, right up to the moment a strange woman set a baby in his lap.

Austin's mother wanted him to raise a family, which he always expected to do, someday. But those plans had always been put off in favor of the next adventure. And lately the adventures were leaving him unsatisfied. Even so, he could feel the likelihood of a quiet, ordinary life slipping away from him with each passing year.

Even if he couldn't remember the baby's mother, Austin wasn't really surprised to find Little Jeffrey in his lap. Quite an irony, considering his own youth. God must have a sense of humor. Either that or he wanted to teach Austin a lesson. At age thirty-two, it was high time Austin accepted some responsibility. And Little Jeffrey was a responsibility Austin couldn't or wouldn't run away from. The baby was a wake-up call, clutching at Austin's shirt buttons and drooling his way right into Austin's heart. It was a new experience, and Austin considered it a challenge. He took to changing diapers, reading baby food labels, and monitoring the child's every need like he had been waiting for it all his life, not running away to the far corners of the world.

As he rode along, Austin tried to remember everything he could about his own father, but there was precious little. If it hadn't been for old Four-of-a-Kind, his beloved maternal grandfather, Austin wouldn't have had any father figure at all. Now he was intrigued by the idea of being in a family again, small as it was, but the critical, missing element was a wife and mother. He couldn't help but think of Sandra. When he first opened his eyes and saw her, he would have fallen off the couch, if he hadn't already been lying down. He didn't know the woman looking down at him, but that didn't matter. Instinctively he felt that, during his long years on the road, he might have been running toward this one moment, this rendezvous with life. Now, all at once, his restlessness had come to an end. How to explain it?

There had been plenty of women in his life, but he'd never found a real *he'eo'o*, or heart mate. And Sandra Coulton was something special. Meeting her felt like divine intervention. Like someone up there was still looking out for him.

All he had to do was convince Sandra.

That wasn't going to be easy. She had already guessed what kind of man he was, before Little Jeffrey. He was willing to fight for his son, if he had to, but how could any court of law give him custody over a stable, professional woman of Sandra's caliber? He would prefer that it not come down to either-or, since Sandra was the woman he wanted, for himself and his baby. But, so far, she wanted nothing to do with him, and the battle for custody was going to be waged on the cool, dry fields of Sandra's scientist's heart.

With that in mind, he spurred his horse in the direction of the lake, where Jake said Sandra had constructed a research blind. He had no trouble finding the small river, and he rode along the path next to it. After thirty minutes or so he crossed an overgrown jeep road. He reined up and scanned it in both directions, looking for tracks, footprints, or other signs of recent use. Nothing.

Before he could spur the horse on, a middle-aged

gentleman dressed in a safari hunting jacket and floppy hat came around a bend in the road, about fifty yards away. The man was walking toward him. He was smoking a pipe and carrying a double-barreled elephant gun in the crook of his arm. Austin waited. When the man got closer, he raised his hat in greeting.

"G'day, mate," the man said in a thick, Australian accent. His wide handlebar moustache drooped over a snaggle-toothed grin.

"Hello yourself," Austin said. "Bag anything?" He pointed at the gun.

"What, with this?" The man looked at the cannon as though he had completely forgotten he was carrying it. "My heavens, no. I shouldn't think I'd have to, really."

Austin was confused. "Aren't you hunting?"

The man looked at him warily. "You're not a member of the local constabulary, are you?"

"No way." Austin grinned at the idea.

"Ah, good." The man rested the rifle butt on the ground and extended his hand in greeting. Austin reached down from his horse and they shook.

"My name's Brisbane, Melborne Brisbane." Only he pronounced it "Brizb'n, Melbun Brizb'n." "I'm currently in the employ of Star Century Studios of Los Angeles, California."

"Really. What brings you all the way up here, Mr. Brisbane?"

"It's Gretchin, I'm afraid." He pronounced the name "Grit-chin." Brisbane took the pipe from his mouth and grimaced. "She's lost in the woods."

"Gretchin?"

"Yes, Grit-chin." Brisbane folded his arms over the

upright barrel of the immense firearm. He looked completely at ease as he stood there, one big game hunter chatting with another in the Outback. "She's been with the studio for years," he said. "We've been filming a picture down the road a few miles." Brisbane gestured over his shoulder with the stem of his pipe, then above his head, as if he were pointing at the words on a theater marquis. "It's an exciting September release called *Fire on the Gambeze*. That's just the working title, of course. Damn titles are always changing. Hard to keep track of them, really."

Odd as it was, Brisbane's story rang true. Leave it to Hollywood to shoot a movie in Alaska that was supposed to be set in Africa.

"What about Gretchin?" Austin asked. "She could be in trouble if she's been lost for very long, even in good weather."

"Gretchin? Oh, yes, Gretchin. No one suspected she was dissatisfied with her work, or her accommodations. She was giving us one of her better performances. Then we found her one night at the catering table eating like there was no tomorrow."

"Is that odd?"

"No, not really. When you film long hours, you don't have time to eat. You can forget all about food until suddenly you're starving. But some bugger served Gretchin a salmon steak. She made short work of that, I'll tell you. After that she simply walked off the set and we haven't seen her since."

"You think she got sick on some bad fish?"

"Bad? My heavens no. Top quality stuff they have around here." Brisbane leaned in conspiratorially. "Star Century isn't as well funded as some of the studios.

They can't afford gourmet catering, so that salmon steak must have been a revelation, compared to what she had been eating. Gretchin's probably out looking for more."

"In the woods?"

"Exactly. But the poor girl hasn't got a clue how to catch a fish. I hope we can get her back to the set. It would be a shame if someone mistook her for a wild animal and shot her."

"Why would they do that?"

"They might, if she frightened a group of campers or something."

Austin's mind reeled. Surely Alaskan campers weren't as careless with firearms as Brisbane made them out to be—then a light came on. "Gretchin's not a woman, is she?"

"Oh, Lord no. She's a grizzly bear, man. A grizzly. A fine specimen, too. But very friendly. Gentle as a lamb on most days. At least when she's been fed. I'm not sure she can even survive in the wilderness. And of course, the film won't be the same without her. They'll have to rewrite the whole damn thing."

Austin scratched his head. "Why don't you call the Forest Service? They might help you find her."

"I suggested that, but the producers don't want to, at least not yet. They're afraid the bloody bureaucrats will revoke their permit to film if they find out we let a bear get loose. Or worse, they might insist on shooting Gretchin themselves before we can bring her in. They don't know how tame she really is."

"Then I hope you find her first."

"Yes, and I'd better get cracking. Be a good lad and let me know if you see her." Brisbane hefted the big gun to his hip. "Three shots into the air. That's the international signal for help. I'll come running."

"Of course," Austin said, even though he didn't have a gun.

Brisbane winked at him and started to walk up the road.

"Oh, Brisbane," Austin called. "How would I know Gretchin from any other bear?"

"That's easy. She's got a distinctive black star, right here on her forehead." He pointed his index finger between his eyes. Easy to see, once you're close enough."

Austin nodded.

"Also, as I said, she's well trained. Responds to all the industry hand signals, if you know those. That's how we get her to act when the cameras are rolling." He tipped his hat and walked away, holding the gun in the crook of his arm. An Alaskan-Australian Davy Crockett.

Austin watched him go. As he spurred his mount lightly across the road, he glanced down and noticed the familiar pattern of bear scat on the path. He'd seen enough of it in Montana to know. But was it Gretchin's or from a wild bear? Either way, he'd have to be careful.

Back on the trail, the spruce trees closed in overhead, darkening the sky. Through the shadows Austin could barely see the narrow path he was following. He imagined Sandra, somewhere up ahead in the gloom, taking notes in her blind as she watched a cute bear cub forage for roots and berries in the mists of the primal forest.

It was no wonder the animals loved this country.

With plenty of food and shelter, they could live out their lives completely undisturbed by man, or any other enemy. A few days ago, he would have envied the bears their solitude.

He traveled another mile before he reined the horse to a stop at the edge of a large, sun-lit meadow. Water spilled from a raised berm on the far side, indicating that a lake, undoubtedly Sandra's lake, lay beyond it, just where Jake had said it would be. He dismounted, to walk the rest of the way without the horse. The last thing he wanted to do was disrupt Sandra's study by riding into the middle of it. He needed her respect, and he hadn't figured out how to earn it, yet.

He let the horse graze and walked across the meadow, taking his small backpack, and wondering what miracle of biology had created the divine Sandra Coulton. He stopped and took a deep, pine-scented breath. Yes, the woman was beautiful, but, after a lifetime spent as a seriously confirmed bachelor, how could he have fallen in love so easily? Was it love, lust, or just the challenge Sandra presented? Maybe he'd never really been in love before, and that was why his feelings all seemed so new. One way or the other, he had to find out.

He came upon the clear, blue alpine lake, about two hundred yards across, dotted with beaver lodges and fallen trees. The spruce forest came down to the banks on all sides, except for the occasional narrow, sandy beach. On the far side, another sparkling waterfall tumbled steadily downward from a height of about fifteen feet. The whole scene looked like a photograph from an Alaska tourism brochure, or one of those old animated beer signs he'd seen in countless smoky barrooms.

Standing quietly, he surveyed the lake, looking for Sandra or one of her bears before he got any closer. At first, he saw nothing. Then, as a cloud slipped away from the sun, he saw a metallic reflection, low in a tree on the far-left bank. Looking closer, he made out some camouflage netting and artificially arranged branches that must be Sandra's blind. Nothing was moving inside.

Staying behind the trees, he made his way carefully around the lake in the direction of the blind. He hunched down and started playing his favorite kid's game. He was no longer Austin Smith. Instead, he was Austin Running Bull, the Cheyenne Sioux Chief of fierce reputation he had pretended to be when he played cowboys and Indians with his friends in Montana. He slipped through the trees like a shadow, trying not to step on dry twigs or make any other sound. He paused every ten yards or so to listen and study the forest.

He stopped short when he heard a shuffling sound. Something was moving around in the bushes ahead of him. A bear? No, he was looking at a man's back. Slight in stature, the man wore a dark green uniform, and a Smokey-the-Bear hat. He was crouching behind a bush, looking at something out in the lake. Something Chief Running Bull had failed to see.

Austin stood silently behind the man and scanned the lake, too. He saw nothing at first. Then his gaze returned to the waterfall. There, under the cascading flow, at the bottom of the falls, he noticed water spraying here and there, hitting something as it fell. Looking more closely, he saw flashes of pink darting in and out of a curtain of water. With shock he recognized a familiar silhouette and certain pleasing, pink shapes moving seductively under the water that he, as a man, had been genetically programmed over the millennia to respond to on a visceral level. In short, he felt a certain tightening in what a romance writer might refer to as his "nether regions."

Sandra Coulton was standing in the middle of the waterfall, apparently taking a shower. Naked. And this joker in the bushes was watching her. Not that he could blame the man. Austin was tempted to watch, too, as Sandra climbed out of the lake and started to dress. But no, even Austin knew that spying on a bathing woman wasn't right. He strode forward, no longer worried about making any noise.

The uniformed man heard him, stood up, and spun around just as Austin grasped him by the neck with one hand.

"Wait!" was all the man could say before Austin's strong fingers closed around his throat. The man beat on Austin's arm with both hands, but Austin held on tight. Not tight enough to completely cut off the man's oxygen, unless he struggled, which he did for about thirty seconds. Then the man lowered his arms and looked up at Austin, pleading with his eyes.

Austin released him and the man fell backward onto a bed of leaves, gasping for air.

"What…on earth…do you think you're doing?" the man gasped.

"I was going to ask you the same thing," Austin said through clenched teeth.

"You attacked me."

"Just be thankful I let you go."

"You're in big trouble, mister," the man gasped.

"You've just assaulted a federal officer. And that's a felony."

"A federal officer?" Austin took a half-step backward and looked again at the man's uniform. "You're just a Forest Service flunky. And a sneaky one at that."

The man rubbed his neck. "I am responsible for...periodically monitoring the progress of Miss Coulton's research."

"That's not all you were monitoring, was it?"

The man climbed to his feet while Austin considered whether he should let him.

"I don't know what you're talking about," the man said, straightening his tie.

"Right."

"Walter? Austin?" Sandra pushed her way through the underbrush, more or less dressed, but still wet enough that her clothing clung to her curves. Her damp, glorious hair splayed down the front of her khaki shirt, soaking it through. Austin ached to look at her, but the "take-charge" sound of Sandra's voice chilled his passion.

"What's going on here?" she asked.

"I was just coming to see you," Walter said, "when this civilian here assaulted me from behind."

"And you saw quite a bit, didn't you?" Austin said.

Sandra shot Austin a hard glance. She stood in front of him with her arms crossed, hiding her breasts and the front of her shirt.

"And what are *you* doing here, Mr. Smith?"

"Well," he said, scratching his head, "I was coming to see you myself."

"I know why Walter would come here"—Walter's

chest puffed up a bit—"but what do you want?"

"I wanted to talk to you," Austin said. He had no idea how he was going to explain his presence.

"What about?"

Austin sighed and hitched his eyes in Walter's direction, hoping to communicate to Sandra that he didn't want to talk about it in front of Walter. The forest ranger stood stiffly, hands on his hips, belatedly affecting an air of authority. Sandra followed Austin's gaze to Walter.

"Walter Boyles," she said. "This is Austin Smith. He claims to be the father of the baby we found on the ranch house roof."

"I *am* the father," Austin said.

Walter's hands came off his hips. His eyes narrowed like a gunfighter's. "A likely story," he said. "If you are the father, you'd would know how the baby got onto the roof at Misha Ranch. How about it, Mr. Smith?"

Austin considered grabbing Walter by the neck again, but he didn't. "If the baby wasn't carried away by a bird, I have no idea," he said finally. "But he was given to me by his mother in Prudhomme Bay."

"You know who the mother is?" Walter asked. He gave Sandra a questioning glance.

"No," Austin said. "Not really. I'm just trying to…help." The word "help" sounded weak, even to Austin. He was bungling his first and perhaps only opportunity to convince Sandra that he wanted to do the right thing for his son. A lifetime of diligently avoiding such responsibility wasn't serving him well.

"Right now, I think the baby needs a little more than your 'help,'" Sandra said.

"You know what I mean." Austin felt his resolve crumbling. Unfortunately, it was replaced by anger. Anger at himself, for not knowing what to do, and anger that anyone else, even Sandra, should decide what he could do with his own son.

"No," Sandra said. "What exactly do you mean?"

Austin stood a little straighter, but his voice lowered to a whisper. "What I mean is that Little Jeffrey is my son and he belongs with me. I'm his father."

"Are you going to let him take the baby away?" Walter asked.

"I don't think so," Sandra said.

"Now wait a minute—" Austin raised his hand.

"No, I think you should wait, Mr. Smith." She pointed at him with one finger, then noticed how her shirt clung to her breasts and crossed her arms again. "I appreciate your sincerity and your desire to help, but I'm not going to give that baby away just because you've gotten it in your head that you might be the father." She gave him a sad smile.

"Why not?"

"I'm sorry, but I haven't seen anything since you dropped out of the sky that tells me you know how to raise a child. I know you disagree, but this really isn't the time or place to talk about it."

She turned and started walking away in the direction of the blind. Austin's mind reeled.

"And you?" he asked. His anger had taken control of him. "What makes you think you can raise a child any better than me? Do you think a college degree in biology qualifies you to be a mother?"

Sandra turned on him, a curious mixture of hurt

and fury burning in her eyes, but Austin couldn't stop himself.

"The boy isn't an experiment. You can't just observe him as he grows up, taking notes on his behavior like you were proving some scientific theory."

The words spilled out of his mouth seemingly unbidden, as shocking to him as they must have been to Sandra. He liked this woman, in spite of what she thought about him, or perhaps *because* of what she thought about him, but he had to draw the line. No one was going to take his child away from him without a fight.

Sandra advanced two steps on Austin, who stood his ground, bracing himself for her wrath. She raised both of her fists, ignoring her damp, revealing shirt, and opened her mouth.

But, before she could speak, all three of them froze when they heard the low rumbling growl of a bear.

Chapter 4

Sandra spun in the direction of the blood-curdling sound. Not more than thirty yards away stood one of the largest grizzlies she had ever seen. It rose onto its hind legs and poked its nose into Sandra's empty research blind, obviously looking for something to eat. Thank goodness Sandra wasn't inside, since she had been taken completely off guard. Now her emotions were spinning out of control. A split second ago, whether she liked it or not, she was bracing herself for a knock-down drag-out fight with Austin. Now her already high adrenalin level shot skyward with the bear's appearance. In spite of all that, she tried to stay calm. She had to think quickly. All three of them were in danger.

Still looking at the bear, she said in a firm whisper, "Walk away, back down the trail. Quickly. Bears don't like to go downhill because they have short front legs."

She glanced back at Walter and Austin, but Walter had already disappeared, and she had no idea in which direction he'd gone. Austin simply stood there, looking at the bear in fascination. Sandra strode past him and tugged on his sleeve.

"Come on," she said. "Let's go before he sees us."

But the bear, which apparently had found nothing of interest in the blind, was now lumbering down the trail directly toward them.

Without taking his eyes off the animal, Austin placed his hand on her shoulder, as if to reassure her. "You go," he said calmly. "I'll distract him."

"Don't be crazy." Sandra knew that, unless the bear stopped to eat him, Austin could distract the beast for no more than three or four seconds.

"Go," he said.

A shaft of fear knifed through her. This crazy man, whom she didn't know from Adam, had decided to risk his life to protect her.

She stood in front of him, to look him in the eyes, except that he was at least a foot taller than she.

"Believe me," she said earnestly. "I've studied these animals for years. There's nothing you can do. Now *come on*." She grabbed his arm again and tried to spin him around, but he gently shook her off.

"You'd better get going yourself."

"Come on!" she begged. "Think of your child!"

That caused him to raise an eyebrow, but he just smiled at her. "Maybe you convinced me," he said. "My boy might be better off with you. I can distract the bear long enough for you to get away."

"It's not worth it. *I'm* not worth it. Really." She clutched his arm with both hands and pulled on him as hard as she could, but he didn't budge. With the beast now only twenty yards away and closing fast, she looked at Austin, then back at the bear, and made a quick mental calculation. She hardly knew Austin, and if he was crazy enough to stand there and let a bear attack him, well, what could she do to stop it?

She released Austin's arm and started walking quickly down the hill, but her feet slowed with each step until she came to a complete stop. Her own father had died at the hands of a bear. She had just been a girl at the time, and there was nothing she could have done to save him. But leaving Austin to the same fate didn't feel right. After all, she was the bear expert, and maybe there *was* nothing she could do to save this foolish man, but if he chose to stand there and die trying to save her, she simply couldn't run away.

"Oh, Lord, help us," she said out loud. Shoulders slumping, she turned to face what might be a horrible death for both of them. Instead, what she saw made her jaw drop in surprise.

****

Geoffrey had been dozing in a bright ray of sunshine that bathed his crib all afternoon. Not a bad life, being a baby. He could sleep all day and talk about any subject that came to mind, without the awful arguments he always seemed to start in heaven. Sure, baby food wasn't *haute cuisine*, and he couldn't keep from soiling himself on a regular basis, but even that gave him a certain sense of freedom. All he had to do was relax and let go. Someone always came by to clean him up.

For hours, he'd slipped in and out of warm unconsciousness, only vaguely aware of the scruffy-faced cowboys who looked in on him now and again.

"Ah, what a life these humans have." Too bad he wasn't in a home with a natural mother. It seemed like a hundred years since he'd been allowed to suckle at a soft, warm breast. *"Mmmm, thanks for the mammories."*

Then the prayer came in. It was just a short one— "Lord help us"—but Geoffrey recognized it immediately. A Two-Twelve. Animal-human confrontation—Sandra was in trouble. He closed his tiny blue eyes and slipped into inter-plasmal space. His consciousness streaked in the direction of the prayer to its origin and instantly registered the shock on Sandra's face.

Looking through Sandra's eyes, Geoffrey saw a bear shuffling down a trail in the middle of which stood a determined but defenseless Austin Smith.

"What on earth is that man doing?" Perhaps he'd misjudged this Austin fellow. At that moment he didn't seem nearly as clever or intelligent as Geoffrey had given him credit. It might be time for the man to return to his heavenly home after all. That peeved Geoffrey a bit, since he'd gone to the trouble of saving Austin's life just that morning. Well, perhaps Geoffrey would let him go this time. The human race might be better off without Mr. Smith's foolishness muddying up the gene pool.

He started withdrawing his consciousness from the scene. *"Sorry, dear,"* he said to Sandra. *"Heaven can't answer all your prayers now, can it?"* Then a troubling thought occurred to him. He still couldn't remember why he'd been sent to the ranch in the first place. Not that he really cared all that much about Austin, but he did have that bet with Gabriel, and saving this man's life might have something to do with it. Was Geoffrey playing into Gabe's hands by not keeping Austin alive?

Geoffrey reinserted himself into the unfolding tragedy and reached forward with his angel consciousness to the bear. Perhaps he could turn the animal aside at the last minute by implanting a thought about blueberries or something. *"Okay...now!"*

Funny, nothing happened. He tried again, harder.

Still, nothing happened. The beast was almost on top of Austin now, and Geoffrey suspected that Gabriel might be intervening on behalf of the bear. Mentally backing up a step, he put a half-twist on his own intervention. It was a trick he'd learned from the Countess of Rosmar, a witch in the court of King Henry, in twelfth century London.

The bear finally slid to a halt with its claws only a few feet from Austin's toes.

"Ah, there we go. The half-twist gets them every time."

Austin had just raised his not-so-puny human arms as though he had the strength to ward off the charging brute. Geoffrey wondered if Austin thought he had saved himself. Pesky non-believers. Someday they would all learn. God would make sure of that. The Archangel quietly withdrew from the scene, only to find that he'd wet his diaper again.

****

The short hairs on the back of Austin's neck stood straight up when he had heard the ugly growl. He had no clue what could have made such an awful noise. Instinctively, he had frozen, not wanting to move until he knew what the danger was and where it came from.

Walter's reaction had been more immediate. He jumped straight into the air, hit the ground running, and dove through the bushes, all in the space of a single heartbeat.

Austin's gaze focused on the rippling golden-brown coat of the animal making the dreadful noise. A bear. His astonished brain formed the word, even as the animal's head turned and its eyes focused on his own. Time seemed to stand still, and to Austin's surprise, he felt no fear at the sight of the hairy bruin. After all, the grizzly seemed much less threatening than Sandra had been a few seconds earlier. The bear could only kill him, and at that moment dying in the claws of a wild animal struck Austin as in keeping with the reckless way he had lived. It would be poetic justice. He probably deserved whatever Sandra was going to say to him before they were interrupted. It didn't take a scientist to point out he had no business being a father, but that realization profoundly dismayed him. Just because he had lived his life on the wild side didn't mean he hadn't dreamed of meeting someone like Sandra and settling down. But, perhaps she was right. Perhaps he was beyond redemption. Except at the hands of a bear.

At least he'd never have to apologize for his unkind words to Sandra. As ashamed as he felt, facing the bear might be the only way he could show Sandra what kind of man he was. If he died, at least she would remember him as the man who gave his life for her and his son.

His son. In the fleeting seconds while he stood his ground, a vision of his son's possible future flashed before his eyes. But something was wrong with the scenes unfolding in his mind's eye. He expected Little Jeffrey to grow up in the care of a loving mother who reminded him daily of the courageous father he once had. But no. There was a twist Austin hadn't expected. Sandra, ever the practical woman, had decided that she and Little Jeffrey needed a living man in their lives, not a memory. So, Sandra had gotten married. To an accountant. And they lived in a tract home in LaDue, a boring, upper middle-class suburb of St. Louis. It was awful, and Austin refused to die with that on his conscience. No son of his was going to grow up in a stifling suburb, never savoring the pungent aroma of a Cairo bazaar, or seeing his own strong jaw reflected in the glittering pools of the Taj Mahal.

"Wait!" he cried.

He had to live! He had to show his son the glory of the Himalayas. He had to... The bear towered over him. Austin instinctively raised both hands, straight into the air, not so much for protection as to stop the charging beast by the sheer strength of his sudden resolve to live.

And the bear did stop. Directly in front of him. It dropped down onto all four paws. Blackness crept into the outer edges of Austin's vision, and he struggled to keep from fainting dead away. But now, as the bear looked at him more or less eye-to-eye, Austin finally saw the small, distinctive black star between the animal's big brown eyes.

"Gretchin?"

"Grr," rumbled the bear.

Austin's knees almost buckled, and he fought the urge to sit down. Apparently, he wasn't in any danger after all, but he couldn't be sure. He didn't know how long it would take a tame bear to revert to a wild animal. It just stood there, licking its muzzle and rocking from side to side on its feet, as if it was waiting for instructions.

He peered into the bear's eyes, trying to think of what to do next.

"Austin?" He heard Sandra's quavering voice, probably ten feet in back of him, but he didn't want to answer. He didn't want to do anything that might spook Gretchin, tame or not. Instead, he waved his arm behind him, motioning for her to keep her distance.

"Stay back," he said as pleasantly as he could. Gretchin licked her lips. "I think she's hungry."

"Of *course* she's hungry," Sandra whispered. "She's a bear. Bears are *always* hungry."

"I think I can help," Austin said. Slowly, he slipped the small backpack from his shoulders and, without taking his eyes off Gretchin, clicked open the buckle. He found the peanut butter sandwich, pulled it from the bag, and unwrapped the wax paper from around it. Dangling the bread between his thumb and index finger, as close to the edge as possible, he took one cautious half-step toward the animal.

"Here you go, girl."

"*Austin, are you out of your mind?*" Sandra sounded like she'd kill him if the bear didn't.

"Are we friends, girl?" Austin asked the bear.

Gretchin simply "Grr'd" softly. Then her nose began to twitch, and in the blink of an eye she snatched the sandwich from Austin's hand with one sweeping paw.

"Whoa!" Austin glanced down at his fingers. He expected to see bloody stumps, but they were all still there, unharmed.

The bear sat down on her rump, holding the sandwich in both paws. She sniffed it. Then licked it. Then ate it in one bite.

Austin turned around, all smiles, and faced Sandra. He raised his fist in a "victory salute" over his head. "Yeah! Friends for life. Just like the movies." A split second before he heard Gretchin roar, Austin realized his fist was still in the air, and he remembered that the bear recognized hand signals.

Slowly, he turned around. Gretchin had risen again on her hind legs and towered over him once more, looking like she had decided Austin was made of peanut butter, and she liked it. Austin stumbled backward, practically in the shadow of the beast. The heel of his boot caught on an exposed root and he tumbled backward. As he rolled onto his back, his hands flew out in front of him, palms open.

The bear emitted a quiet "Grr," dropped down onto all four paws, and ran away, back up the trail. Sandra sprinted to where Austin lay on his back and jumped up and down as she watched the bear retreat into the woods.

"Oh my God," she gasped. "Oh my God. Did you see that? Did you see that?"

"I had a pretty good view." Austin got up and dusted off the bottom of his jeans. If he owned a gun he would have fired it three times in the air to signal Brisbane.

"I can't believe it," Sandra said. "Do you realize you just stopped a bear attack cold?"

"No. Really?"

"It was more than that. You practically drove it away. How did you do that? You must have some sort of scent or smell or something." She put her arm around his waist and started sniffing his shirt. "This is sensational."

"Now that you mention it, other than a recent dip in the ocean, I haven't bathed in two or three days."

Austin realized Sandra had forgotten the sacrifice he had just tried to make. But, as a champion bear fighter, he was a lot more interesting to her than as an itinerant bush pilot claiming to be the father of a child she wanted to keep for herself.

"You simply stood there and raised your hands," Sandra said. She put both hands in the air, mimicking what he'd done. "That's the kind of thing you're supposed to do if you're attacked by a mountain lion. Making yourself look bigger than you are." She crooked a finger on her chin, thinking. "This could change everything."

He assumed she meant everything about bear attacks. But then, how many people got attacked by a trained Hollywood bear?

He opened his mouth to tell her about Gretchin, but the nearness of her tantalized him. He hesitated. That hair. Those marvelous breasts. He liked being her hero, and he didn't want the feeling to end. No hurry. He could tell her about Gretchin later.

Her now-drying auburn-brunette whatever-it-was hair bounced seductively as she spoke, and her soft brown eyes flashed with excitement. Who was this woman who got so turned on by a life-threatening encounter with a wild beast? Austin figured he was a wild beast, of sorts. Could she ever get as excited about him?

This thought intrigued him while Sandra talked effusively about the event, breaking down and reviewing each step of what had happened, until Austin bent forward and gave her a quick kiss. She looked startled, but then she smiled and hugged him tightly around his chest and went on talking. Apparently, she saw the gesture as nothing more than an emotional reaction to the excitement of the moment. Acceptable behavior, not motivated by any deep, lasting feelings. Oh, well, that was a start. Ten minutes earlier she would have slapped him for doing such a thing. Or gotten a restraining order.

"Don't you think we've had enough science for today?" he asked.

"What? Sure, maybe. But, oh, what a day. What could happen next?"

"I was wondering that myself." His too-broad smile was apparently lost on her.

"Where's Walter?" she asked, looking down the trail. "I'm sorry he didn't get to witness this. They'll never believe me at the Forest Service. Or the university."

"The way he was running, I suspect Walter is half-way back to Washington, D.C. by now."

Sandra did a double take, looked at him, and laughed. Then she gave him another friendly hug. "Let's go back to the ranch."

Only then did they remember their horses. Sure enough, Austin's horse, which had been loosely tethered back on the trail, had wisely run away once she heard or smelled the bear. Sandra's, too, had escaped.

"It's okay," Sandra said. "They both know where to find dinner, and I'm sure they'll end up at the ranch long before we do."

"It's a fine afternoon for a walk," Austin said, presenting his elbow. "Shall we?"

As they started down the trail, Austin glanced backward, over his shoulder. In the middle of some underbrush, just on the edge of the trees, a pair of coal-black eyes peered back at him through the leaves.

He sincerely hoped it was Gretchin, but he kept walking anyway.

Chapter 5

As she walked down the trail toward Misha Ranch, Sandra's head still swam with adrenalin. She looked up at Austin. "We could publish a paper about you in my university's journal of wildlife biology. If we did a little more research."

Austin glanced over at her, raising an eyebrow. "You mean you'd have to stick me in front of some more bears to see if the same thing happened?"

"That would be the proper way to do it."

He looked at her with plain disbelief. She laughed and playfully punched him, her fist bouncing harmlessly off his rock-solid shoulder.

"I think I can wait a while before I meet another bear so up-close-and-personal," he said.

She laughed again, but she wondered what he must be thinking of her at that moment. After all, before the bear arrived, she was winding up a haymaker that might have taken his head off. Now, all she wanted to do was laugh and hug him, or dance down the path with him singing, hand-in-hand. All of her senses had come alive as she glided along next to Austin. Her toes were barely touching the ground.

"But seriously," she said. "All we—I—would have to do is collect some background literature, so other biologists who read the article would know we put some thought into the experiment. Or at least into interpreting the results."

"There's no scientific validity in reporting a freak accident?"

"Sure, I suppose so. It's called 'anecdotal evidence' in the world of science. But we should investigate whether you actually did something specific that stopped the bear from attacking. It could be important. It might save other people's lives in the future."

"That would be nice," he said. He put his arm around her shoulder and drew her close to him. She slipped her arm around his narrow waist and held on tight. He felt so good her skin raised goose bumps. She could feel her heart beating in the pressure where they held onto each other. She felt woozy, giddy, and excited, all at the same time, just like a school girl. Was she still excited by the bear, or was something else going on here? The bear was gone, the animal one anyway, and now she was simply walking through the woods, alone with Austin Smith.

Austin the ne'er-do-well. Austin the bush pilot. Austin the hunk from out of nowhere. Austin, Austin, Austin.

Who was this man, anyway, who literally dropped out of the sky and stopped a bear, all in one day? Was she really going to have to fight him for Little Jeffrey, or...? Unanswered questions buzzed back and forth in Sandra's brain like a bumblebee she couldn't shoo away.

Gradually her excitement dimmed, and Sandra's training began to reassert itself. She decided her giddiness was caused by the adrenalin pumping through her veins, a physiological reaction to the highly emotional encounter with the bear. Nothing had changed, really. She still wanted to keep Little Jeffrey, and she still had to convince Austin that she would be the better parent.

Even so, she may have been a little harsh with the big guy. After all, any man willing to face down a hungry grizzly to save Walter and her had to have some good qualities. Didn't he? Even if what he had done was completely reckless and unnecessary? From the looks of him, she'd bet money he had been reckless his whole life, the complete opposite of her. In spite of that, she somehow found herself attracted to the man. She knew there wasn't any future in that. She wasn't about to throw away the quiet, steady life she had built for herself and run away with Austin to the other side of the world. She shook her head. How long did she think that arrangement would last? No, that was crazy talk. She wasn't going to run away with Austin, but maybe she could give the man a break. Maybe.

"That was a pretty brave thing you did," she told him.

"Ah, shucks, ma'am," he said. "It weren't nuth'n."

"It also wasn't very smart." She hadn't wanted to say that, but it was true.

"At the time," he said, "I considered the bear to be the lesser of two evils."

"Oh, yeah." She had almost forgotten how angry she had been when Austin questioned her qualifications as a parent. She slowly dropped her arm from around his waist. Sure, being a competent scientist didn't automatically mean she would be a good mother, but motherhood was instinctive with women, wasn't it? No, that couldn't be true. She only had to look at her own mother to understand how wrong that idea was.

She hadn't gotten along with her mother in years. When Sandra's father had been killed, her mother was left alone to raise Sandra all by herself. She expected her mother to be proud of her when she went off to college. But, in the end, Martha had resented the fact that Sandra chose the same profession as her deceased husband, the man who had abandoned her, even if it wasn't his fault.

What's more, Sandra had chosen a career that isolated her for long periods of time in the middle of a forest. Had she subconsciously wanted to do that? Either way, she was hardly in a position to judge Austin. So, she decided to give him the benefit of the doubt.

"I think I owe you an apology," she said, looking down at the dry leaves, pine needles, and twigs littering the trail.

"For what?"

"I've been too hard on you. I shouldn't have assumed you would never be a good father."

"Oh, that. For a scientist, your instincts were pretty good, even if your conclusions were questionable."

"What do you mean?"

"I mean you were right, at least about the old Austin. The last thing in the world he ever wanted to be was a father."

"And now?"

"Now the old Austin is gone."

"Where did the old Austin go?"

"I think the bear got him."

She thought about this and then stopped walking. Austin took two more steps before he turned to see why she'd stopped.

"Hello, new Austin Smith," she said. "My name is Dr. Sandra Coulton, and I'm very glad to meet you." She held out her hand for him to shake.

"Dr. Sandra?" He gave her a weak handshake.

"Yes. I'm still the old Sandra, after all. The bear didn't get me."

He started walking again, and she hurried to catch up.

"What's wrong with the old Sandra?" she asked.

"Nothing, Doctor. I was just hoping to meet a 'Sandy,' I guess."

****

They walked the rest of the way to the ranch more-or-less in silence, except for Austin's occasional off-key whistling. Sandra couldn't tell if he really lacked any musical ability, or if he was intentionally trying to irritate her. Either way, a new kind of frustration grew inside her with every step. Her mother had advised Sandra long ago that all men fell into one of two categories. They were either "nice guys," or they were "characters." Women were always attracted to the characters, she said, but it was the nice guys who made good husbands.

Austin Smith was a character, that was certain. Definitely not husband material, which seemed to confirm that he wouldn't make a good father, either. Except, of course, that he was determined to be the child's father. She was tempted to let him try single parenting for a month or so, so he would find out how much work it really was. That might cure him. Of course by that time he could be on the other side of the world again, and what would become of the poor child?

They were both dusty and tired by the time they reached the ranch. But to Sandra's surprise, Austin immediately went to check on the baby. Perhaps he genuinely loved the child. She had a momentary vision of Austin flying a rickety cargo plane over snowcapped mountains in bad weather with Little Jeffrey sitting on an apple crate, buckled into the co-pilot's seat next to him. No safety seat. She sighed and followed Austin into the room where Little Jeffrey lay in his crib.

Geoffrey looked up at the man who claimed to be his father.

"Boo Bah Waa Ta." "*Hi Dad.*"

"Hi, son," Austin said. "For a while there I thought I'd never see you again."

"Yeah, we almost lost you there, didn't we?" As usual, this came out as more baby babble. *"I may not be able to save you every time you get yourself in trouble, so I strongly suggest you be more careful in the future."*

Sandra leaned on the door jamb with her arms folded.

"He's a real talker," Austin said.

"That he is."

Austin placed his palm over the baby's forehead, apparently checking the child's temperature. He used his thumb to lightly pull down the skin under the baby's eyes and examine their clarity. He softly squeezed the skin on the child's arm.

"He could use some more liquids," Austin said.

"What?"

"I think he's a little dehydrated. We should feed him again."

Sandra looked at him with a cocked eyebrow. "So," she said. "You're a pediatrician now, in addition

75

to being a pilot?"

Before he could answer, the front door opened. Sandra and Austin did tandem double-takes. Standing in the doorway, Sandra saw what looked like a Christmas tree at first, green with red and white lights. It turned out to be Walter. He still wore his uniform, including short pants and the Smokey-the-Bear hat, but he had unbuttoned his shirt and applied white ointment to numerous red blotches that were swelling up all over his chest, arms, legs, and fleshy pink face.

Geoffrey gurgled, stifling a burst of laughter.

"You're alive!" Walter blurted.

"Yes, but what happened to you?" Sandra asked.

"I've discovered poison oak in Alaska." He waived one of his thickly bandaged hands in the air. Only the tips of his fingers were exposed. "I didn't think we had any here, but I must have rolled through fifty yards of it coming down that hill."

"Oh, Walter." Sandra rushed over to him, but at the last second, she stopped short of hugging him. "Come in and sit down—" She meant to say "on the couch," but she realized it would get covered with the white lotion, not to mention the poison oak. She pulled a wooden, straight-backed chair from a corner of the room and offered it to him.

Austin and Walter eyed each other warily.

"Let me make you a cup of tea, Walter," Sandra said, and she went into the kitchen. She could hear the men talking as she filled the teapot.

"Kind of humorous, isn't it?" Austin asked.

"I don't know what you're talking about."

"I thought you so-called federal agents were supposed to protect people from wildlife."

"Actually," Walter said, "we're supposed to protect the forest."

"From what I can see, the forest can take care of itself."

"Protecting God's forest is everybody's job," Geoffrey burbled from his crib.

Walter's eyes narrowed and he sat a little straighter in his chair. "You didn't kill that bear, did you? That would be illegal."

Austin gave him his best "Who are you trying to kid" look. He turned away and went to the kitchen to look for some baby formula, mostly to get away from Walter, but the walking Christmas tree followed him. Walter stopped in the doorway with his arms folded.

"I'd have to report it, if you killed that bear," he said.

Sandra looked up from the teapot. "Did what?"

"Mr. Natural here was just paying me a compliment," Austin said. "He thinks I killed that grizzly bear with my *bare* hands."

"I don't know," Geoffrey said in baby-talk. *"Is that any less believable than the fact that a baby stopped a bear from attacking you?"*

Sandra held out a tin cup full of steaming tea to Walter. When he took it from her, his eyes snapped open wide. He shifted the cup to his other hand, holding it by the handle, and setting it down on the kitchen countertop.

"Walter, you wouldn't *believe* what happened to us out there," Sandra said.

Walter blew gently on his burned finger tips.

"I thought we were all doomed," she said. "But Mr. Smith here raised his hands up and commanded the bear to stop."

Walter looked from her to Austin, disbelief plainly written on his face. Austin smiled at him. No need to mention that the bear was Gretchin. Not at that moment, anyway.

"It stopped cold," Sandra said. "Just like that. Then it turned around and ran back up the trail. I was right there and saw the whole thing." She turned to Austin. "What you did was really quite brave."

The sparkle in her eyes was bright enough to jangle something at his core. Bright enough to illuminate a corner of his soul that had been darkened much too long. He almost lost his balance.

Just then they all heard a rapid "thwump—thwump—thwumping" sound, coming from somewhere over the cabin, and growing louder.

They went back to the living room as Jake burst in through the front door.

"I think the Great Stork's a'coming back!" he yelled as he ran past them.

Walter looked toward the ceiling, as if he expected whatever was making the sound to come through the roof. Sandra looked at Austin.

"Helicopter," he said.

They walked outside to the porch and, sure enough, a bright yellow and chrome helicopter circled the ranch, not far overhead. It descended, setting down lightly in a large, empty corral and kicking up clouds of brown dust. The engine idled for a few seconds, then revved up as the helicopter lifted off. Everyone watched as it circled again, then set down, this time on the grass next to the beach by the bay. The motor stopped and a man in an orange jumpsuit dropped out of the pilot's side door. He stepped briskly around to the passenger side, opened the door, and helped a woman step out. She wore close fitting designer jeans and a shimmering gold jacket. There were rhinestone-studded cowboy boots on her feet.

"Well," Walter said. "I guess I'd better get going. I've got to file a report on that bear attack, you know." With that he hopped off the porch and ran in a direction opposite that of the approaching couple.

Sandra looked at Austin. "My mother," she said. She crossed her arms, turned around and walked back into the house, leaving Austin alone on the porch.

Austin watched Sandra's mother stepping carefully over the grassy field toward the ranch house, while the helicopter pilot walked a few respectful steps behind her. Austin didn't want to be the only one on the porch to greet Mother Coulton, so he followed Sandra inside. He found her standing in the middle of the living room, her arms folded, lightly tapping her left foot. She did not look pleased.

Chapter 6

"Maybe I should find out what the cowboys are up to," he suggested.

"No. It's all right."

Just then the pilot, still dressed in his orange jump suit, opened the front door, stepped in, and stood to one side. Her mother took three steps into the room, glanced at the surroundings, and dropped herself into a stuffed chair. The pilot stood next to her.

"Hello, dear," Mrs. Coulton said.

"Mother." Sandra struggled to keep her voice deferential.

"Don't look so happy to see me, dear."

"After our last visit I thought it might be best if we never saw each other again."

Mrs. Coulton waved her hand dismissively. "Pooh," she said. "Don't be so dramatic. You were angry. I would never hold that against you. But that was months ago, and I had to see how my baby girl was doing, here in this...this wilderness." She looked around her as though she could see the dark, dangerous forest right through the walls of the house.

"I'm doing just fine, Mother."

"Yes." She gave Austin a long, appraising look. "From what I can see, you're doing much better than you were on my last visit."

"Austin Smith," Sandra said. "Meet my mother,

Congresswoman Martha Coulton."

"Congresswoman? Pleased to meet you."

"And I you," Martha said, smiling. She extended her hand without getting up. Austin stepped forward and they shook hands.

"Ooh, goodness. A member of the United States Congress." Geoffrey wriggled a little in his homemade crib. Finally he'd run into someone important enough to merit the attention of an archangel. *"This woman must have something to do with my mission."* He would pay close attention.

Austin and Martha eyed each other warily.

"A boyfriend, Sandra? Are you ready to try that again?"

"Mr. Smith is just an acquaintance."

"Right. I understand. You don't want to rush back into anything serious, even if it does get pretty lonely up here at night." She flashed a set of perfectly capped teeth at Austin, who smiled back. Martha gestured at the man in the orange jump suit without taking her eyes off Austin. "This is Mr. Johnson." Johnson nodded almost imperceptibly behind his mirrored aviator sunglasses, but his blank expression didn't change in the slightest. "He's my pilot, and, well…my assistant."

Johnson stood more or less "at ease," with his hands clasped behind him. Sandra couldn't guess where her mother had found him and what the full extent of his duties included. The man's gray, unhealthy complexion made him look vaguely sinister, and his pallid skin contrasted sharply with his orange flight suit. A few beads of sweat were forming on the man's forehead, and she wondered if he was nervous. Who wouldn't be around her mother?

"What exactly *are* you doing in this part of Alaska, Mother?"

Martha didn't answer immediately. Instead, her gaze swept from the soles of Sandra's hiking boots to the collar of her plaid, western shirt.

Sandra idly brushed her hair with her hand, knowing it was a useless gesture. Her mother had already passed judgment on her appearance. She knew her mother's next comment would have been— "That's no way to attract a man." But Austin's presence stifled that.

"Can't a mother drop in for a simple visit to see her daughter?"

"Not if that mother is a congresswoman. A congresswoman whose last four visits outside of Washington, D.C. were to beaches in the Virgin Islands."

"Oh, nonsense." Martha dug into her handbag and brought out a pack of cigarettes. Before she could rummage around for a light, Johnson produced a yellow disposable lighter from nowhere and snapped it lit in front of Martha's face.

"Mother, please. Not in the house."

"What's the matter dear? Are you afraid I'll burn the place down?" She glanced again at the rustic furnishings. "From what I can see, that would be an improvement."

"We have a baby in the next room."

Her mother gaped at Sandra wide-eyed, then at Austin, who simply smiled and shrugged.

"A grandchild, Sandra? You really should have said something."

"He's not mine, Mother."

"Ah, I should have known. When you were a child, you brought home every stray dog in the neighborhood."

"She found this one on the roof," Austin said, pointing upward.

Martha looked sideways at Sandra as she lit her cigarette with the lighter in Mr. Johnson's still outstretched hand.

"Mother. You sat on the House Sub-Committee that investigated big tobacco. And you *know* about the health effects of secondary smoke." Martha looked to Austin, perhaps to see if he felt the same way. But he looked as though he wouldn't mind having a smoke himself.

"Health nuts," her mother said. "Sometimes I think they make up those statistics just to scare the rest of us. I've been smoking for years, and I don't see anyone dropping dead around me." As she exchanged a knowing smile with Mr. Johnson, Sandra stepped forward and deftly pulled the cigarette from between her mother's fingers while she wasn't looking.

"I can take that," Austin said.

Sandra frowned at him. She looked around for something she could use as an ash tray. When she couldn't find anything suitable she handed the cigarette to Austin, who strode into the kitchen, presumably to dispose of the offending item. Sandra watched him go and noticed that he took a quick puff before he stubbed the butt out in the sink.

Martha also watched Austin leave. "You must tell me, dear, where did you find him?"

"He came in the airplane you saw upside down in the bay."

"My, my. The most marvelous things fall out of the sky here in Alaska. Perhaps we should set out some baskets."

"Mother."

Watching Austin come back into the room, Martha said, "I hope you're not going to run away from this one, dear." Then to Austin she said quietly, "She has a history of running, you know."

"Mother."

Martha winked at Austin. "From what I can see, I don't think that's going to be a problem for *you*, but get her to tell you about that someday, before you get too attached."

"Mother!"

"But first, let's have a look at this mysterious baby of yours."

****

Martha Coulton looked down at the baby in his makeshift crib and then at her daughter.

"You say you found him on the roof?"

"*Yes, the roof*," Geoffrey said. "*And not a very dignified entrance*." He made a mental note to register a complaint about that with Gabriel. That little trick wasn't helping him blend in as an ordinary child. Hardly fair.

"I didn't find him. The cowboys did. I just got him down."

"Any idea how he got there?"

Sandra looked at Austin, fearing he would tell his story about a giant bird, but all he did was smile.

"No, I have no idea how he got there," Sandra said.

"Perhaps the stork stopped to rest while he was making his rounds and forgot about him."

Austin shrugged at Sandra, who rolled her eyes.

"Hello, little pumpkin," Martha said. She waggled her fingers at the child.

"Oh boy, another finger waggler." Geoffrey smiled up at Martha. *"What is it that compels grownups to wave at infants? It's not like I'm going anywhere."*

"What a talkative little darling." Her mother bent over and lifted Little Jeffrey from his crib. She inspected the bandana diaper and looked at Sandra. "Perhaps I've underestimated your abilities."

"I may not be a mother," Sandra said, "but I am a woman." She took the baby away from her mother and cuddled him a moment before putting him back in the crib. "You still haven't told me what you're doing here."

"My, aren't we suspicious?" Martha walked back into the living room. Johnson, Sandra, and Austin followed, in that order.

"Well?" Sandra prompted.

"Fine," Martha said, "you might as well know. As you probably have not heard, since you are out here in the middle of absolutely nowhere, there is an election next year."

"So?"

"I am up for re-election."

"Oh, yes." Geoffrey waved his stubby arms. *"I'll bet I'm here to help this Congresswoman get re-elected. That would be a suitable task for an angel of my stature."*

"That baby has a set of lungs on him, doesn't he?"

Sandra ignored her mother's attempt to distract her. She was beginning to worry about the reason for her visit. "You're a member of the House of

Representatives, Mother. You're always up for re-election."

"Precisely."

"So?"

"Elections cost money."

"And?"

"Some of my constituents have money."

"And so?"

"They want to give that money to me."

"And then you'll get re-elected."

"I knew you'd understand." Martha started for the door. Johnson almost stumbled over himself to reach it and open it before her.

"Wait, Mother!"

Martha stopped and turned to face Sandra.

"What's the catch?"

"Well…we might have to cut down a few of your trees."

"What?"

"The forest is so big. Surely you won't miss a little corner of it."

"Who are these constituents of yours?"

Martha eyed her daughter in silence for a second, then rolled her eyes.

"Huntington Mills," she said at last.

"The paper company?"

"And United Metals."

"The mining company?"

"They're some of my biggest supporters."

"They can't mine or cut timber here, it's a protected national forest. Congress is proposing that it be given wilderness status."

"For the moment."

"So. You're going to take away its national forest status, just like that?" She snapped her fingers.

"Heavens, no, Sandra. I would never do that. I have a responsibility to the American people to investigate first, then do the right thing. That's why I'm here. I'm on a fact-finding mission, you see. I'm going to find out all about this wonderful forest of yours firsthand. Before they fire up the chain saws."

Sandra resisted the impulse to choke Martha into unconsciousness. Instead, she threw up her hands. This woman couldn't possibly be her mother. They had so little in common.

"How can you *do* that, Mother?"

"Oh, I don't do it, really. Congress does." She inspected her nails. "In fact, I intend to issue a scathing press release opposing the bill, right about the time it's too late to stop it from passing."

Sandra's mind reeled. "How can getting reelected be more important than preserving a forest, not to mention my research?"

"But, darling, how many people are ever going to come up here and see your precious trees?"

Sandra opened her mouth to answer, but her mother continued, cutting her off.

"And what about all those people back in civilization whose jobs depend on the timber industry, construction, and manufacturing? What would you tell them?"

"I'd tell them to work somewhere else."

Sandra glanced at Austin for support, but Martha spoke first. "How about you, Mr. Smith? Do you think jobs and the economy are important?"

"A man's got to take care of his family," he said.

He looked at Sandra, but the look she gave him back could have wilted plastic roses.

"Yes, that's right, Mr. Smith. Where would we be without family values?"

"You seem to have done fine without any," Sandra said to her mother. Austin winced. Even Martha finally seemed to be moved by Sandra's comment.

"I'm a special case," she said coldly.

"I don't care," Sandra said. "I won't let you do it."

"Well, dear, you've got about two weeks to stop me. That's how long it will take me to get a bill to the House floor.

"I'll stop you. Somehow. I won't let you callously destroy this beautiful place."

"You sound just like your father, you know."

"I consider that a compliment."

Martha looked at Austin and spoke as though her daughter were a thousand miles away.

"That man might have been a brilliant scientist, for all I know. All I remember is that he spent very little time at home with *his* family. Perhaps he simply wasn't interested, I'll never know which." She shook her head slowly.

My, how bitter. How sad. Geoffrey's mind churned. This driven woman, a member of the most powerful government on earth, had lost all interest in what makes life special. Now she was planning to destroy the very thing on which her daughter's career depended, just to get reelected. Or was it to spite her dead husband?

Deciding that Martha's subconscious might not be too hospitable, Geoffrey gently probed Sandra's memory for the name of her father. *Ah, there it is.*

Harvey Coulton. He made a mental note to check the Heavenly Roles for Harvey. From Sandra's fond memories of her father, Geoffrey felt certain the man had easily slipped through St. Peter's Gate. Not to say it was all that hard anymore. Pete had been in charge of the Gates forever, and lately he spent too much time on some social media site and wanted everybody to be his friend. A lot of angels thought the old fart had lost the ability to discriminate. But, the Boss steadfastly refused to assign the aging saint to any other duty. "This is not a democracy," he would say.

Considering Martha, Geoffrey guessed that Harvey was one soul who found some relief in the "'til death do us part" portion of the marriage ceremony. Maybe Geoffrey could coax the man away from Paradise long enough to discuss his wife's poor spiritual condition.

"Mother," Sandra said quietly. "Father loved you very much. I will not listen to you talk about him like that."

Martha Coulton said nothing. She simply looked at her daughter a bit sadly, then turned to Austin.

"Do you have a wife, Mr. Smith?"

"No."

"That's too bad." A shadow of a smile crossed Martha's face as she glanced at Sandra. "My daughter almost had a husband, once."

"Mother."

"Oh, you haven't told Mr. Smith about your hair?"

"Mother."

"Well, you did what you had to do, I suppose. And, your hair still looks so marvelous, so…"

Sandra glared at her mother, who seemed to be gauging how much more she could say. Austin looked at Sandra with renewed interest and raised eyebrows.

But Sandra wanted to know more about her mother's plans for the forest.

"Mother," she said one more time.

"Sorry dear. I do have to go." Johnson opened the front door. "I'm going out to commune with nature now."

Nature? The idea that Martha Coulton would ever consider communing with Nature sent Geoffrey's mind spinning. *"You shouldn't go. I've got to help you."* Should he let Martha get away, or should he think of some way to keep her close to her daughter, and Austin? What was he to do?

Martha stopped in the doorway and looked around the room one more time. "Don't tell me. I don't even want to know if the taxpayers' money is helping pay for any of...this." She stepped outside. "And don't worry. I'll give you at least twenty-four hours warning before the bulldozers come through your front door." Then she was gone.

Sandra and Austin looked at each other.

Austin sighed. At least he knew where Sandra had gotten her stubborn streak. He wanted to take her into his arms and hug her, but she would have none of it, not while she was fuming about her mother.

"Oh, go on, you big lug," Geoffrey said. *"She needs you. Even if you can't see her aura, it's written all over her face."* Geoffrey inspected the swirling, vividly-colored emotions that everyone had produced. Clouds of it lingered, drifting about the room. It would take minutes, perhaps hours, for such a strong and impressive display of emotions to dissipate back into the ether. *How can people function in such a chaotic*

milieu? It's enough to make me want a hug.

"An unbelievable woman," Sandra hissed.

Austin took a step toward her but stopped. "How can you say that about your *nescko*?"

"My what?" Sandra looked at Austin sideways.

"Your *nescko*. It's a Cheyenne word for mother, but it's more than that. Your mother's a woman who knows what she wants and knows how to get it. You have to admire that."

"Admire her? I'd like to strangle her. And you deserve the same, if you support her. Whatever she's doing, it's just to spite my father. Or me."

It's so sad. Geoffrey saw much more in Martha than either of his current human parents could. He saw the pain that lurked just below the surface. Pain over feelings Martha desperately wanted to share with her daughter.

"That's really holding a grudge," Austin said.

"That's my mother."

"And now she's going to take revenge against your father by hurting you?"

"She was right, you see. I am just like my father."

"What does that mean?"

Sandra looked at him. He could see her appraising him, trying to decide how much she could open up to him. She looked away and crossed her arms.

"I guess," she said, "it means that I never had much time for her, either, after I grew up. Just like my father."

Or any family, for that matter, Austin decided, as he sadly finished the thought for her. "I guess we're a lot alike in that respect, too. I haven't had much time for a family, either. Up to now."

Sandra turned away and looked out a window. "You can't compare our lives," she said stiffly. "At least I've had some direction. Some goals. And I'm not compromising my principles for some job, or money."

Austin wasn't sure if her comments referred to him or her mother. Probably both.

"I think I'd give everything I own to have my mother back, and a family," he said.

"I'm sorry, but from what I can see, that wouldn't be giving up too much. Besides, I'm not you, am I?"

Sandra had barely finished speaking when she strode from the room. Austin saw the pain in her eyes, and he knew she didn't mean her hurtful words. He exhaled slowly and looked out the window. As he had so often in his life, he fought down the familiar loneliness that crept into his bones. It was loneliness as vast as the rolling grass plains of the Montana reservation he had fled. When he left he vowed he would never be lonely again, but nothing in the bazaars of India or the jungles of Indonesia kept the loneliness away, and it had been an empty vow—until he met Sandra Coulton. When he regained consciousness on her couch and set eyes on her it was like being reborn. He knew at once what he needed in his life, and he steeled himself again in the face of what looked like an ever more difficult challenge.

This woman he was so drawn to may have had an easier life than he, but she had experienced her own pain. Whoever or whatever had injured her so badly had given her some steel, too, and she wore it like armor around her emotions. She wasn't ready to let down her defenses and accept him into her life. She would be a tough nut to crack. He prayed he was up to the task.

Chapter 7

Uh, oh. The electromagnetic waves of the incoming radio message traveled at the speed of light, waking Geoffrey from his nap long before the call reached Misha Ranch.

Something's wrong. I'd better let this message go through.

A stony, awkward silence between Sandra and Austin lasted most of the following day, but it was finally broken by the electronic crackle of the radio speaker. Sandra was surprised to hear a familiar voice breaking through the static.

"—dra? Sandra? Damn it, Sandra, why don't you answer me?"

"That's my mother," Sandra said. The fact that her mother was personally using a radio, not to mention the urgent tone of her voice, told Sandra something must be seriously wrong.

Austin looked up from his game of solitaire. "Is she always that friendly on the phone?"

"She must be in trouble." Sandra dropped the notes she had been studying and bolted from the couch to the radio.

"I'm here," she said, almost before she had pushed the microphone button. But her mother couldn't hear her.

"Sandra-a-a," Sandra heard when she released the

button. Then she faintly heard someone else, speaking in a slow, halting voice. It sounded like Mr. Johnson had been drinking.

"Let go...the button. Can't hear—"

Sandra jumped in. "Mother. You have to let go of the microphone button when you aren't talking. Otherwise you can't hear me."

"—damned radio anyway. Why couldn't we have brought a cell phone? What? Oh."

"Mother?"

"Yes, dear." Her mother suddenly sounded as calm as if she were sitting in the next room.

"What's going on?" Sandra asked.

"Hmmm? Oh, yes. It seems that we've gotten stuck out here in your little forest."

"How's that?"

"Mr. Johnson chose today of all days to contract some sort of illness. Can you imagine that? Right in the middle of the wilderness."

"Mother, are you still in the air? Or are you on the ground?"

Austin appeared at her shoulder. Sandra turned to look at him as she spoke and felt an odd sense of security as she looked into his eyes. The simple fact that he was there comforted her.

"—believably inconsiderate, if you ask me."

"Mother."

"Of course this is your mother. Haven't you heard a word I've said?"

"Let go of the button when you're not talking."

"Oh, all right."

"What's wrong with Mr. Johnson?"

"He's sick. I told you that."

Austin took the microphone gently but firmly out of Sandra's hand. His touch sent a delicious electrical spark skittering up Sandra's arm. The sensation surprised her, especially since they had been giving each other the cold shoulder for most of the afternoon.

"Mrs. Coulton. This is Austin Smith. Please describe Mr. Johnson's symptoms for me." He spoke in tones that would have served any doctor well at a patient's bedside, and Sandra studied him closely. She wondered if he had starred in an episode of General Hospital, or some other medical soap opera on television. She didn't have a television, but against her better judgment, her respect for this wayward Adonis grudgingly inched up a notch.

"What are you, some kind of doctor?" Martha asked.

"Just tell me what his symptoms are, please."

"I don't know. He's sick. When he talks he doesn't make any sense, and he can hardly stand up. Right now, he's lying on the ground muttering nonsense."

"That would be fever," Austin said. "Does he have a headache?"

"Oh, yes. I've had enough migraines to recognize a splitting headache when I see one."

"How does his skin look?"

"I beg your pardon?"

"Does he have any rash?"

They heard silence for a few moments, apparently while Martha inspected Mr. Johnson's complexion.

"I'll say. He's breaking out like fireworks on the Fourth of July."

Austin held the microphone against his chest.

"It could be Rocky Mountain Spotted Fever," he

said. "A bad case."

"Rocky Mountain Spotted Fever?" Sandra had heard of the disease, of course, transmitted by ticks. "That can be fatal if it's not treated, right?" What was she doing asking Austin, anyway? She was the biologist.

He nodded. When she took the microphone back from him, her hand lingered imperceptibly longer in his than it needed to. Spark. Spark.

"Mother, how are *you* feeling?"

"Other than being very put out right now, I feel fine, dear. But Mr. Johnson had better get well soon."

Sandra could imagine the scathing looks her mother was giving the hapless pilot.

"I'd like to get out of here before the sun goes down."

"Mother. We think Mr. Johnson may have contracted Rocky Mountain Spotted Fever."

"What? We're nowhere near the Rocky Mountains, are we?"

"That's just the name. He may have been bitten by a tick. That's what made him ill."

"Oh, my."

****

Geoffrey stirred in his crib. *I've heard of it, too. It's a rickettsial disease. Chances are he won't die—I don't see any aural indications that he's due in heaven, anyway. But Mr. Johnson may be in for a rough time.* Geoffrey considered whether he should do something to help the poor man. Humans were such a frail species, and prone to mishaps. Even the multitude of heaven's minions couldn't help them out of every misfortune.

Then it came to him. *Gadzooks! What if this was*

it—his reason for being here? After all, it wasn't just the pilot who needed his help. A Congresswoman, too, was stranded in the middle of the wilderness. Important legislation could be affected. A whole forest might be at stake.

"Ah, Gabriel you devil."

As if on cue, the air above Geoffrey shimmered, and Gabriel's face appeared, lips pursed.

"I'm not giving you any hints," the vision said. "You do what you think you have to."

"Don't play coy with me. I've got you now, and you know it. So what if I have to save the congresswoman as an infant? Did you think being a child out in the big bad woods would keep me from winning our bet? This will be cherub's play."

"Pride, Geoffrey," Gabriel said. "I've always said that pride would be your downfall."

"Right. By the way, what did we bet? I still can't remember that."

"Don't worry. I'll let you know when I win," Gabriel said. His smile held no warmth. The air shimmered and he was gone.

"Like...heck you'll win!" But his nemesis had disappeared.

Geoffrey reached out with his heavenly consciousness and, swirling over the forest, he found the bright yellow helicopter in a meadow at the base of a craggy peak. Its painted metal skin shone brightly in the clearing where it had come to rest.

Slowly, carefully, he located the life signs of the small insect on the back of Albert Johnson's neck and caressed the creature's aura gently. *"Come on, little fella. You've done enough."* The animal stirred but then hesitated.

"Headstrong little bugger, eh?" Geoffrey caressed the tick a little more forcefully. Once again it hesitated but, slowly, eventually, it crept down Johnson's shirt collar and fell off, disappearing into the bug-sized jungle of grass. Geoffrey was a little annoyed that it had taken the tiny creature so long to get the message, but he shook it off. *At least that's a start.*

****

Sandra could tell from the edge in her mother's voice that her skin crawled at the thought that ticks could be anywhere within a hundred yards of her.

"Just how long will Mr. Johnson be this way?" Martha asked.

Sandra didn't have a good answer. She let Austin slide the microphone smoothly back out of her hand. Spark. Spark. Spark. Was he getting the same sensation? Somewhere deep inside her, a tiny, long-extinguished flame re-ignited. She smiled, but she considered a physical attraction to Austin silly. She hadn't been seriously attracted to a man in years, so she was likely to be more susceptible than usual to any fluctuation in her hormone levels. Too bad the energy mankind generated in its sex drive couldn't be captured to keep the lights on. If it could, she might have more interest in it. As it was, she shook off the feeling. Her mother was in trouble and her body only wanted to snuggle against Austin's chest.

Geoffrey watched Sandra's aura sparkle around the edges and unfold, slowly coming alive with delicious flavors and hues.

Ah, yes. Amour, lieben, love. God's ultimate gift to mankind. After all these millennia, it's one of the few things I'd be willing to trade my wings for. He sighed once, then concentrated again on the problem at hand.

"Mrs. Coulton," Austin said. "Mr. Johnson needs treatment. The sooner the better."

"Treatment with what?"

"Antibiotics."

"Okay," Martha, said through clenched teeth. "I'll just call the pharmacy and have them deliver."

Austin chuckled diplomatically.

Only then did Sandra realize that someone might have to rescue her mother. The helicopter might carry some emergency supplies, but would it have antibiotics? Either way, she couldn't imagine her mother walking out of the forest with a sick man.

"Can we go get your mother and Mr. Johnson?" Austin asked.

"Only on horseback. Even if there was a decent road, we don't have a vehicle that could make the trip."

Austin's eyebrows shot up.

"We haul hay around the ranch in a junky truck, but I wouldn't trust it in the backcountry," Sandra said. "And you can only get to the ranch by boat or float plane."

"Mrs. Coulton," Austin said into the microphone. "Please look under the passenger seat and locate the helicopter's first-aid kit. It will be in a red or yellow plastic box." Martha did so and read the labels of the contents to Austin. There were no antibiotics. But there was aspirin.

"Give Mr. Johnson some of the aspirin and keep him hydrated," he said. Then he looked at Sandra. "That's about all she's going to be able to do for him, right now."

"Someone's going to have to go get them, aren't they?" Sandra said. "And take the antibiotics to Johnson."

"Yes."

Sandra mentally inventoried the cowboys for a list of men who could make the trip. All of them could ride a horse but none of them had much medical training. More importantly, none of them could fly a helicopter.

"Where are you located?" Austin asked Martha.

"How on earth would I know?"

Sandra took the microphone back from Austin, pausing to catch her breath as she did so. So much electricity. She was surprised they didn't burn out the radio circuits every time she and Austin touched hands.

"Mother, look around you. Do you see any significant landmarks?"

"Well…there's an awfully big mountain we've landed next to."

"Does it have snow on the peak?"

There was staticky silence while Martha apparently looked out of the helicopter and up at the mountain.

"Yes, it does."

"That would be Mount St. Lawrence. It's the highest peak in the region, and it would still have snow on it, even this late in the season."

Geoffrey rubbed his chubby hands together. *"They'll rename it Mount St. Geoffrey when I get through."*

Austin smiled. Sandra smiled back, proud of her resourcefulness. "In what direction is the sun?" She asked.

"How on earth would I know," Martha said.

"There will be a compass on the, uh, dashboard,"

Austin said.

"Did you hear that, mother?"

"Yes. Give me a minute." Sandra looked at the sun out the window and noted the time on her wristwatch.

"It's to left of the mountain from where I am. The dashboard says that's west."

"Is there a stream nearby?"

"Yes, a very pretty one."

"Good." Sandra looked at Austin. "That means they're on this side, on the southern slope. I think I know where, more or less. It shouldn't be too hard to find them."

"Mother," she said, "keep the radio turned on so we can call you back if we have to. We're coming to get you."

Austin gave her a look that said, "What do you mean we?"

"Of course," Martha said. "I'll just dip my sore feet in this nice creek here and wait for you."

Sandra ignored Austin's questioning look. She could tell from the sound of her mother's voice that she expected to be rescued in the next thirty minutes.

"Mother."

"It's really quite beautiful here, now that I look at it."

"Mother."

"Yes, dear."

"It will take us two or three days to reach you," Sandra said. "Maybe more. We'll have to send someone on horseback."

"Two days! You don't expect me to stay in these awful woods with a sick man for two days. Where will we sleep? What will we eat?"

"You can sleep in the helicopter. And look around the cockpit. Most of the aircraft in Alaska carry survival rations."

"Survival rations? Good Lord. How do you expect me to live on survival rations?"

"If Mr. Johnson can't fly, it's the only way," Sandra said.

"Hold on a second," Martha said. Sandra heard muffled scuffling in the background, including her mother's frantic voice saying, "you...right now...fly this thing...damn it!" Then her mother spoke into the microphone again. "He's seems to be sleeping at the moment," she said with some annoyance. Then, more quietly, she said, "Please hurry, dear."

"We'll get started as soon as we can."

Sandra set the microphone back in its cradle and looked at Austin. "Can you fly a helicopter any better than you can an airplane?"

"If I said no, would I still have to go?"

"You're the only pilot we have."

"*I can fly.*" Geoffrey wanted to get off the ranch, even if it was only for a day or two. And he wanted to win his bet.

Austin sighed and listened to Little Jeffery, cooing and gurgling. A look of concern crossed his face.

"It won't be that bad," Sandra said. "I can show you on the map pretty much right where they are."

"You're not going?"

"Do I need to?"

"She's *your* mother. Besides, I probably wouldn't find her without you."

"Someone has to stay here with Little Jeffrey. I can send one of the cowboys with you."

"*But I want to go, too!*" Geoffrey pouted. Clearly Gabriel thought putting Geoffrey in a baby's body would keep him from going on the rescue mission. But Geoffrey could see where things were going and, with a roll of his eyes, he flicked the tiniest dab of angel dust at Austin's forehead. A pinch of friendly combativeness—not quite hostility—but mixed with some decisiveness. Just a little something to move the conversation in the direction he wanted it to go.

"Oh, no," Austin said. "If I go, my boy is going with me."

"What? You can't take a baby out into the woods."

"Why not?"

"Well, for one thing, as you now know, it's full of bears."

"Ah, but I have the touch. Remember?" He held both hands in the air and wiggled his fingers. "The big bad bears don't mess with Austin Smith."

"Just because one bear decides not to eat you for lunch doesn't mean they all won't."

"Why not? Yesterday you thought I had invented a pretty good defense against bear attacks."

"That hasn't been proven, and in any case, I'm pretty sure you're not Saint Francis of Assisi."

"*That quack!*" Geoffrey tried to cross his arms in indignation, but they were still too short. "*I am so tired of Frank getting credit for being a friend of the animals. Any cherub can pet a squirrel. And Frank never had to work with animals like these.*" He gestured a chubby hand in the direction of Austin and Sandra.

At that moment Little Jeffrey's biological imperative took Geoffrey by surprise. "*Oops.*" *I guess I should watch these emotional outbursts.* He applied another angel trick to keep the smell to a minimum.

"He's my son," Austin said. "And I can protect him like, well, he was my own son." His eyes narrowed. "Besides, if I go into the forest without him, how do I know he'll be here when I get back? I won't take that chance."

"What, you don't trust me?"

A semblance of a smile crept onto his lips. "Look," he said. "In spite of what you think, I can take care of the baby just fine. So make up your mind. If you want someone to fly that helicopter, I can do it, but I won't go without my son." He went back to the kitchen table to resume playing solitaire.

Sandra felt her jaw lock as she thought about the situation. Austin simply had to go. The only question was who was going with him? The cowboys knew the country reasonably well, but if even if one of them went, Austin would still want to take Little Jeffrey.

Her gaze took in Austin's strong arms and broad shoulders. She realized there wasn't much she could do to stop him from taking Little Jeffrey with him whenever he wanted to go. And yes, there were bears in the forest, but a hostile encounter wasn't all that likely. Lots of people went camping with their kids. Even so, she wished Austin could be a little more sensible in his new role as a parent.

She sighed. She knew she couldn't leave the poor baby alone in Austin's hands, no matter how well-meaning the man was. Her mother and Mr. Johnson needed to be rescued, so it wasn't a good time to fight over Little Jeffrey.

"Let me know when you've decided," Austin said without looking up from his card game.

She saw him put a red queen on a red king, cheating to keep from losing the game.

"You're not exactly helping," she said. Then she sighed. "I've been up that trail before, and I know we can find them if I went along."

"So, you want to go with me?" He grinned.

"It looks like I don't have any choice." Plus, the ride might give her enough time to convince Austin that the baby needed a mother, not a bush pilot.

Austin scrunched up his face.

"Maaa, Ta Pa Buaagh," Little Jeffrey said.

The odor of his boo-boo reached Sandra's nose, too. She crooked her thumb in the direction of the crib.

"Your turn," she said to Austin. "Let me see what kind of parenting skills you have."

"Gaa Pa Ta, Bow." *"Oh, boy! Road trip!"*

Chapter 8

Sandra insisted that they have their "wheels-in-the-well" and be on the trail by "oh-dark-thirty," which reminded Austin of his stint in the Marines. Before they left, they started arguing over who should carry Little Jeffrey in the makeshift backpack, the one with two holes cut in the bottom to accommodate the baby's legs. Austin quietly listened to Sandra explain why she, or just about any woman, was better suited to look after a baby than he, or just about any man, and in the end, he didn't put up much of a fight. He simply looked at her while she talked, marveling at the soft texture of her lips, the peaches-and-cream complexion of her skin, and the bounce of her art-project hair as she cocked her head sideways whenever she made a point.

He knew Sandra wouldn't have it any other way. When she was done talking he handed her the pack and said, "Okay." He hadn't expected her to let him take the baby on the trail at all, and he felt a little guilty about that, even though old Four-of-a-Kind had taken him into bear country on horseback many times when Austin was a mere child. If Sandra wanted to ride all day with a wiggling baby boy on her back, she was welcome. At least that way he could keep an eye on the both of them at the same time.

Sandra gave Austin a surprised, sideways look when he gave in so quickly. She wondered if he'd be as compliant about other issues for the entire trip.

"Traveling by horseback isn't as fast as by helicopter," she said, stating the obvious. "It will take us days to find Mother, and then, only if she's where I think she is."

"That's okay." Austin kneed his horse lightly in the ribs and tugged on the saddle cinch one more time. "I'll try to enjoy the scenery."

"With any luck we won't encounter any bears, but if we do, I'll let you take care of them." She gave him a wink.

"My pleasure," he said, but he sincerely hoped his services as a bear fighter would not be necessary. "Before we go, tell me why your buddy Walter can't go get your mother. Doesn't the Forest Service have a truck or something?"

She looked at him and rolled her eyes. "Would you want to depend on Walter in this situation?"

"I see your point. There isn't anyone else nearby?"

"Sunspots are messing with the radio and I can't call anyone else. Besides, there are no roads and if we took a truck we might run out of gas. Horses are the quickest, surest way to get Mother out of her predicament, not to mention helping Mr. Johnson. And we shouldn't leave a perfectly good helicopter sitting in the middle of the forest."

"Okay, okay." He held up his gloved hands, surrendering again. "Let's do it."

****

Leading the way on horseback, Sandra forded Deadhorse Creek, crossed into a small grassy meadow, and found a trail that wound into the nearby pine forest. The treetops were shrouded in early morning fog. She and Austin each led one of two spare horses. The extra horses carried supplies, and they would be needed for her mother and Mr. Johnson to ride if the helicopter couldn't be flown out of the forest. Sandra prayed the helicopter would fly. She couldn't imagine her mother camping out on the trail, much less riding back to the ranch on a horse.

They traveled at a modest but steady pace, stopping only for quick snacks or to feed and change Little Jeffrey. Apparently Austin knew his way around a horse, but Sandra was curious to know whether the long ride would punish him. By mid-afternoon, she was impressed by the way he kept up. It was a pleasant day, and her concerns about bringing the baby along seemed groundless. The forest surrounded her like a comforting old friend.

By late afternoon, a cool breeze rustled the spruce tops, giving the woods an empty sound. Sandra knew it was anything but. All around them nature was stirring to life, anticipating the night. Everything from beetles to mule deer stalked underbrush, looking for dinner or a mate. Or both.

Dinner for Sandra would consist of dried soup and some bread she'd baked at the ranch. Hearty, even if not gourmet. As for a mate, the only available man within miles was Austin Smith. She remembered the electricity tingling her fingers when they passed the microphone back and forth the day before. She wrote that off as a purely physical reaction, and the sheer newness of him. She admitted an immediate sexual attraction to the man, but what kind of catch would a man like Austin make? Their lives were utterly different. She had her research, which required her to carefully plan things in advance and pay close attention to every detail as it progressed. Austin, on the other hand, could take off every morning—literally, since he was a pilot—and fly to some new, exotic location whenever the whim struck him. No plan. No obligations. Nothing to tie him down.

How could one woman satisfy the needs of such a drifter? Indeed, what woman had spent the night in Austin's strong arms more than a year ago? With a twinge of jealousy, she tried to think of any likely candidates in Prudhomme Bay. She knew a few of the women there, and for the most part they didn't seem like the type for a one-night stand, even with a man as attractive as Austin.

Women who migrated from the lower forty-eight states to Prudhomme Bay were not much different than women anywhere else. There was the usual mix of professionals like herself, who still looked somewhat out of place in the wilder parts of Alaska. Then there were housewives and waitresses, and other workers. There were even a few who worked on the oil rigs. Some women were still plying the world's oldest profession, attracting the oil patch men who filtered back and forth from the rigs and pipelines in the production fields farther north. Austin might have spent the night with one of them. She would probably never know.

****

Geoffrey didn't mind the ride at all. He used his angel skills to subtly lighten his baby body and dampen some of the jostling as he rode along on Sandra's back. He also lightened Sandra just a wee bit. If she noticed, she didn't give any indication, and Geoffrey spent the day chatting with birds and admiring God's beautiful creations as he rode along. He was confident that saving Congresswoman Coulton was his goal for this mission, and he was well on his way to winning his bet. What could Gabriel possibly do to stop him now?

****

For Austin, it was the longest he'd been on a horse since he roamed the Montana hills as a teenager. His rear end had turned to stone, and his legs might be too stiff to bend by the time they stopped for the night. But he wasn't about to complain. There was much to be thankful for. All day long he rode behind Sandra, where he couldn't help but admire her ability to sit a horse. Her square shoulders and the arch of her back accentuated the thrust of her hips and her heart-shaped bottom, which undulated with every hoof-step. The sight of all those womanly parts sensuously rolling back-and-forth and side-to-side took his mind off of his own growing soreness.

And then there was his son. Little Jeffrey talked up a storm, waving his arms from the pack on Sandra's back like he was directing an orchestra. It was easy for Austin to imagine that the three of them were a family, out for a Sunday picnic. That idea pleased him, even if it was only a fantasy. And if he wanted a different kind of fantasy, he could go back to watching Sandra ride.

What would she be like in bed? Probably nothing to write home about. After all, the woman's brain was likely filled from wall to wall with statistics, experiments, and data. Could she let herself go long enough to make love? It might be like making love to a computer. But Sandra's perfect body argued otherwise. Her gently curving hips and firm breasts spoke volumes about the pleasure in store for any man lucky enough to be let in through her defenses.

Sex had never been hard for Austin to get, if he wanted it. But he wanted more than sex from Sandra Coulton, a lot more. Unfortunately, he didn't have much experience at forging long-term relationships with women, especially when the woman in question wasn't interested. He couldn't blame her. Before he met Sandra the word *relationship* made his skin crawl.

Most of the time he could endear himself to a woman, at least enough to be on friendly, if not intimate, terms. But Sandra was more cautious than most of the women Austin had met. At some point in her life, she must have been deeply hurt. Unfortunately, it was probably by a guy much like himself. The last thing in the world he wanted to do was hurt Sandra Coulton, but how could he prove that? That problem kept him fully occupied when his fantasies didn't cause his thoughts to stray into more erotic territory.

They stopped at last to make camp in a small clearing next to a bubbling creek, swollen with spring runoff. At Sandra's insistence, they brought along two small pup tents to camp in, one for each of them.

Austin chuckled. "Wouldn't we be warmer if we both slept in the same tent?" He asked this in part hoping she'd say yes, and in part because he knew his question would get a rise out of Sandra.

"It won't get that cold," she said. "Besides, except for privacy, we won't need the tents at all, unless it rains."

Geoffrey eyed the heavens. He didn't relish the idea of sleeping outside on the ground. He preferred the downy soft pillows of the passing clouds, but he'd settle for a tent, if that was all they had.

Austin felt a bit helpless, like he had lost his touch. Sandra had ignored all of his feeble come-ons during the day, but maybe she had been out of circulation so long, she might not have recognized them for what they were.

Sandra looked up from her map. "Hey," she said. "Don't look so glum. We rode hard and put a lot of miles behind us today, but I had another reason for stopping at this particular spot. I think you're going to like it."

The fact that she would do anything he liked piqued his curiosity. He watched her rummage around in one of the bags her spare horse had carried and pulled out what looked like a black silk scarf, wadded into a small ball.

"Swim suit," she said.

"That?"

She looked at it too, nestled in the palm of her hand. "It's lightweight," she said. "For backpacking."

His crooked smile did little to mask his confusion. Even in summer, the water in an Alaskan creek would be freezing cold. Then again, he remembered seeing Sandra bathe at the waterfall, but that was downstream and at a lower altitude, where the water would have been a little warmer. Still, most of the Marines he'd served with would have shriveled to the size of figs if they swam in a frigid Alaskan creek.

"Okay," he said tentatively.

"No, I'm not crazy," she said. "There's a hot spring, right beside the river, just downstream. The water comes out of the ground at around eighty degrees Fahrenheit. It's perfect for soothing saddle sores."

Geoffrey waved his chubby little arms. "*Oh, boy, a hot tub!*"

"But I don't have a suit." Austin's smile turned impish. He envisioned the two of them playing naked in the water, their skin glistening under the late afternoon sun.

"No problem," Sandra said. "You'll just have to wait until I'm done."

Austin's smile vanished, then reappeared. "I'll use my boxer shorts," he said. "They need washing anyway."

Sandra ignored him as she gathered up Little Jeffrey, a towel, and a small pack. Then she started walking down the trail. "I'll be back in about thirty minutes." She gestured at the knife lashed to Austin's leg. "See if you can do something useful with that thing, like starting a fire and fixing supper." Then she was gone.

"Well, I'll be damned," Austin said to the surrounding trees. He sat down and leaned against his saddle, which he had propped against a fallen log, and stretched his legs out to their full length. "That woman is a one-off." He tried to ignore the fact that she was undressing a few yards away. What would she really think if he joined her after ten minutes or so? Would she let him jump in if he went for a little walk and accidently stumbled on the hot springs? He shook his head. He'd end up in a lot more hot water than he bargained for. Still...

He set about starting a fire, then poked through Sandra's saddle bags looking for dinner as she instructed. What he found did little to stir his appetite. Dried fruit, powdered soup, and instant oatmeal. The only thing that interested him was a loaf of home-made bread. He grabbed that, tossed her bags aside and reached for his own. Somewhere near the bottom of one of them he found the half jar of peanut butter he had taken from the ranch kitchen.

"Ah," he said. "Dinner is served."

****

The hot springs pool was one of Sandra's favorite places in the forest. Its waters seeped from a rock outcropping and spilled into a basin next to the frigid mountain stream. On earlier visits she had enlarged the pool by stacking flat stones until they formed a low wall, partially damming the water at the point where it flowed into the stream. The pool was about fifteen feet across now, and its steaming waters were surrounded by trees on three sides and had a stunning view of the nearby mountains. She'd have built a cabin on this spot if it had been more accessible.

She drank in the beauty of the site and started to unbutton her dusty shirt. Then she remembered the incident at the lake where she conducted her research. Austin could have been spying on her then. Or Walter. Or both of them. They had never quite cleared up that little incident. Suddenly cautious, she moved behind some bushes as she stripped off the rest of her clothing and put on the swimsuit.

Ever the gentleman, Geoffrey averted his gaze at, well, more or less the right moment.

"*Hubba hubba!*"

Once Sandra had her suit on, she turned her attention to the baby, who was overdue for a bath. In a moment of genius, she brought along an old folding camp stool. The seat fabric had worn out long ago, but the short metal frame was still solid. She had draped sheets of strong plastic loosely across the seat opening. Now the unit made a handy portable baby bath or small crib. She lifted Little Jeffrey out of his pack, took off his diaper and placed him gently down into the plastic sling. It held him perfectly.

"Every bit as comfortable as the old Roman baths," Geoffrey observed. He even had a handmaiden to attend him. He would enjoy this. Just like the good old days. He waited expectantly for his ablutions.

But Sandra couldn't resist taking a dip first. She set Little Jeffrey and his makeshift bathtub on the only level surface, a broad, flat stone on top of the dam at the edge of the pool. Water overtopped the stone, but it passed through the thin metal legs and just under the bottom of the plastic forming the baby's tub. It seemed safe enough. Then she slid into the water up to her neck. She closed her eyes and let the soothing warmth work its magic on her sore muscles. A gentle mist rose around her and caressed her face. Nothing felt better after a long day's ride. Normally she wouldn't have needed the swimming suit, but with Austin nearby, she wouldn't go in the buff.

After a few minutes her muscles relaxed and her mind began to wander. She thought about the man waiting for her back at the camp, and she wondered what it would be like to have him next to her. Naked? Yeah, naked. Why not? She wriggled her toes on the sandy bottom of the pool as she let her imagination go. In her mind's eye, she could practically see him striding through the mist, standing at the edge of the water, unashamed, bare muscles rippling. She giggled. The image almost took her breath away.

She smiled, but it was only a fantasy. She wasn't the kind of woman who had casual sex. She wasn't even looking for romance, but just the idea of slipping between the sheets with a man built like Austin Smith kindled a warm glow inside her. It was just a harmless daydream, even if she couldn't seem to forget it. In her mind's eye, Austin appeared through the mist again. She imagined him pausing long enough for her to notice him, standing at the edge of the pool, challenging her to say something. The nerve of the man. She smiled, ever so slightly, but her heart raced. Otherwise, she tried to remain cool and show a certain indifference. She turned her head away to rub her shoulder, but not before giving him a teasing glimpse of her breasts. She closed her eyes and giggled again. She hadn't fanaticized about a man in years.

Across from her, she heard water gently lapping as Austin lowered himself into the steaming pool. Funny, her daydreams never came with audio before. Maybe she had been in the hot water a little too long. She opened her eyes and saw the real Austin Smith grinning back at her through the fog, sitting a few feet away.

"Thirty minutes is up," he said.

"What?" She leaped up in surprise and indignation. Or at least she tried to leap up, and it wasn't very dignified. She rose out of the water so quickly she lost her footing on the slippery bottom of the pool and immediately fell backward. The wave she created raised Little Jeffrey off his perch. To her horror, the baby, still in his cradle, slid with the wave into the current of the swift mountain stream and was swept away.

"*Man overboard!*" Geoffrey yelled. He managed to keep the crib upright. Once afloat, he and his makeshift boat dashed between rocks and under overhanging branches. He slowed the rushing water as much as he could without making it look like pancake syrup, then he searched frantically for a plausible means of escape, some way to save himself without making it look like divine intervention.

Back at the hot springs, Austin sprang to his feet, leaped over the rock dam and past Sandra, a blur of flesh, racing after the baby. Sandra hopped up, too, and scrambled out of the pool. She knew a shortcut downstream, and she pushed her way through the underbrush, praying that she would find Austin holding Little Jeffrey safely in his arms. In her haste she slipped again and dove forward. As she went down a protruding branch caught the shoulder strap of her swimming suit, temporarily slowing her fall. When the thin, skin-tight fabric had stretched to its limits, it snapped and tore off of her chest with a "whoosh."

She landed heavily on her hands and knees, now with her breasts exposed. She stood up and snatched the remnants of the top of her swimming suit from the branch, but there wasn't much left of it, so she dropped it and ran. She could see Austin's naked body darting through the trees like a Greek Olympian. He rounded a bend and went out of sight. She followed him, praying again that the baby was okay.

She pushed her way through some bushes and found Austin standing motionless, thigh deep in the middle of the stream with his impressive back and tight bottom facing her, but without the baby. Water rushed around his legs as he stood with his hands at his sides. He was looking down over a small waterfall. She had the sickening realization that Little Jeffrey must have gone over and…no, it was unthinkable.

She stopped next to Austin, only slightly more aware of his nakedness than her own, ignoring the freezing water and the goose bumps covering her body. She looked at the water spilling away in front of her and heard it splashing in a pool, fifteen feet or so below them. Tears welled in her eyes. She couldn't see the baby. A sob escaped her throat.

"It's my fault," she gasped. "I shouldn't have—"

"But he's okay," Austin said.

"What? Oh. I suppose he is." She assumed Austin meant that Little Jeffrey had gone on to a better place—heaven, of course. She sobbed and let the tears stream down her already wet face.

"But we'll need to get him out of there pretty soon," Austin said.

"What?" She wiped her nose with the back of her muddy hand and stared at him. He pointed down over the falls. She leaned farther forward, her gaze following his arm until she finally saw what he had been looking at. A few feet below them, Little Jeffrey's cradle had landed on the thin branch of an aspen tree that hung over the stream.

"Oh, my," she sobbed. The baby was indeed okay, so far at least. The momentum of the stream must have thrown him clear of the waterfall. He wasn't even wet, and he looked up at them, waving his short arms and smiling.

"Pretty clever, huh?" His mortal caretakers had no way of knowing that he had frozen local time just as he plunged over the falls. Then he coaxed a tree next to the stream into growing the still flimsy branch on which he now rested. From his perspective, the lengthy

interruption had also given him a chance to review a volume of 14th century Italian literature, in the original Florentine, a treat he'd promised himself for quite a while. Now refreshed and feeling *molto bene*, he was ready to resume his duties as Little Jeffrey.

"We have to get him out of there," Austin said. "I don't know how long that branch will hold."

"Yes, but how?"

The two of them stood there, almost as naked as Adam and Eve, looking down at the baby. Austin seemed lost in thought, unaware of his nudity, and it took all of Sandra's concentration not to stare at his, well, *considerable* nudity.

She forced herself to focus on the problem of the branch. The stream was narrow, but the branch was high enough that it couldn't be reached from either bank, or even from the middle of the stream.

"Can we climb out on the limb and get him?"

"That branch looks too weak," Austin said. "If we try that, he'll fall off."

"Shouldn't we take the chance?"

Geoffrey had been so caught up in debating the inaccuracies of Dante's "Inferno" with some colleagues from the Long Term Prayer Fulfillment Division that he'd failed to realize these two poor mortals might have trouble reaching his perch when the time came.

"Maybe we can build some kind of ladder," Austin said.

"How can we build a ladder without tools?" Sandra asked. She tried hard to keep her gaze above Austin's shoulders.

"Good point. One way or the other, we need get down below him." Austin reached out and placed his hand on the small of her back, just above the swell of her bottom. The gesture appeared unconscious since he didn't seem to notice her at all as he studied Little Jeffrey's precarious perch.

Instinctively, Sandra leaned into the smooth wet skin of his chest for comfort and almost swooned at his slippery touch.

"For crying out loud." Geoffrey watched their two auras mingle together in a bright, electric cloud of carnal steam, much as their bodies would entangle if things were ever allowed to go their natural way. The situation looked like it could quickly get out of hand. Why did they have to see each other in the buff? They're so distracted now it could take all night to get him down. His mind raced. What could he do?

I don't suppose a little advice would hurt. He put in a quick mental call to a couple of guys he knew in heaven's Natural Resources Division.

"Alphonse, Dimitri, are you there?"

"Yo, Chief. Wassup?" The two *paisanos* were forever calling him "Chief," for reasons Geoffrey never understood, but he put up with it. In spite of their undignified behavior, Geoffrey couldn't help but like the two former restaurateurs. At least they said they had been restaurant owners during their time on earth. Geoffrey thought it was suspicious that they had shown up in heaven late one Friday night, both at the same time and quite a bit before it was natural. But Geoffrey had always been too polite to question them about their past. After all, they had gotten into heaven. And once you got into heaven, what you did on earth stayed on earth. Besides, The Big Guy found their talents useful in a lot of circumstances, even if they were not ones related to their assigned duties in the Natural Resources Division. But this seemed like a natural resource kind of issue, so Geoffrey had paid a call.

"I hate to bother you," Geoffrey said.

"No bother at all," Dimitri answered for the both of them. "We just got done convince'n a former brudda of ours of the error of his temporal ways."

"Yeah." Alphonse chuckled. "It was very satisfy'n woik, if you know what I mean."

Geoffrey didn't know what they meant, but he didn't ask. It was always better that way.

"Well, now that you're free, perhaps you can help me with a little problem?"

"Our pleasure, Chief. Who's the troublemaker?"

"No, no. It's nothing like that. It's just that I seem to be, well, up a tree, and I can't get down."

"Eh? Let's have a look."

The celestial curtain parted and the two battered faces—more appropriately described as "mugs"—appear in the sky overhead.

"You the one in the dirty diaper?" Dimitri asked.

"What? Oh, yes, I suppose so. You try living as a baby for a couple of weeks."

"Whatever floats your boat, Chief."

"It's an *assignment*, of course. Anyway, I had to put myself in this tree to keep from harming the poor child whose body I've borrowed. Now I have to get down and on with my mission. I can't do it on my own, and my mortal caretakers need some help."

"Yeah," Alphonse said. "They've got some very impressive equipment, but it's all the wrong kind, if you know what I mean."

Geoffrey heard their snickering but ignored it.

"Come on now. You two are supposed to work with nature. Got any ideas?"

"Why don't you jump?"

Geoffrey held his temper. After all, he was in a delicate situation, and he needed help. He tried to put his chubby baby hands on his hips.

"Look," he said. "With advice like that, I'll be up here all night."

"Well then, perhaps we should sing you a lullaby!" Before Geoffrey could protest, the two old New Yorkers began to sing, in two completely different keys.

"Rock-a-bye baby, in da tree top."

"When da wind blows, da cradle will rock."

"When da bough breaks, da cradle will fall—"

"Wind!" Geoffrey shouted. "That's it!"

"And down will come babeeeee, cradle and aaalllll…"

"Thank you, thank you," Geoffrey said, anxious to get rid of the pair. "You've been a great help. I can take it from here. So long. Goodbye." He waved them away.

The sound of singing faded as the celestial curtain drew closed, but Geoffrey had the solution he needed. Within seconds a breeze picked up and the leaves of the surrounding aspen trees began their trademark quaking. His own branch began to sway ominously.

****

"Look," Sandra said. She pointed down at Little Jeffrey. "The wind's come up. I think he's going to fall!"

"There's nothing left to do then," Austin said.

"What do you mean?"

With his hand still on the small of Sandra's back,

Austin, stepped closer to the precipice of the rushing water, pushing her closer to the edge, too.

"You mean—?" Before she could finish her sentence, he jumped, forcing her to jump with him.

Chapter 9

With her eyes shut tight, Sandra dropped through the air and plunged feet first into the pool next to Austin. Icy water enveloped her, further taking her breath away. Her feet touched the shallow bottom and she sprang to the surface, wiping water and hair away from her eyes. The first thing she saw was Austin, standing in chest-high water. At that very moment, the baby's crib slipped off the branch and fell. With his arms out, Austin caught Little Jeffrey, cradle and all, as neatly as he would a football.

"You got him!" she cheered.

"*Nice catch,*" Geoffrey said.

Sandra splashed toward Austin and Little Jeffrey, ready to hug them both. Then she glanced down at her bare breasts. Oops! She dropped down into the frigid water up to her chin. Goose bumps had hardened into pebbles, all over her body. Austin started to wade over to her.

"Don't bother," she said, waving him off. "I'm okay."

"The baby looks fine, too," he said, "but don't you want to check him yourself?"

"Sure, but uh, I can do that back at the campsite. Thanks."

"*I'm good to go,*" Geoffrey said. "*I've had quite enough adventure for one day.*"

"Okay," Austin said. He waded to the far edge of the pool and climbed out. In the late-afternoon light, Sandra stared at the stark contrast between Austin's tanned, muscular thighs and his tight but much whiter buttocks. Cradling Little Jeffrey and the camp stool in his arms, he strode into the trees without looking back, melting into the forest like a goat-footed Pan who had just stolen a sheep. Sandra's heart fluttered a beat and she caught her breath, but she shook it off, assuring herself it was only a reaction to the freezing water. Still, she couldn't deny the urge to leap up and run after him. In a few moments the warmth she had been feeling inside started to fade. She began to shiver.

"Hello?" she called.

She was alone, half-naked, and floating in a pool of water cold enough to raise permanent chicken skin on a bowling ball.

"Hellooo," she called again. "A little help here, please?" Foolishly, she had expected Austin to come back with a shirt or a blanket or something she could use to dry off and cover up with. He may have been preoccupied with the baby, or perhaps the sound of the waterfall drowned out her calls. More likely he figured that since she had stood next to him nearly naked once, she shouldn't care whether he saw her again. Just like a man.

She waded to the edge of the pool, but still no Austin.

"So much for chivalry," she muttered. She clawed her way up the muddy bank on hands and knees, slipping back into the water twice and skinning her knee before she got all the way out. Stooping over in the cold, with her arms folded over her breasts, she

125

stepped gingerly into the trees.

Her teeth were chattering by the time she found a red and black checked blanket, hanging on a tree branch next to the path. She snatched up Austin's offering and wrapped it around her shoulders.

Back at camp, Geoffrey was in reasonably good spirits. He waved his baby arms in the air while Austin duct-taped a dry bandana diaper on him. Geoffrey had managed to put the mission back on track, even if the incident might cause some hard feelings between his two human care-givers. It looked like his temporary parents were keeping each other at arm's length once again, but their auras still swirled together in a cloud of erotic blues and reds whenever they were near each other. A few orange and purple swirls of irritation intermingled, now, too. Typical, he thought. Mortals found it hard to acknowledge their true feelings. And, being only human, Austin and Sandra would likely need to sort out who was to blame for his unscheduled cruise down river before they could treat each other with civility again.

Austin had pulled on some blue jeans but he was still bare-chested when Sandra returned. Sandra wanted to scold him for causing the incident they had all just survived, but the sight of Austin's glistening pectorals reminded her of her own nakedness and struck her unexpectedly shy.

"Thank you...for saving Little Jeffrey," she said levelly as she pulled a dry shirt from a saddlebag.

"You're welcome," he said as he, too, found a shirt.

Oh, no. Here it comes.

"But next time." Sandra dropped the blanket and

flipped the shirt over her shoulders at the same time while she talked. "I think you should be a little more careful around the baby."

Austin looked up and his dark steady gaze met hers. She tried to keep her gaze above the fading view of his chest as he buttoned up his shirt.

"I'm sorry things got out of hand back there," he offered. "But nothing would have happened if we had all stayed together in the first place." He slipped into an open smile, almost a grin.

"Please," she said. "I'm not ready to go skinny-dipping with someone I hardly know."

"Hey, that was before we jumped naked from the top of a water fall. And we've changed the same baby's diapers. You can't do all that and still be strangers. I bet if you gave me half a break we might become friends."

"Give you a break?" Sandra struggled to keep her voice calm and matter-of-fact. "I am trying to save my mother, who is alone in the wilderness with a sick man, and all you're trying to do is hit on me, like we were in one the bars you seem to frequent."

Austin and Geoffrey winced at the same time.

"So," she said more quietly. "You'll forgive me if I haven't had time to 'give you a break.'"

"Yeah, I suppose you're right." Austin was silent for a moment, apparently thinking. Then he said, "I didn't mean to make light of our problem here. I just thought…I mean I can tell that…"

Against her better judgment, Sandra couldn't stay mad. She was tired and her heart went out to him. "Go on," she said. But she cringed a little. She sounded like a school teacher prompting a student who was having difficulty expressing himself.

Austin stood up and started pacing in a small circle. "There's something I want to say to you, and I don't want you to take it the wrong way. I mean I don't want you to think I'm trying to pick you up, even though…"

"What is it?"

Austin looked off into the woods, like he was trying to remember what it was he wanted to say, or to get it just right.

"It's just that, in the short time we've known each other, I've grown…to…like you. A lot." He held up his hands as if he expected her negative reaction. "And respect you, of course. Yes, I respect you, too." He looked at her wide-eyed, but wary.

It was such an obvious attempt to rehabilitate himself in her eyes, but surprisingly, something deep inside Sandra relaxed, like she had been mentally holding her breath. He liked her. That wasn't news, but now he was making a formal confession of his feelings, and this didn't help Sandra control the low-grade panic she had felt growing inside her ever since Austin's arrival.

She took a few deep breaths and tried to clear her mind. She appreciated his affection, but she wasn't going to encourage him. He couldn't be serious. She wasn't going to put herself on Austin Smith's list of available women in every port-of-call.

"Thank you," she said finally. His smiled broadened. "I guess I like you too, in a way."

His smile faded.

"Did I say something wrong?" she asked.

"No, no. I only thought perhaps we could, I mean, something more could…oh, forget it."

They looked at each other for a second and Sandra sat down, wary of whatever Austin might say next.

He slapped the palms of his hands on the back of his legs and said, "Hey, I should make you some dinner. Don't you think?"

"Dinner. Now there's a thought. I'll help you, just so, you know…"

"So it's more than peanut butter?"

"Yeah." She was grateful he had changed the subject.

They worked together to set up camp and prepare a simple meal, carefully talking about this and that. Austin was a little more forthcoming on his vital statistics. Thirty-two years old, in good health—as if Sandra couldn't tell—and between jobs—again, as if she couldn't tell. And, as it turned out, he did have a pilot's license, at least at some point in his life. Sandra didn't catch whether it had expired or been revoked for some reason.

He had been in a couple of relationships he described as serious, but none of them had ever come close to marriage. Not surprising. Sandra wondered what kind of women could make Austin consider the confining bonds of matrimony. Then, off hand, she wondered what her father would think of the man. He'd probably like Austin, but then he always saw the best in people, even in Sandra's mother.

For the rest of the evening the two of them worked fairly well around the campfire, doing separate tasks. He set up the tents and sleeping bags while she did the cooking. She insisted on this. At one point he helped her lift a heavy pot off the fire, holding his hands over hers as he did so. As before, Sandra felt the silky, electric sensation whenever their hands touched, as if an electrical current ran between them. It was the pure sensuous pleasure of flesh casually touching flesh, even though they had practically embraced each other's naked bodies earlier in the creek. She wondered what it would be like to kiss him. Not the peck on the cheek she had given him before, but one of those long, slow kisses, perhaps with some tongue. It was a notion that persisted, no matter how she tried to ignore it, no matter what else she thought of him.

Little Jeffrey lay on a blanket, playing with his toes.

"Hey, I can almost reach them now. I seem to be getting bigger. I must be growing up."

Geoffrey grew quiet, awed by the miracle of life. It was something he seldom got to experience first-hand, not being a mortal. He waved his stubby arms at Sandra and Austin. *"You people are so lucky. Your only real job is living. How come so few of you understand that?"*

Sandra involuntarily tensed when Austin reached down and took the baby into his arms.

"Whoops!" Geoffrey, who had recently achieved a small measure of success in controlling his bladder, suddenly had to hold himself back, lest he foul himself and Austin at the same time.

"Hi, there, you little pisser," Austin said.

"You know me too well."

"Does he talk like this all the time?" Austin asked Sandra.

"I don't have a lot of experience with babies," she admitted, "but I've never seen any who talked as much as this one."

Austin's eyes twinkled. "Maybe he's singing."

"*A wonderful idea,*" Geoffrey said. *"I'll have you know that I held first chair in the Junior Triumphant Choir, during my days as a cherub. I'm still called upon to perform a solo, every now and then."* He hummed a few bars from the second act of *La Traviata*.

"Listen to him go on."

"Maybe you should sing to him." Sandra reclined a little onto her sleeping bag. To her surprise, Austin cocked his head and smiled, apparently considering the idea.

"I don't know if I can remember any lullabies."

"Surely you can think of something."

With a surprisingly melodic baritone, Austin began to sing, all the while looking at Little Jeffrey.

"Come along with me,

And I'll sing you a song,

Of a crusty old sailor named Rick,

Whom the ladies knew well,

Who'd wrestle with hell,

And who'd boast of the size of his—"

"Hey!" Sandra sat up straight. "That's your idea of a lullaby, some kind of bawdy sea chantey?"

"That's pretty much all I've heard lately."

"Well, I don't think it's suitable for a young child. Choose something more appropriate."

"What's the difference? He's too young to understand the words." He set the baby down on his sleeping bag.

"*I'm* old enough to understand the words. Besides, studies have shown that babies *do* remember things, in a way. Not verbatim, but words and images get imprinted on their young brains, making it easier for them to recall things when they get older and hear them again."

Austin frowned. "Is there anything they haven't studied?"

Sandra arched an eyebrow at him.

"Sorry," he said. "All I can rely on is my own experience. And I don't think it's ever been studied."

Sandra laughed. "We're going to change that, remember? To see why you have a way with bears."

"Oh, yeah." He grew silent, remembering that he still hadn't told her about Gretchin. Now it seemed too late, but that was okay, so long as she never got the chance to put him in front of another grizzly. In the meantime, watching the firelight dance off the colors in Sandra's hair, his thoughts drifted back to the events of the day. He had practically strained his eyes, trying not to stare at her tight, goose-bumped flesh as they stood at the top of the waterfall. Were her breasts always that firm and pert, or was it only an effect of the cold? Either way, it was all he could do to keep his swelling manhood from standing at attention and betraying his desire, even in freezing water and with the baby in danger.

He took a deep breath. "I have an idea I'd like you to study for a while."

"What's that?"

"You remember what I said before, I mean before dinner?"

"No, what's that?" Sandra lied. They had done so well for the last hour or so, talking about themselves, but just in a friendly way. Why did he have to go and spoil it?

"I think we should study some way to make

ourselves a team," he said.

"You go boy! Now you're talking." Geoffrey tried to roll over, to get a better baby look at his parents.

Sandra froze. For a second her "fight or flight" instincts kicked in and she wanted to run. But there was nowhere to go, so she pushed the fear down and looked back at him steadily. "What do you mean, a team?"

"I mean, I think we'd be really good together."

"Good at what?"

"You know, doing things together."

"Doing things together? Like what? Like going to a movie? Are you asking me for a date or something?"

"I suppose I would, if there was a restaurant or a theater within a hundred miles."

"You don't really mean it, do you?" She almost laughed, but she was afraid he was serious, or as serious as a man like him could be. For all she knew, the guy only wanted a woman to take care of his baby. Either way, a cold wave of fear swept through her chest, making it difficult for her to breathe. She had to nip this attraction in the bud.

"Please, Austin. I know you can't be serious."

"Why not?"

"Let's just say I'm not looking to date anyone at the moment."

"People tell me that's exactly when you find somebody you like. When you least expect it."

"People say a lot of things that don't make any sense. You've got to look at things from my perspective. Just two days ago I was spending a nice, quiet afternoon organizing my census data, when all of the sudden you fall out of the sky, looking for your baby. Of course it looks like the baby fell out of the sky, too, but that's a different problem. If my mother hadn't gotten into trouble, we would have settled the matter of Little Jeffrey and you'd have been on your way." She didn't say that Austin would have been on his way without Little Jeffrey. No sense stirring up that controversy right then.

"In any case," she continued, "I'm on a rescue mission for my mother and my nice, calm scientist's life has been turned completely upside down."

He smiled. "On behalf of all the quirky cosmic fates, I apologize."

"Thanks, but things are still pretty messed up."

"True, but it's not like I planned to be here."

"Yes, and if you had done a little more planning on your first visit we wouldn't be in this fix, would we?"

"Okay, you've got a point there."

"And now there's a child."

"I'm not trying to get out of that fix."

"Maybe not, but that brings me back to my real point. I don't know much about you, other than the fact that you apparently spend most of your time gallivanting around the world, getting in and out of fixes like this."

"*Lady, please,*" Geoffrey said. "*If you'll slow down for a moment, you'll see that the man loves you. That's gotta count for something.*"

"You can't just drop into my life, turn everything into chaos, and expect me to start dating you with open arms." She rested her chin in her hand. She wasn't as upset with Austin as she thought she'd be. "Besides, I'd want to know a lot more about you or any man first, before I start teaming up with him."

"I'm an open book."

"Yes, a mystery. You say you have—or had—a pilot's license, although I've seen your questionable flying skills. But you're willing to fly a float plane out into the wilderness to find a baby who may or may not be your child."

"And that's a good thing, isn't it?"

"Don't interrupt me, I'm on a roll."

He put up his hands in surrender.

"From the way you look at Little Jeffrey," she said, "and the way you diagnosed Johnson's illness, you could be a doctor, for all I know. On the other hand, it's entirely possible you've been running guns or God knows what in Kathmandu for the last year."

"Yeah, well, maybe you don't want to know about that part, young lady."

"Now you show up at Misha Ranch and you want to sweep me off my feet."

"Pretty much."

"I just might be attracted to you, Austin Smith, but even if I was, I can't let that happen."

"You could try."

Sandra paused, embarrassed that she had admitted any kind of attraction to him. She rambled on, trying to put that statement behind her. "Maybe I do like you, sort of, but I have responsibilities. I have a job to do. I can't go off to Cambodia and run guns for the fun of it."

"You could try."

"No, I can't. And neither can you, now. You have a child to consider."

"I can change. Do the right thing. It can't be that hard."

"Even if I believed you wanted to," she said,

"people can't make fundamental changes in their personalities that easily."

"A study showed that, too?"

Her glare faded into a wan smile. Let's see if Mr. Smith has the qualifications to settle down, she thought. "What exactly *were* you doing last year, besides being an accidental father?"

He ran his fingers through his hair and sat back. "I've been shipping supplies."

"Supplies? Who needs supplies? Only…oh my God. You *are* a gun runner!"

"Not guns."

"Bombs, then? Ammunition?"

"No. Nothing like that. At least not lately."

"Then why all the secrecy?"

He squinted, obviously uncomfortable. "I might lose my pilot's license…again."

"Drugs?"

"No, not drugs! At least not those kind of drugs."

"Then what kind of drugs?"

"More like medical supplies. And food."

"How can someone lose their license for shipping medical supplies and food?"

"I was flying them into Burma. To some people the government doesn't like."

"To rebels?"

"No. Not to rebels. There's an orphanage there. In the countryside. It's run by my uncle. When things got unstable, both the government and some bandits were intercepting every scheduled shipment worth stealing. It was hard for regular flights to get anything through. I was just helping out."

"For a price, of course."

"What I did was supposedly illegal, at least according to the State Department. Some treaty violation, or something. The local government didn't like it either, but they were pretty corrupt."

"Is that where you learned about medicine?"

"No, um, for that I went to medical school."

"You? You really did go to medical school?"

"For two years."

"Oh. So, you're not a doctor."

"No. Not quite."

"You couldn't cut the mustard?"

"It's not that. I can go back, in a year."

"What? Why in a year?"

"That's when my suspension will be over."

"Did you get into academic trouble, or what?"

"It's more like 'or what.'"

"Okay, what happened?"

"I was in a clinical program. I got into it early, since I'd been a medic in the Marines—"

"The Marines?"

"Yeah, well, I served for a couple of years there, too."

"Only a couple of years?"

"I can go back—"

"When your suspension is over, I know. Let's go back to medical school."

"Yes. I was working in the ER one night when a man staggered in from the restaurant across the street. Things had been pretty quiet, so the doctor in charge was out of the hospital, at a movie, if I recall."

"A man after your own heart."

"I got hold of the doctor by cell phone pretty quickly, and he decided the patient was having a heart attack. He ordered a whole bunch of counter-measures based on that diagnosis. Anyway, this guy couldn't speak, but he kept pounding his chest and holding his throat, like he couldn't breathe."

"What did you do?"

"He was moving around too quickly, so I figured he wasn't having a heart attack. He was simply choking on his dinner, so I gave him the Heimlich maneuver. I guess I saved his life."

"And for that you got expelled from medical school?"

"No. Just suspended. The man turned out to be the mayor. Which was okay. But when he left the restaurant in such a hurry, a photographer followed him into the hospital. The guy managed to take a picture of the mayor just as he expelled half a baked cod. It landed on the front page. So to speak."

"And for *that* you got suspended."

"Probably, but they said it was for not following my supervising physician's orders. My instincts were right, but when you're only a second-year medical student, doctor's orders trump your instincts."

"Of course. I'm sorry about that."

Sandra sighed. At least Austin wasn't a gun runner. Not lately anyway. A sense of relief settled over her.

"So, what made you go to medical school in the first place?" she asked. "You'll pardon me if I say you don't seem like the kind of guy who'd thrive under that kind of discipline."

He arched an eyebrow at her. "You're right, I suppose. I never had much of a family structure growing up, but my mother encouraged me to go to school, and I liked it. I guess I was looking for something more stable." Like you, he didn't say. "Why did you become a biologist?"

"That's easy," she said. "My father was a biologist."

"And you want to be like him?"

"Yes, he was my hero when I was growing up."

"Do you like it?" he asked.

"I like it, although biology can be hard work."

"No. I mean do you like being like your father."

His question puzzled her. "I'm not really like him, except for my profession."

"What was he like, your father?" Austin poked at the fire with a stick.

"I remember him being very handsome, and very professional."

"Like you."

"He was a very important scientist."

"Like you?"

"Much more so than me, at least so far. Dad's work made him fly all over the world."

"Like me?"

She laughed. "I don't think my father broke any State Department rules doing his research."

"Did you miss him?"

"You mean do I miss him now?"

"No, I mean did you miss him when he flew all over the world."

"Yes," she said quietly. A tear stung the corner of her eye. Since she had admired her father, she always struggled not to miss him when he left home for work. Then one day he was gone forever, and she never had the chance to say goodbye. She fought back new tears and changed the subject.

"I'm sorry," she said. "You're nice, in your own way, but I'm sure you see my point about the two of us. Our lives are so completely different. Like my father, I believe in the scientific method, following doctor's orders, if you will. Or at least keeping things orderly. You know, thinking things through before you act, following the plan, doing things rationally. That sort of stuff. You believe in your feelings, your...your gut instincts."

"Ah," he said. "If someone did a study, they'd find out that my instincts are almost always right."

She laughed. "Maybe so, but let's stick to one thing at a time. For the moment, we should focus on the rescue mission, even if it is my mother we have to rescue."

"And later?"

"Later can take care of itself."

"Fine," he said. "Can I ask you another question?

Sandra stiffened. It seemed like every time he asked a question, it was about her, and it always pointed out some kind of flaw.

"Different subject," he added.

"Do you have to?" she asked.

"No, but I was wondering. When you were a kid, before you decided to be like your father, what did you want to be when you grew up?"

She laughed. The question seemed innocent enough. He could hardly criticize her for having dreams when she was young.

"I had this crazy notion," she said.

"Those are the best kind. Tell me about it."

She thought back on her childhood and smiled. "I read a lot of the old classics when I was young. You know. Nancy Drew. The Hardy Boys. When I was a girl, most of the kids had never heard of those old books or wouldn't touch them if they had. But my mother had saved them all for me."

"Okay, so…?"

"In high school I read most of Hemingway and Faulkner, long before they got assigned as homework. I even worked on the school newspaper. Anyway, I had this idea that when I grew up I would move to Paris and be a foreign correspondent or something."

"Doesn't sound so farfetched. What happened to that idea?"

She didn't have to think much to answer that. "Oh, c'mon. Grownups get real jobs."

"Like research scientist?"

"Wait just a minute, mister. You've been criticizing my profession the whole time I've known you. What exactly is wrong with being a research scientist? It's a lot more respectable than being a…whatever you are at the moment." She waved one hand at him in dismissal.

Austin just looked at her. Where she expected to see confrontation, he was simply wide-eyed with sincerity, which scared her more than seeing him angry, more than when he was simply hitting on her.

"That's it," he said. "I think you put your finger on it."

"Well, of course I have," she said. "Put my finger on what?"

"Respect. What you need is respect."

She threw up her hands and looked at him sideways. "Everybody wants respect. What's wrong with that?"

"Nothing, in and of itself. But it can be misplaced."

"All right, Mr. Know-it-all. How is my need for respect misplaced? This I've got to hear."

He looked at her a little sadly. "Are you sure you want to hear it from me?"

"Why not? Apparently, *you're* the expert."

He stood up, walked to her side of the fire, and sat down. Then he reached out and gently took one of her hands in both of his. This wasn't proper psychologist's protocol, as far as she knew, and it took her off guard. She almost drew her hand back, but didn't, and some of her irritation dissipated as she waited to hear what he would say.

"I think it's all about your father," he said quietly.

"What?" She pulled her hand away from his. "What are you talking about?"

"Listen to me," he said without raising his voice.

"I don't think so. I've heard just about enough. I don't need you to—"

"Your father was a great man," he said.

"What?" This confused her even more. "You never knew him."

Sandra's head swam. Her anger at Austin was real, but it felt misplaced somehow. His quiet insistence and sincerity gave him a moral superiority she didn't think he deserved, and she was afraid that whatever he was saying might be true.

"I only know one thing about your father," he said, "and that's all I need to know."

She didn't want him to go on, but she felt compelled to listen.

"All I know is that your father had you for a daughter."

Sandra laughed.

"No, I mean it," he said. "I am grateful for that, even if I never get to be your friend, or whatever. It looks to me like your father did a damn good job of raising you, at least as long as he could."

Tears stung Sandra's eyes once again and she clenched her fists. "What difference does that make to you?"

"The thing is this," he said, still maddeningly calm. "You still want your father's respect, even though he's gone."

"No." But an electric shock jolted Sandra's chest. She stared at Austin, not knowing what else to say. Was it true?

"There's nothing wrong with that," he said. "Nothing at all. It's just this. I don't know how much of the life you lead now is yours, and how much of it is because of your father. You may not know either."

"But…" Sandra's mouth dropped open and, in her indignation, she couldn't think of any quick rebuttal. It was as if everything she had known about the decisions in her life threatened to melt like cotton candy, leaving a light, airy, empty space in her chest. She was afraid the emptiness might be filled by confusion and uncertainty, but she was totally unprepared to feel…fine. What did that mean?

Mercifully, Austin stood up and smacked the dust off his backside with both hands. "I'm sorry if I made you mad," he said. "It's just the way I see it, and I could be completely wrong."

Speechless, she waved one hand at him to show him she was okay.

"I think I'll go for a little walk," he said. "Maybe

clear my head."

She was the one who needed to clear her head, but the blank look on her face and tear-fogged eyes made her feel foolish when Austin smiled down at her. She was baffled. She didn't know whether to thank him or throw a stick at him.

"I'll try not to get lost," he said.

Sandra just nodded.

He stepped away from the light of the campfire and disappeared into the darkness. She hugged her knees and stared at the fire. Orange and blue flames were quickly consuming the dried pieces of wood she had carefully arranged within the protective stone circle. She lay down on her sleeping bag and closed her eyes tight.

Geoffrey had been only half listening. He was practicing blowing saliva bubbles and watching them drift away until they popped. He casually examined Sandra's emotional aura, tortured as it was by the mixture of love, fear, and confusion, especially where her parents were concerned. She had loved her father, but that love had come to an untimely end with her father's death. Her mother had never recovered from the loss of her husband either, and, making matters worse, she was simply too hurt to fill the empty space in Sandra's heart. On that ill-fated day, their mother-daughter relationship began its downward spiral.

Geoffrey inspected some glitches in Sandra's aura a little more closely. Then he realized she had never finished grieving for her father. She wasn't about to put herself in a position where someone she loved so much could leave her again. It was too painful. Austin, the poor sap, didn't have a chance under these circumstances. The more he loved her, the more she'd run away.

Geoffrey tried to pose a thoughtful finger on his chubby chin. What would it take to calm Sandra's heart and set her back on the right path?

"Her father! That's it!" He knew what he had to do. Mentally he filed a petition with the heavenly Office of Emergency Soul Communications. Thankfully, his archangel status meant he didn't have to sit through their dreary answering system. "If you wish to locate a soul, conceive the number two. If you know the name of the soul, but the soul is lost, conceive the number—" that sort of interminable thing.

"You want what?" An administrator's voice boomed. You'd think she was sitting at the Right Hand, not administering a mid-level, service-oriented office.

"Please," Geoffrey said, trying hard to keep a friendly tone in his voice, "I need an emergency three-way tele-soul conference. Heaven and Earth."

"Across the inter-plasmic barrier?"

"Yes, that's it."

"That's highly unusual."

"There's no other way to do it. And, I should add, I have Senior Archangel level authorization."

"Hmmm. What did you say your name was?"

"Almaric. Archangel Geoffrey Almaric Behir de Giverny. You know, Geoffrey of Jericho? Geoffrey the Avenger and all that?"

"Yes, yes, of course Mr. Almachek. Will you hold please?"

"Actually, I just need to—"

They hadn't waited for him to answer.

Geoffrey hummed along through six minutes of

Gloria Patri, the Boston Pops version, Arthur Fiedler conducting, before the ESC administrator came back to him.

"And in which century will you be needing this, Mr. Almatick?"

"That's Almaric. And I was hoping I could do it now."

"Now? Heavens!"

"Yes." Geoffrey was getting desperate. Of course there was a certain amount of bureaucracy, even in Heaven, but this was setting a new standard. "And by the way," he added quickly. "You tell the Archangel Gabriel that if he interferes with this conference in any way I'll pluck every feather off his back until he looks like a naked roasting hen."

There was an awkward pause. A shorter one, this time.

"Well, well, Mr. Almaric, you're in luck. I see we've had a cancellation, and some interplasmic space has just become available. Are your parties ready?"

They'd better be, Geoffrey thought as he gathered up their aural essences.

****

"Sandra? Sandra?" a man called out.

Had she really heard her father's voice? It drifted to Sandra through a dream-like fog, faint but urgent.

"Sandra, honey, I'm here," he said.

"Dad? Is that you?"

"Yes, honey, it's me. I'm right here with you."

"Oh, Dad, Dad. Is that really you? I've missed you so much. Where have you been? Where are we?" It was hard to see through the misty colors swirling around her.

"None of that matters," her father said. "The only important thing is that we're together, for a little while, anyway."

Sandra wanted to run to her father, wherever he was, but some unseen force held her back. Then the cold steel of her mother's voice cut through the fog like a hack saw.

"Harvey Coulton? Is that you?"

"Yes, dear, it's me."

"What are you doing in my dream?" Martha asked.

"It's not a dream," Harvey said.

"I don't want to dream about you anymore," Martha said.

Sandra couldn't help but notice the word 'anymore.' "I dream about him, too, mother."

"Sandra? What's going on? Where are we?"

"We're in a special place," Harvey said.

"It's got to be a dream," Martha said. "Look at all this fog. And the colors."

"It's a dream if you like. We've been given a rare opportunity to talk."

At this, Martha seemed to sense a challenge. "Talk about what?"

"Us. What we meant to each other. What we still mean to each other."

"What good would that do?" Martha said. "You're dead. And if you weren't dead you'd probably be away on some lecture tour."

"I'm sorry my work kept us apart. It was a terrible mistake. I would do things differently, if I had the chance."

Sandra tensed at her mother's pain and anger, both familiar to her, as if she had harbored them all along

147

herself. But now she felt them fading, if only a little.

"Can you forgive me?" Harvey asked.

"It's too late for that," Martha said. "You're gone."

"Maybe, but I'm not dead to you," he said quietly. "And I'm not dead to our daughter."

"I'm still here," Sandra said. "Why did you have to leave us, Dad?" She sounded like a child again, like she had never fully comprehended death.

"I'm sorry about that," he said, "but on that score, I didn't have much choice, if you'll recall."

"What do you mean?" Martha asked. "You chose to study those damn bears, didn't you? And just look at what that did to our daughter."

Sandra stirred in her sleeping bag. "Come back, Dad," she murmured. Then she drifted into a dreamless, forgiving sleep.

"Hey, Central," Geoffrey said. "We've lost our connection! We weren't done!"

"Sorry. We had to bump you for a Priority One request. I'm afraid we won't have another opening for, uh, it looks like fifty-six years. Would you care to make a reservation?"

"Thanks, but no thanks."

So much for helping Sandra and her mother. Priority One came straight from the Front Office. Someone up there wanted him to get back to his mission.

Chapter 10

When Sandra blinked her eyes open she found herself in her warm sleeping bag, with sunshine lighting up the inside of her pup tent. It was morning. She mentally clutched at the fleeting fragments of her dream before they got away. It was no use. All she remembered was her father comforting her, and the annoying sound of her mother's voice. That and the familiar loneliness of growing up without a father. Then she remembered she was on the way to rescue her mother, and that she had almost let Little Jeffrey drown. And that she had been half naked in front of Austin. She groaned out loud and unzipped the sleeping bag. She dreaded what the day might bring.

Austin was already dressed and set a pot of coffee on the fire to boil. She had slept much later than she usually did, and Austin had let her.

Sandra insisted that they break camp as quickly as possible, and she got them back on the trail with the same efficiency as she had the day before. That left little time for conversation. She didn't want any more dime-store analysis from Austin, even though his opinions from the night before seemed to strike a chord inside her. She wasn't ready to believe what he'd said, but it had caused her to think.

As she had on the first day, Sandra rode in front with the baby, finding their way up the trail with a map,

149

and with her pack horse and Austin trailing behind her.

In addition to Austin's impromptu psychology, nearly losing Little Jeffrey in the creek still weighed heavily on her mind. She blamed Austin, of course, but in hindsight she knew she shouldn't have put Little Jeffrey's crib so close to the water. It seemed perfectly safe at the time, and how was she to know that Austin would slip into the hot springs pool without her permission? She tried to hold on to that thought but she knew she was as much to blame as he.

On that score, she feared she might not be any more qualified to be a parent than her mother, or Austin. Sandra was supposed to be the responsible one in the outfit. Even Austin seemed to understand that. And, since she was a woman, taking care of an infant was supposed to be second nature. Wasn't it? So what she had done at the hot springs was inexcusable, even if Austin had triggered the near disaster.

It didn't help much that Austin was the one who saved Little Jeffrey, not her. She was beginning to feel her moral superiority slipping away, and that meant Austin was gaining ground in their subtle contest for custody of the baby.

On top of everything else, Sandra was mortified about running half-naked through the woods. She didn't know much about Austin, but she figured sexual attraction is what prompted him to confess, in his own awkward way, that he had feelings for her. He was simply a man at the mercy of his testosterone. Men joked about women being controlled by their hormones, but men usually had only one thing on their minds around women. Sex. She didn't want to succumb to an attraction that was biochemically motivated.

Even so, now that they were on the trail she couldn't forget standing next to Austin's sculptured pectorals, washboard chest, and magnificent... manliness. She shook her head and tried without success to stifle the images that kept flashing through her brain.

She remembered the feel of Austin's strong hand on the small of her back, low enough to set off impromptu fireworks as they stood at the waterfall. That, in turn, triggered some completely unrelated fantasies that, if left unchecked, were quite breathtaking. These short vignettes were usually set in her bedroom at the ranch, or on a bed of soft leaves in the middle of the woods. Once, she imagined sitting naked in Austin's lap, facing him on a galloping horse. When her eyes focused again she had to dive for the map as it slipped from her fingers. Such fantasies continued unbidden throughout the morning. Then she'd remember that Austin had snuck uninvited into the hot springs. That would irritate her and she'd start the emotional merry-go-round all over again.

Round and round she went. It was impossible to settle on a single way to feel, and she didn't want to confuse things even more by talking to Austin. Not until she could sort out her feelings about a man she had nothing in common with, except a baby who surprised them both.

****

Austin listened to the slow, clomping rhythm of the horse's hooves on the dry trail. With each step he mentally kicked himself for sneaking into the hot springs. Such an idiot. Then he'd turned into a complete sap, trying to tell Sandra how he felt and talking about her father. No one liked being psychoanalyzed. Whatever small bit of progress he'd made at bonding with Sandra was slipping away. How could he regain the initiative? He wanted to say something, but they were riding single file up the narrow trail and it was difficult to carry on a conversation. With each passing minute, Sandra's silence was killing him.

"Hey," Austin called out. "Are we there yet?"

"Not by a long shot," she said without turning around. "Do you need a potty stop?"

"I'm okay." They rode another ten minutes in silence.

"Hey," Austin said again.

"What?"

"Read any good books lately?"

Sandra held the map over her head for him to see. "Just trying to keep us from getting lost."

He rolled his eyes, which she wouldn't see. After that he gave up and tried to take more of an interest in the scenery. He watched the distant peaks, the spreading green forest, and the burbling creek that ran beside the trail. All very beautiful but, inevitably, his gaze returned to Sandra. They had talked so much the night before, Austin hadn't expected Sandra to be so quiet now. As the minutes turned into hours, the distance growing between them tortured Austin in ways he never knew he could suffer over a woman.

****

By the time Sandra decided to stop for the day, neither one of them had said much to the other. It was mid-afternoon, and still several hours before nightfall, but she wanted to rest the horses. She let Austin set up the tents again and gave him some other, relatively easy tasks, to keep him busy. And to minimize any discussion.

While Austin worked, Sandra made a show of studying her map. Turning it this way and that, half-heartedly studying details that she had already memorized, having stared at them all day long. They were making good time, but she was still preoccupied with the incongruous Mr. Smith. Placing a finger on the map at what she believed was their location, she glanced up at him where he was stacking wood for a fire. He was the notorious diamond in the rough. A tarnished silver dollar lost under a mountain of pennies.

She hadn't decided what to think about needing respect from her deceased father. So what if Austin believed that. It didn't seem like such a bad thing. For all she knew there could be an afterlife; and, if there was a heaven and her father was watching everything she did, she wanted him to be proud of her.

Her only real problem at that moment seemed to be Austin, who claimed he was seriously attracted to her. All she had to do was tell Mr. Smith, "Thanks, but no thanks," and that should be the end of it. Shouldn't it?

As she watched Austin work, the dragon tattoo on his arm flexed ominously. His strength was such a contrast to the tender way he handled the baby. Sandra remembered seeing his tattoos at the waterfall, slick and glistening from the water. Tattoos did not belong in her world. Nor did love at first sight.

****

For his part, Geoffrey decided he had done about all he could for Sandra and Austin. Sooner or later they would have to take responsibility for their emotions. For now, however, he would be happy if they could just reach Martha Coulton's helicopter without any more distractions. Then Sandra and Austin could fall into each other's arms like they were meant to, or they could go their separate ways. if they chose. It made no difference to him, really. Saving Martha Coulton was his mission. What else could it be?

****

Folding up her map, Sandra finally broke their awkward silence. "You're holding up pretty well for a city boy," she said.

"I wasn't always a city boy." Austin poked at the fire with a stick.

Sandra reached into a stuff sack and tossed him a plastic bag of trail mix. "Have some hors d'oeuvres before dinner," she said. "You deserve it."

He started to speak, but she stood up and turned her attention to one of the horses. Standing on the opposite side from Austin, she loosened the animal's cinch and slipped off the saddle. All day long she had yearned to break the silence between them, but eventually it was obvious she was ignoring him. The longer it went on, the harder it was to stop, but now it was time to ease them back into some harmless conversation, if she could.

Austin chewed a mouthful of nuts, raisins, and M&Ms. "Not bad. What did you call this stuff?"

"Trail mix. Some people call it gorp."

"Gorp? Is that the sound you make when you swallow it?"

"I can't believe you've never heard of gorp. Wherever you've been living lately, you haven't been reading yuppie outdoor magazines."

"The last time I went camping I was sixteen years

154

old. I had T-bone steak for dinner, which I cooked in a cast iron skillet, and a tray of cinnamon rolls for breakfast."

"Apparently that was before nutrition was invented."

Austin laughed, but then he said, "Reservation kids don't think much about nutrition, especially when they're camping. Hell, we never even considered it camping. It was more like a way of life."

"Reservation kids?"

Austin eyed her carefully. "Didn't I tell you? I'm one-quarter Cheyenne."

"Maybe you did. I don't remember." That would explain his complexion, the color of Morrison sandstone, but up to now he hadn't done anything to give her the impression he was Native American. Other than stop an angry bear in its tracks with his bare hands, perhaps.

"You're just one quarter Indian?"

"Yeah. Most of the time I don't even think of myself as an Indian. Not a real Indian, anyway. But I know that I am. As a kid I listened to my grandfather tell me stories about the battle at Little Big Horn. Stories he learned from his own grandfather, told to him by his father who fought there. I wanted nothing more than to become a great warrior chief." He laughed at the idea. "After all, I could be Sitting Bull's great-great grandson." Then he winked at her. "But of course, no one really knows."

"Your father didn't keep any records?"

"He might have, but the old man didn't hang around much, you see?"

"Oh." She blinked at him. She wasn't going to

pursue that topic unless Austin wanted to. If he had grown up without a father, that might explain why he felt so strongly about being a father for Little Jeffrey.

"*Good guess*," Geoffrey said. He inspected the motivational lobes of Austin's aura and found them rich with responsibility, at least where his loved ones were concerned. "*You should pay attention to this guy, lady*," he said to Sandra. "*Once you get him on your side, you'll never get rid of him.*" Of course Sandra heard only the baby's soft cooing.

"What about your mother?" Sandra asked.

"My mother was a saint. She was the one who pushed me to go to medical school. At the time I thought she just wanted to get me off the reservation, do something with myself, and that would have been a worthwhile goal, too."

Sandra waited as he poked at the fire again, thinking he had more to say.

"You know," he said. "As much as we Indians like to tell stories about our great chiefs, it's really the women who hold the tribes together. Especially these days, but maybe they always have. They're quiet, but they keep the cultural fires burning while the men, like me I guess, are out shouting war cries and trying to find bigger buffalo to kill. I've always admired the women. That's why I don't understand why you don't appreciate your mother."

"The fires my mother lights tend to be more destructive."

He nodded.

"The famous chiefs must have been a great inspiration to you," Sandra said.

"Yeah, I suppose so."

They fell into another awkward silence. Sandra regretted how critical she had been of his footloose ways. Instead of being a complete ne'er-do-well, he may have clawed his way up from a hard childhood to make something of himself in an unsympathetic world. She felt her heart go out to him again.

"I'm sorry," was all she managed to say.

"For what? I made my choices, just like everybody else." He smiled. Then he slapped his thighs and stood up. "I think I'll go for another little walk before it gets dark. Work out some of the kinks from our ride."

Sandra was about to say she would go with him, but he said, "Do you think you can keep an eye on my son for a little while?"

"Of course." Apparently he wanted to be alone. "Don't get too far away," she added. "Two rescues in one week is all I can handle."

"Hey," he said, "when I'm in the woods, I'm not Austin Smith anymore. I'm Chief Running Bull, a fierce Cheyenne warrior." He put the flat palm of his hand over his eyes, mocking the stereotype of an Indian watching an approaching wagon train. "No way can the great chief get lost in the forest."

She smiled as he started walking down the trail, his cowboy boots kicking up small clouds of dust. She intended to keep an eye on him as long as she could, but she glanced down at Little Jeffrey, and when she looked up again Austin had disappeared into the trees. Maybe there was something to that Running Bull stuff.

She picked up the baby and gently started rocking him in her arms.

"*Ah, yes.*" Geoffrey sighed. *Once more at the bosom of my mother. This is tough duty, Gabe. Tough duty indeed.*

She hummed a lullaby her father had taught her, and the baby drifted off to sleep.

"Why, oh why?" she whispered. "Why has God…dropped you and Austin Smith…right into my lap?" She smiled when she remembered again the advice her mother had given her about "nice guys" and "characters."

"If only the characters could be nice guys, too."

She tried to imagine what life would be like with Austin. She thought of the two of them attending a dinner party at the home of her university's president. All of the distinguished faculty would be there, spouses in tow, and when she and Austin arrived, she would hear the women whispering among themselves about the man on her arm. Eye candy for sure. The wives would be jealous that their own husbands hadn't taken more of an interest in physical fitness.

Later, over cocktails, she imagined Austin standing in a circle of full professors, regaling them with stories about opium dens in Shanghai, or the houses of ill repute he had visited in Kathmandu. Even if he had been a medical student once, Austin's openness and honesty would seem naive to a group of stuffy, back-stabbing academics, all fighting each other for tenure.

Nope. It would never work. Mentally she rolled her eyes and growled. Maybe Austin was trainable, like Liza in *My Fair Lady*. It was easy to imagine that scene. She would be Professor Higgins, of course. Austin would be the street-wise, diamond-in-the-rough Liza.

"Concentrate, Austin," she heard herself say. "And try again. I know you can say it. Gorp."

"Gurp?"

"No, no. Gorrrp."

"Garp?"

Sandra throws up her hands. "Someone tell me why, oh, why can't the smugglers learn to speak?" Cue the music and she would break into song.

No, no. The music in her head screeched to a halt and the image vanished from her mind. She had no future with Austin Smith. There was no point in fantasizing about it.

Austin was definitely a character, even if he wasn't completely irresponsible. But it was the nice guys who made good mates, and that idea reignited the familiar fear in her chest. The more comfortable she became with Austin Smith, the more the fear grew.

It was the same fear she had felt four years earlier when she almost got married, and that really confused her. Austin and her former fiancé, Todd, had absolutely nothing in common. But Sandra wasn't going to marry Austin. Sure, she was attracted to the man, what woman wouldn't be? They might even become good friends after they finished rescuing her mother. But deep inside, some persistent itch suggested that she was on the verge of throwing herself into the man's arms. He was like a drug calling to her.

Logically, it was irrational. She had just met him. So, it must be something else. In order to figure out what, she gave herself permission to carefully, very carefully, explore her feelings for Austin and where they might take her. One step at a time, she told herself. One step at a time. She decided to get up and find him. She was sorry she had ignored him all day, and a short walk together might get them back on better terms. She slipped the sleeping baby into his backpack, careful to get both of his legs through the openings and hoisted him onto her back. Then she set out in the direction Austin had gone. He couldn't have gotten too far.

After a few minutes in the forest, she could barely hear her own footfalls. The trees around her and a thick padding of detritus on the forest floor swallowed up any sound she made. The late afternoon sun sent shafts of light knifing through the shadowy tree canopy. The gentle whistling of the wind overhead was broken only by the occasional chirping of birds.

She wondered whether Austin Smith wanted her to find him.

****

Austin stuck his hands in the pockets of his jeans and scuffed the dirt in front of him with the toe of his boot. Things weren't going all that well. The day before could have been disastrous, but he had saved Little Jeffrey and nimbly side-stepped any more serious trouble.

But the incident seemed to open Sandra up. When they talked over the campfire, he thought he was chipping away at her hard, scientist's shell, and he could have filled the forest with a Cheyenne victory cry. Then she'd given him a cold shoulder for most of the next day.

It was simply the way of some women, he told himself, but he wasn't ready to give up. Sandra wasn't just another woman, another conquest. Oh, no. She was the woman of his dreams, and finding her could only have been a gift from a Great Spirit, *the* Great Spirit, whichever one that was. And he didn't want to blow it. He only wished he had listened more closely to his grandfather's spiritual stories, and not so much to the exciting warrior stuff. Ah, well, he was who he was.

Lost in his thoughts, Austin didn't immediately notice the warm puff of air that tickled the back of his hand. Gradually, he realized that something was behind him, something warm, soft, and wet. Something began to nuzzle and sniff the wrist of his left hand, still in his pocket. When he glanced down, he saw a big black nose. An animal's nose. A bear's nose. He pulled his hands slowly out of his pockets and froze. The nose puffed more hot air and he fought the urge to sprint away like a deer, a deer that would quickly become dinner for a much swifter bear.

Austin's life should have been flashing before his eyes, but he had done that once recently, and it hadn't been as interesting as he had hoped. Besides, he slowly realized that this bear meant him no harm. Not yet, anyway. If it had, Austin would already have been eaten. Carefully, Austin reached out his hand and stroked the length of the big furry nose.

He heard a low throaty rumble, but it didn't sound like an angry noise. It sounded more like purring. He turned his head just enough to see the small black star on the bear's head, right between the eyes. Right where Austin prayed it would be.

"Well, hello, Gretchin. Nice to see you again."

"Grrr," Gretchin purred. She continued to nuzzle his pocket. He smoothed his hand along the short fur of her nose, then he scratched her head lightly.

"Are you having fun out here in the wilderness?"

"Grrr," Gretchin rumbled again.

Austin remembered what Melbourne Brisbane had said, that Gretchin responded to all the usual hands signals, whatever they were. He turned all the way around to face her, but she sat down, then rolled over onto the ground and lay there, looking up at him.

"What's the matter girl? Have you gotten a little lazy on your wilderness vacation? Are you forgetting your training? Let's see if I can help you get back into shape."

****

As she pushed her way through a swath of underbrush, Sandra wondered whether she could find an Indian in the woods if he didn't want to be found. She knew that was stereotyping Austin, but he *did* sound like he wanted to be alone. And she had expected to find him before now.

She cupped her hands over her mouth to call out for him, but she heard a rustling sound and some low grunting, coming from the other side of a rock-studded hillock. It sounded like a wild pig rolling around on the forest floor. It wasn't like any sound she had ever heard a wild bear make, so she was pretty sure she and Little Jeffrey weren't in any immediate danger. It could have been a big hairy moose, scraping the winter fur off its antlers against a tree. Whatever it was, the feral noises thrilled her. Finding Austin could wait. She crept forward, hoping to catch a glimpse of the animal without frightening it off.

She drew closer to the grunting, careful not to step on a twig or make any other noise. Then, just on the other side of a large boulder, she spotted a flash of thick, brown fur. She drew back. She hadn't gotten a good look at it, but she immediately knew she had stumbled upon a bear!

"Cripes!" she whispered. If she had suspected a

162

bear in the slightest, she would never have snuck up on it, but she had never heard a bear make such noises. Fortunately, it had been looking away from her, and her hiding place was downwind. The bear hadn't seen her, and it might not smell her if she got away quickly. She started to back up, but she decided to risk peeking at the animal one more time to find out whether it had detected her presence, and to see why it was making such unusual noises. She peered around the rock again with one eye and saw a towering grizzly drop down onto all four legs and roll over onto its back. Then it waggled paws as big as dinner plates back and forth in unison, like it was swimming on its back. Sandra smiled. In spite of its size, the bear acted like a big cute, stuffed animal. Without warning, the bear leaped to its feet. Sandra sprang backward, thinking it must have smelled her.

Before she could turn and run, the beast stood on its hind legs and pirouetted in a full circle. Sandra gasped. Even a playful bear could be dangerous, and she should be frightened, but she had never seen a bear act so oddly. The grizzly leaned over sideways, like it was trying to touch one foot. It was an utterly bizarre display. The animal continued to lean over until it had one big, furry front paw on the ground—and executed a perfect cartwheel.

"What?" Sandra gasped. She never imagined that wild animals would do such things, outside of a circus. She shifted Little Jeffrey on her back and stared at the feral acrobat, which rose back up on its hind legs. It appeared to be clapping its front paws together, in time to some unheard rhythm. Then it rolled onto its head and did a somersault.

"I don't believe it!" Sandra said out loud. This time the bear heard her. It came up on its feet and turned to face her.

"Uh, oh," she whispered.

Deep in the midst of his nap, Geoffrey stirred. *"Babies sure need a lot of sleep,"* he mumbled. But he didn't mind. He was dreaming that he was lying on a lounge chair on a white sandy beach in Bermuda. A young cherub intern had gone off to fetch Geoffrey another piña colada. He snuggled into the backpack, his eyelids sank like the tropical sun over the distant, watery horizon. Surely his parents could get along without him for a few more minutes.

Sandra knew she couldn't run, and the tactic all the experts recommended, playing dead, would be dangerous with Little Jeffrey in the pack on her back. The bear took a step toward her, and Sandra desperately tried to remember exactly what Austin had done when he had faced down a bear two days ago. Boldly, she leaped out from the rock and raised both of her hands in the air.

Geoffrey snapped awake and realized what was happening. *"What are you doing, young lady?"* His arms flailed helplessly. *"Do all you mortals have a death wish?"*

But the bear stopped, just like the bear Austin had faced. It rose onto its hind feet and let loose a chilling roar. Sandra's vision blurred, but she forced down her panic and kept both arms straight up in the air. To her surprise, the bear dropped onto all fours and turned away. She staggered backward a couple of feet, gasping for breath.

"Wow," she said. "It really works!" She had just

recreated Austin's experience, and she had gotten pretty much the same results. That was evidence of its scientific validity. She imagined the editors of the most prestigious scientific and nature journals bidding furiously for her story about the encounter. Perhaps someone would produce a television mini-series about her research, like they did about Jane Goodall, who studied gorillas.

Who knew? They might even name a chair in her honor at the university. Maybe—but the bear didn't scamper in the opposite direction, like Austin's bear had. This bear came back and stood there, looking at her and flashing a menacing row of teeth. Sandra's eyes grew wide. It wasn't going to run away. Then, to her amazement, it rolled forward and performed another neat little somersault. When it came back to a sitting position, it played with its toes. Sandra could swear it had a grin on its face.

"Neat trick, huh?" Austin stepped out from the other side of the boulder.

"What the—?"

"Her name's Gretchin."

Apparently he had been leaning against the opposite side of the same rock she was hiding behind. Confusion swept through Sandra's brain like a dust storm.

"Wait a minute," she said. "Did *you* stop the bear from attacking just now?"

"No. You did that. I stopped her from running away, and I threw in the somersault just for fun."

"What?"

"Want to see it again?" He whistled at Gretchin, then held up three fingers on one hand.

"No, I don't want to see it again."

Gretchin rolled into a somersault anyway. Austin tossed her an after-dinner mint from his pocket, which she caught in her mouth and swallowed without chewing.

Sandra felt hot fury rushing into her veins. "You tricked me!"

"Not exactly. I didn't know what I was doing the first time I met Gretchin. I didn't know that first bear was her."

"But you didn't use some kind of Indian trick to stop the bear, did you?"

"Nope. I don't know any Indian tricks, really."

"And you never said a word to me about this Gretchin bear, did you?" She stepped closer until she was toe-to-toe with him as she spoke. She looked up with her chin thrust forward, surprising both of them with the strength of her anger.

"I was going to," he said.

"Before or after I made a fool out of myself by publishing all this in a journal article?" She threw her hands out to her sides for emphasis. She didn't wait for an answer, but she and Gretchin, having gotten the signal from Sandra, spun simultaneously on their respective heels and stalked away from each other.

"Whoa!" Geoffrey's arms flew out straight in front of him when Sandra spun around.

Sandra stopped dead in her tracks when she saw a group of men running toward her. One of them carried a very large gun.

Chapter 11

"Stop her!" a man yelled.

Sandra braced herself, thinking the men were talking about her, but they swept by her and ran past Austin. All but one of them. A short, bearded man in a "Hard Rock Café, LA" baseball cap staggered to a stop in front of her. He bent over with his hands on his knees, breathing hard. After a few deep breaths he looked up at her.

"Damn," he said. "We almost got her this time."

Sandra turned and realized the rest of the men were running after Gretchin. Each of them waved his arms in the air, giving the bear different hand signals. Undoubtedly Gretchin would be confused, but she had a good head start, and it didn't look like she wanted to be caught.

Sandra looked back at the man in the Hard Rock hat. "You're after the bear?"

"Yes, the bloody bear," the man wheezed. "If we ever do catch her I think I'll shoot her myself."

Sandra mustered as much indignation as she could, even though she wasn't sure what they were talking about. "You're not allowed to hunt bears in the national forest."

"We're not hunting her," the man said. Breathe, breathe. "We're just trying to catch her."

"I don't think you're allowed to catch bears,

167

either."

"And we *would* have caught her if you hadn't given her the signal to run off." He said this as though Sandra had chased the bear away intentionally, which she had, in a sense.

"Okay, mister," she said. "Next time your bear attacks me, maybe I'll shoot it for you."

The man straightened up and waved his hands. "No, no, don't do that. I was just kidding. She cost us a lot of money."

"Just what is going on here, anyway?" Sandra asked.

"Allow me to introduce myself. My name is Leonard P. Spinelli. The director."

"Oh, boy. Movie people. Things are looking up." Geoffrey tried to brush back the few dark strands of hair on his baby head, but the best he could do was slap his cheek.

"Director of what?"

"Of what?" Geoffrey asked. *"Lady, haven't you seen "The Martian Melodies" or "Purple Passions of the Popes"? Now there was a piece of work. If only the real popes were so lively."*

"Films," Spinelli said. "I make films."

Sandra heard the disappointment in Spinelli's voice when she failed to recognize him. "We don't get many movies up here," she said by way of an apology. Then she got suspicious. She didn't like seeing wild animals in captivity. "What do you mean she was your bear?"

"We are, or were, making a movie with that bear," he said. "Until she ran off."

"Smart bear."

"Very smart. She's been trained by the best. But

there's something else. She's in heat. Managing one bear is problem enough. I don't know what we're going to do if she finds a mate."

Sandra put two and two together just as Austin walked up. "So, you have a trained bear running loose in the woods?" She was speaking to Spinelli, but she was staring daggers at Austin.

"Yes," Spinelli said.

"Why don't you just whistle or something and get her back?"

"Gretchin only responds to silent hand signals," he said.

"There's a hand signal I'd like to give you," Sandra said, still looking at Austin. Then she stalked away before anyone could reply. Geoffrey rolled his eyes, bouncing around on Sandra's back, practically forgotten.

"I think I'm going to be sick."

With her head swimming, Sandra stumbled blindly in the direction of her camp. Just a few minutes earlier she had decided to make up with Austin. Again. And she had almost opened her heart to him. Again. Almost decided to throw caution to the wind. Again. Only to find out that he had lied to her about their first encounter with the bear. How could she have been so easily fooled? How could she trust a man who would lie to win her affections?

Austin caught up with her, but Sandra didn't slow down or even look at him.

"I'm sorry," he said, walking along beside her.

"Why didn't you tell me it was a trained bear?"

"Do you mean now, or earlier?"

"Now. No, earlier. Now *and* earlier."

Austin stepped in front of her, turned, and put his arms on her shoulders, stopping her forward progress. He stepped close to her and she felt her anger begin to dissolve, against her will. But she wasn't ready to forgive him. Deliberately, she shook his hands away from her arms and stepped back.

"You lied to me," she said with icy calm.

"No. Not exactly."

"No? What do you call it when you don't tell the truth? I thought we had almost been killed by that bear and you let me go on thinking it. Didn't you?"

"Well, we *might* have been killed."

"Only if it had accidently tap danced on top of us."

He laughed, but his brows knit, and Sandra could tell he was at least trying to be serious.

"Truthfully," he said. "At the time, the first time I mean, I didn't know the bear was tame."

"Sure. And that's why you stood your ground, Mr. Macho, holding your hands in the air, commanding the bear to stop." She had half a mind to take a swing at him.

"No. I honestly thought I might be killed."

"Then why did you do it?"

"I did it for my son," he said calmly. "And for you."

Sandra stood with her arms folded, tapping her foot in the dirt, considering this. He sounded sincere, but the idea of it was preposterous. No man she'd ever known, except perhaps her father, would ever have faced down a charging grizzly for her. It just didn't happen. In one of Spinelli's damned movies, maybe, but not in real life.

No, she was dealing with Austin Smith the

Character now, not Austin Smith the guy so nice that he would give his life for her. But the idea that irked her most was that she might never know the truth.

"I can't believe I didn't see right through you from the start."

"You did." He cupped her hands in his. "You did. I'm everything you think I am, or at least I was. But I'm trying to be a different person. I keep telling you that." His eyes searched her face, his expression earnest. Whatever else he might have said was lost when Spinelli came up, his troop of movie makers bunched up close behind him. Walter Boyles was with them.

"Walter, what are you doing here?" she asked.

"I'm the official Forest Service liaison to Star Century Productions." He beamed at Spinelli, who took no notice. "The Service is dedicated to the wise use of our nation's resources, and if 'Fire on the Gambezie' is successful, Hollywood might make a lot of movies in Alaska, right?" He looked at Spinelli, who was still concentrating on Sandra.

"Oh for God's sake," Sandra said. "Is that what the Forest Service calls a "wise use" of our nation's resources? Turning a national forest into a movie set?"

"Have you ever had a screen test?" Spinelli said. He was closely inspecting Sandra's hair.

"No. I must have been playing hooky that day," she said. She wanted to swat him away like a horsefly.

"Excellent," Spinelli said, as if Sandra had said just the right thing. He looked at her like he was sizing up a used car.

"Sandra's doing some very important research on bears," Walter said.

"Hmm," Spinelli said. "Do you ever go by Sandy?"

"No, I don't. My name is Sandra."

"That's okay," Spinelli said. "There have been others. Sandra Dee, Sandra Bullock. But not so many that it wouldn't work."

"My name is Dr. Sandra Coulton."

"Right. Are you represented?"

"Only by my mother. And that isn't going the way I'd like."

"Can she do lunch?"

"What are you talking about?"

"Your contract."

"My contract?"

"Guild rules, you know. We can't even open a film can without a contract."

"I'm not going to make a movie with you."

Spinelli looked at Walter, seeming to notice him for the first time. "I thought you said she was available."

"Of course she's available," Walter said. "What else has she got to do in the middle of an Alaskan forest?"

"How about all that research you just mentioned?" Sandra said.

"We can use that as back story," Spinelli said. "But it would be more interesting if we made you a police investigator."

"Police investigator?"

"Yes, but one who works as an exotic dancer at night, to make ends meet. Have you ever taken your clothes off?"

"What?"

"I mean for the camera, of course."

"That's it. I've heard enough." Sandra started to

walk away, but when she turned away she stopped short when she came up against Austin's chest.

"She's perfect," Spinelli said to no one in particular. Then, to Sandra, "We still haven't caught Gretchin, so it looks like we're going to need a place to, how do you say it here in the west, "bed down" for the night? We have some tents."

"Not in my camp, mister." Sandra glared up at Austin. "It's a little too crowded there already." She spun on her heels, still having forgotten about Little Jeffrey.

"Whoaaa!" Geoffrey's baby arms flung outward.

She walked away without looking back, but she still heard Spinelli say, "What a little spitfire. The tabloids are going to love her."

****

Forty-five minutes later, out of the corner of her eye, Sandra saw Austin tiptoe into camp. She paid him no attention and busied herself with Little Jeffrey in his camp-stool crib.

"Hey, Lady," Geoffrey said. *"How many times are you going to check my diaper? Don't worry about it. You'll know when Nature calls again."*

The air next to Sandra's shoulder began to shimmer and Geoffrey growled. The last thing he wanted was a needling visit from his rival. Sandra noticed nothing.

"Howdy, cowpoke," Gabriel said once he fully appeared. "How's life on the trail treating you?"

"Great." Geoffrey put on a wooden smile. "It reminds me a lot of the Hotel Flambé in Paris. You should try it."

"I'll pass." Gabriel noticed the clashing red, green,

and purple auras swirling around Sandra and Austin and hooked a thumb in their direction. "They say you don't really know a person until you've traveled with them. Looks like these two have had about all the sightseeing together they can stand."

"I don't know about them, but I have." Geoffrey waved a chubby, dismissive hand at his foster parents. "They just need to come to some kind of understanding, that's all."

"Lordy, what part of sexual tension don't they understand?" Gabriel looked a little closer and whistled softly. "Looks like it's more about denial. And a lot of it." He winked at Geoffrey.

Geoffrey did a double-take and glanced over at Sandra and Austin again. "It's a lot more than sex, that's for sure. But I doubt they'll ever appreciate that. I just hope their frustration doesn't boil over until I finish my mission. Then who knows what they'll do?"

"You know who knows, Geoffrey."

"Yeah, yeah, yeah. The Boss knows all. Speaking of that, isn't it time you told me more about my mission? Why is this congresswoman so special? You can tell me that, at least, now that I know why I'm here."

"Hmmm, why *is* she so special?" Gabriel tapped his chin. "For the most part, I don't really know. But I can tell you this much about your mission. Part of it's about chalk dust."

Geoffrey blinked. It took him a second to understand that Gabriel was referring to something their mentor, Antonitis, used to say. "What's Antonitis got to do with any of this?"

"It's not about Antonitis, exactly," Gabriel said.

"And if I tell you any more, it might endanger one of your more important goals."

"But—"

"Anyway, I've got to run. A choir of angels in the Asia-Pacific section wants a piece of our bet. I'm going over there to find someone I can trust to hold the stakes."

"In that case, you'd better hurry," Geoffrey said. "I'm sure they're betting on me, and I'll be done here before you know it."

Gabriel shook his head lightly. "So much chalk dust, Geoffrey. So much chalk dust."

"What?" But Gabriel was gone, leaving Geoffrey to wonder about chalk dust and Antonitis.

Geoffrey had fond memories of his mentor. Antonitis was much older than Geoffrey, in a sense. Angels didn't age like people. They simply grew wiser with knowledge of the Truth. As they learned and understood more, the additional Truth tempered their auras, giving each of them greater colors, hues, and shades. That, in turn, gave them the appearance of being older and wiser, which, in a sense they were. Humans came with the same feature, but, with a few exceptions, most people couldn't actually see each other's auras. They could read them, though, if only subconsciously. People called it intuition. If someone said, "I liked that man from the moment I met him," it really meant, "That man has a nice aura." Everyone was attracted to the Truth, whether they knew it or not. Of course the reverse of Truth, Ignorance, was also true, in its own way. For that reason, it was strictly forbidden for an angel to judge anyone or anything,

"That duty is above your pay grade," El Jéfe would

say.

Geoffrey sighed. He remembered his days as an innocent Cherub, sitting at the feet of Antonitis, learning his lessons. His young, unspoiled aura was almost clear back then, free of any temperament or knowledge, good or bad. "A clean slate," Antonitis would say. "Ready to be clouded by chalk dust."

Geoffrey never quite understood the analogy, if the Truth be known. He preferred to think of himself as a vessel into which the Truth was poured. He considered his job was serving the Truth to others like a fine wine. When he was frustrated, Antonitis said Geoffrey spread the Truth around like a drunken waiter on St. Patrick's Day. Another observation Geoffrey didn't quite appreciate. Still, he gave Antonitis credit for teaching Geoffrey much of what he knew, at least in the beginning. Back when the old man was still around, his aura fairly glowed with the Wisdom of the Ages, an affect Geoffrey hoped to achieve someday.

If an angel performed his duties well, he got good performance evaluations and his aura improved. And performance was Geoffrey's specialty. Few of the Heavenly Host garnered as many brownie points as he. It was just a matter of time before he earned a stunning aura he could swirl around his shoulders like a cape. He imagined himself strolling along the Avenue of Clouds, catching the jealous eyes of all the other angels.

He sighed, then he remembered where he was—about as far from the Avenue as you could get.

Time to clock in again.

When Geoffrey came out of his reverie, Austin was rummaging through his gear. He went over to look at Little Jeffrey.

"How's the little guy doing?" Austin asked.

"See for yourself," Sandra said. She lay the baby on a blanket and stepped away to search the bottom of a stuff sack for baby food. She desperately wanted an evening without excitement, without a bear, and definitely without talking to Austin Smith, if that were possible. Austin took a quick look at the baby and wisely moved to the other side of the campfire, where he sat down on his sleeping bag.

After ten minutes, Sandra's mood had calmed down from nearly murderous to simply stewing. Since their first encounter with Gretchin, she had almost finished outlining a journal article in her head about bear attacks and how to prevent them. All she could see was her name in bold print as the primary author at the top of the page. What a fool she had been.

She started to feed the baby from a jar of homemade apricot puree. With every spoonful, her feelings about Austin ebbed and flowed, like a tide that washed back and forth over the campground. One minute she might have laughed about the whole thing. But the next minute she was convinced that men like Austin were boys like Peter Pan. They never grew up and thought the world was a playground. The people in it, like her, were just their playthings. If he had any interest in her at all, it was only because he needed a woman to take care of his child.

Austin's silent presence did nothing to lessen the tension. At high emotional tide, she was coiled and ready to lash out at him if he said anything clever. The weight of the baby food jar in her hand felt good. It would make an excellent projectile. Silently she dared Austin to say or do the slightest thing to provoke her.

Austin cleared his throat.

Oh, no, here we go. Geoffrey tried to curl up into a tight little ball.

Sandra poked the spoon into the puree and looked at Austin. She said nothing. "You know," he said. "I'm sorry about all that." Once again, he sounded contrite, but of course contrite wasn't nearly good enough.

"To which *that* are you referring? The lying to me *that*? The making-a-fool-of-me *that* or one of the many other *thats* I could mention?"

"All of them. You don't need to make a list."

It pleased her to see Austin squirm. "So, you're *really* sorry now."

"*Careful,*" Geoffrey cautioned Austin.

"Yes. Yes, I am."

Mentally, Geoffrey tried to dive for the bottom of his crib.

"So, everything's okay now, isn't it? Because you're sorry?" Sandra's smile held no warmth, but a look of relief crossed Austin's face. *Foolish man,* Sandra thought.

"I knew you'd understand," he said.

Her fingers tightened around a baby food jar, but, to her disappointment, she held her temper in check.

"I've got to finish feeding the baby," she said, as if that explained why she wasn't going to talk to him anymore.

There were a few more minutes of silence. Sandra fed Little Jeffrey from a jar of apricot puree, and then fussed with her GIS equipment and a map, planning their route for the next day. Austin seemed to be lost in thought and, with all of that masculinity lounging by the fire, he looked like a model for Camping

Magazine—Women's Calendar Issue. He was the one who could be a movie star, and she wondered what had happened to the film crew. She wasn't about to ask.

Austin noticed her when their eyes inadvertently met. "I really don't mean to make things difficult for you."

"Sure, thanks." Things weren't entirely Austin's fault but, in a remote, not-quite-conscious corner of her mind, she knew she had an advantage. She could cut off Austin's misguided efforts to win her heart once and for all. If she wanted to.

He took a deep breath. "Look. Things are pretty confused right now. I understand that."

"I'm not confused. I'm not happy, but I'm not confused."

"For what it's worth, I'm not happy about our situation either. I really want things to be okay between us."

"Things? You want things to be okay? Whatever do you mean, Mr. Smith?"

"You know, things. I didn't mean to *not* tell you about Gretchin. But, after that first day, things were going so much better between us, and I didn't want to change that."

"So, you let me think you were some kind of hero, when you weren't."

He grimaced and snapped a twig in half. "I liked being your hero."

"I didn't like being your fool."

"Well, I'm—"

"I know, I know. You're sorry."

"Yeah, well, in spite of my lapse in judgment, I still think we can still work something out here."

"What?" Sandra looked at him in bewilderment.

He held up his hands to stop her and continued. "I know you're *not* looking for romance. You've made that much plenty clear."

"Well, now. It's hard to believe, but maybe we're making progress."

"Right," he said. "But we still have the baby to think of."

"*We?*"

"Yes, we. And rather than fight over custody, I think we should settle things, come to an agreement and make it permanent. For the baby's sake, if nothing else."

"What? Are you suggesting shared custody? You and me? Like a divorced couple?"

"I suppose, if you put it that way."

Sandra rubbed her temples. Then she stood up and paced back and forth on her side of the fire, building up steam and waving her arms. "After what I've just been through I can't imagine what kind of agreement you think we could have. First of all—"

She didn't see Austin until he took her into his arms and kissed her. She was too stunned to understand what was happening, but her anger dissipated like it was a foreign language, the meaning of which she no longer understood. She accepted his lips eagerly, without thinking, as if she'd been waiting years for his kiss. But her arms were still frozen in place, in mid-air, where she'd been gesturing. A small moan escaped her throat, half the end of her sentence, and half pure pleasure from his kiss.

"*Wow!*" Geoffrey felt his baby face flush red. He watched the sensuous, roiling colors unleashed by their two auras, embracing in a space that normally was occupied by one.

Sandra's arms slowly dropped onto Austin's shoulders, but the feel of his hard body sent a shiver through her that broke the spell.

She pulled away and stamped her foot on the ground, which made no noise at all on the soft forest floor. "What on earth are you doing?"

"I thought it was obvious."

"You have to stop that," she said. Her eyes were still half-lidded.

"Why?"

Sandra looked at him with sympathy but held him at arm's length. "Because I haven't given you permission," she said. "Don't you get it? You can't just decide you like someone and have them automatically like you back."

He rubbed the back of his neck. "No, I suppose I can't."

"That's right, and I can't let you." She held up one hand to keep him from saying anything. "Austin. All I really know about you is that you stole an airplane—"

"Borrowed—"

"To find a baby—"

"My son—"

"Who may or may not be your son."

"But that's a good thing, isn't it?"

Sandra shot him a "don't interrupt me" glance.

He crooked his index finger on his chin and spoke up anyway. "This isn't really about me, is it?"

"Why do you say that?"

"Your mother said something about a history of running away, and I should ask you about that."

"I don't know what you're talking about."

"So, if you're not running away, then it's possible things could work out between us."

"Reverse psychology? Very clever, but you didn't finish medical school, so I know you're not a psychiatrist."

"It doesn't take a doctor to know what's going on here," he said. "I thought I was the one who was supposed to have a fear of commitment."

"Fear of commitment? Please. I'm not going to have a relationship with you just to prove you wrong. You've got to want to make a commitment. And I don't."

The smile on his face faded.

"Look," she said. "I know that, in your own Austin Smith way, you think you like me. But let's review the reality of this situation *one more time*, so you'll get it. You show up at Misha Ranch out of nowhere, and you want to—and maybe you have, in some small way…"

"What?"

"Swept me off my feet." It was only a whisper, and she held up the palms of her hands to stop him from saying anything. "But," she continued with more strength, "as much as I might—or might not—be attracted to you, I just can't let that happen. I can't run off to the other side of the world on a whim." She paused, embarrassed that she had admitted liking him, or that running off to the other side of the world was even a consideration.

"And besides," she said levelly. "As you say, there's a child to consider. Even if I were attracted to you, and even if I wanted to run off with you—and I assure you I don't—you and I both know you're in no position to take care of Little Jeffrey, even if he *is* yours. And, let's get real, we are not going to share custody of Little Jeffrey. It doesn't work all that well, even with real divorced parents. You and me, well…"

She stopped to catch her breath, fearful of what he would say, finding it hard, even at that moment, to resist his dark gaze and his gentle strength. All he had to do was kiss her again and she might forget everything she had just said, throw her career and her calm scientist's life out the window, maybe forever. She backed up and leaned against a small tree, trying to regain her sense of equilibrium.

"Why do you keep insisting that we're so different?" he asked. "I'll make you a deal. From now on, every time you let yourself go and enjoy life, in any small way at all, I promise I'll do something dull and responsible."

She laughed. "It's like I said before. People can't make changes in their character that easily."

"You and your damned studies." He turned away and looked up at the evening sky. "Was it some kind of study that told you to go into hiding in Alaska?"

She laughed again, but it sounded unconvincing, even to her. "As little as I know about you, you don't know anything about me."

"I recognize somebody who's on the run."

"Unlike you, I have nothing to run from."

"Really?"

"And besides, my life is none of your business."

"Maybe not. But I like you, Dr. Sandra Coulton, and somehow…"

"Please don't finish that thought."

The by-now-familiar waves of panic, dread, and

excitement swept through her, all at the same time. She wanted to leap up and kiss him again, or run away from their little camp at full speed. Just get away, a small voice inside her said. Just get away and give yourself time to breathe. To think. She felt the blood draining from her face. She took a few deep breaths but decided it was a good time to put her head down between her knees to keep from fainting. She sat down and waved a hand at him.

"I don't want to talk about this anymore," she said. "We have a hard day ahead of us and we should get ready."

"I wasn't the only one kissing a few minutes ago. You were there, too. All in."

"Never mind that," she said. "I don't know what that was. I was just caught up in the moment."

Austin turned away and stalked to the other side of the fire. He threw up his hands in frustration. "Sandy," he said, pointedly using her unwanted nickname. "Sometimes the moment is all we get."

Chapter 12

Twenty minutes later, Geoffrey surveyed the scene around him from his makeshift crib. An uncomfortable silence had fallen over the camp. Austin was carefully repairing a strap on the pack in which they carried Little Jeffrey. The strap had frayed a little but didn't really need fixing. He appeared calm enough, but his aura swirled in a confused mixture of greens and yellows. Sandra's aura didn't match her outward demeanor, either. She inventoried their supplies and reorganized the packs that were carried by the spare horses. When she looked up, it was usually to check the stars, or the weather. The two of them occasionally stole glances at each other out of the corners of their eyes. To a casual observer, everything might have appeared normal, but Geoffrey wasn't fooled.

He watched the vivid colors of his two temporary parents' auras eddy and swirl so brightly they almost blotted out the light of the fire. They were thinking hard about each other, not the tasks in front of them. So much yearning. So much fear and loneliness. And all the while they were close enough to reach out and touch what they might need most in life.

Austin's hand slipped, causing him to stick his finger with a needle.

"Ouch!"

Sandra looked over at him. "A little out of practice

with our domestic skills, are we?"

"I'll manage." Austin sucked the end of his finger and squinted at the strap.

Geoffrey shook his baby head, as much as he could. *These two might not exchange a kind word all night.* The behavior of mortals never ceased to baffle him. He tried to put his chubby hands on his hips with indignation and let out a baby-like "harrumph!"

"The baby sneezed," Sandra said. "I told you the forest is no place for a child. If he comes down with a cold…"

"He'll be fine," Austin said.

"How do you know that?"

"I've looked at him."

The confidence in Austin's voice kept Sandra from pointing out that he was practicing medicine without a license. She had read stories about people who pretended to be professionals they were not. Simply by showing an abundance of confidence, they were able to convince others they were doctors, lawyers, or airline pilots, when they actually had no formal training at all. She had even heard of an auto mechanic who once performed an appendectomy so well his fraud wasn't discovered until well after the operation.

She watched Austin surreptitiously for a minute. If he ever applied himself, he could easily be the "whole package" women always talked about. But her shoulders sagged. All of her instincts said Austin would move on as soon as he got bored and take Little Jeffrey with him. She had a vision of Austin leaving Misa Ranch in a rickety old Gypsy wagon, with Little Jeffrey, now a two-year-old, waving goodbye to her from the back door.

****

Austin peered at a bit of fraying fabric in the dim fire light. The old pack strap would hold well enough, not that Sandra Coulton would take his word for it. She had so little faith in him, he wondered why he was attracted to the woman. But he knew the answer. On those rare occasions when she smiled, the light in her eyes shone right through him, igniting his very soul. He only wished he could spark the same reaction in her. Most of the time she treated him with as much warmth as a thermometer, the kind they'd use on Little Jeffrey. Such a shame, too, since she raised his own temperature more than a few degrees. Sandra didn't want to give him an inch of slack when it came to him or his parenting. You'd think he was stealing the boy from her. If she felt so strongly about children, why didn't she have some of her own?

He stole a sidelong glance and found her peering into a large-mammal classification manual. Austin decided that now that a baby had literally dropped into her lap, Sandra could skip marriage, the husband, and all the preliminaries and get right down to mothering the boy to death. But no son of his was going to grow up to be a mamma's boy, if he could help it.

He may or may not convince Sandra that two parents for Little Jeffrey are better than one, but he was going to be the baby's father, come hell or high water. He had never backed down from a challenge before, and he didn't figure on doing so now.

"Brother," Geoffrey moaned. He looked toward the heavens, where undoubtedly He was watching. "Dear Lord, I think I finally understand your fascination with mortals. They're learning tools, aren't

they? You've been watching human beings for thousands of years because you're confused by them, too. You know they're messed up and you don't want to make the same mistake somewhere else in the universe."

"You tricky old bast—" A peal of thunder rumbled across the clear, star-filled sky, like cannon fire, forcefully cutting him off. "Just a term of endearment! No need to get huffy!" *You spend a dozen millennia together and you think you know someone. But no, the Old Man never told all, not even to the angels.* The thunder gradually rolled away to silence.

"Thunder," Austin said. "Is it going to rain?"

Sandra scanned the cloudless sky. "I don't know."

"Well," he said. "Will wonders never cease?"

"I beg your pardon?"

"That's the first time I've heard you admit you didn't know something."

Sandra scowled and they both went back to their separate tasks.

Geoffrey rolled his baby-blue eyes. *At the rate these two are going, they'll end up killing each other before I can save the congresswoman. And speaking of her, I need to find out how things are going at the helicopter. There's got to be something I can do for these two pathetic creatures before I go.* He thought about it for a moment. *I've got it. A modest Harmony Blessing. Just a temporary one. That should nudge them a little closer together and keep things nice and cozy while I'm gone.*

He waved his tiny arms in the air and then hesitated. He didn't get into the field as much as he used to, and it had been some time since he'd invoked a

Harmony Blessing, even on a small scale. *How does it go again? Oh, yes. "Deus Benedictus Harmonius Maximi." Or should that have been 'Minimi'? Ah, whatever.* He was only tweaking the positive natural feelings they had for each other. He waved his arms, as much as he could, in the sign of the Cross, the Star of David, and the Crescent and Star to set the blessing. *That should do it. Now, off to see how Mother Coulton is doing.*

He extended his angel senses and let his consciousness drift away over the treetops. He soared toward the snow-capped peak, now a lot closer than before. Even though night had fallen, the deer, squirrels and other animals on the ground gazed up at him as his essence flew over. Migrating birds watched him with interest. He smiled at them all and continued on his way.

Homing in on Martha's flashing aura and the sad colors surrounding Mr. Johnson, he had no trouble spotting the helicopter. They both sat in the cockpit of the silent aircraft. Beads of sweat glistened on Johnson's forehead as he slumped back in his seat. He moaned, and Geoffrey felt thankful that angels didn't have to experience such mortal suffering.

Not in the ordinary course of business, anyway. Every hundred years or so the Big Man would tap an angel on the shoulder and send him down to earth, where he would have to take the place of some poor sap who was about to get accidently electrocuted or something. The kicker was, as far as anyone knew, taking the place of a dying mortal meant the end of the angel's life as well. Some said there was a special heaven for angels, where they went when they died, if that's what they did. The only thing anyone knew for sure was that no angel ever came back from one of those missions.

Geoffrey assumed he was too important to the Old Man to be disposed of so perfunctorily. The closest he ever came was the time God called upon Geoffrey's mentor, Antonitis, to switch places with the Apostle Paul, kneeling before the captain of the guard outside the gates of Rome. He shuddered at the memory. *Good old Antonitis.* Geoffrey hoped for his friend's sake there actually was some kind of angel heaven.

Johnson moaned again, and Geoffrey gently stroked the man's aura, suppressing his fever and slipping him into a deeper, less tortured, sleep.

Martha Coulton sat stiffly in the passenger's seat with her arms crossed, trying not to listen to Johnson's groans and feverish mutterings. She wondered whether her daughter would find them before the poor man expired completely. The thought of sitting in the small helicopter next to a dead man for two or three days made her shiver.

Sandra was certainly taking her sweet time getting there, but Martha knew the joke was on her. She, the woman who had promised to convert the forest into lumber at the first opportunity, now found herself lost and alone right in the middle of it. She practically growled at the irony but, instead she sat straight up, listening. Something else was growling out in the darkness. Or was it just a little thunder?

She relaxed a little and wanted to get some sleep. She bunched up her jacket to use as a pillow and stuffed it between her shoulder and the Plexiglas helicopter window. She snuggled up against it and closed her eyes, but it was tough getting comfortable under these conditions. At least the helicopter had more leg room than the airlines gave you. That was something. She sighed and opened her tired eyes for one last peek at the dark woods surrounding her. Then she screamed.

Peering back at her through the window, not more than six inches from the end of her nose, was another nose, much bigger than her own. A muzzle with two big, coal-black eyes behind it. A bear!

As soon as she screamed, the bear stood up on its hind legs, waving its paws in the air, and roared. This took away what little breath Martha had left in her lungs, and she sat up, gasping. The mammoth beast dropped onto all four legs and rocked back and forth, silently watching her. As soon as she had recovered her breath, Martha screamed again, and once again the bear rose up on two legs and roared.

Martha passed out. Or tried to, anyway. It was really one of those faints she was so good at contriving in someone's Washington drawing room, when it seemed necessary. She had gotten so proficient at it she almost believed she could faint at will. When she realized she hadn't passed out, she scrunched up her face in fear and squinted her eyes open, hoping the bear had gone off into the woods. It hadn't. It stood on its hind legs, with its front paws resting on the flimsy curved Plexiglas door of the helicopter looking down at her. It licked its lips. Then it licked the Plexiglas next to her face. Martha closed her eyes tight and shuddered, still as death.

After a moment, the bear ambled around the front of the helicopter and over to Johnson's side. With a start, Martha realized she had left the door open a crack to give the sick man some air. Desperately she flung herself across Johnson's unconscious form, reaching for the latch. How do you close the damn things anyway? She had never really learned, since Johnson had always been there to open and close the doors for her.

She snatched her arm back when she grabbed a handful of fur.

The bear had deftly pried opened the door with one paw, as though it had been doing it all its life. Johnson began to fall out of his seat, but his still sleeping head came to rest on the bear's shoulder. Martha flattened her body back against her own side of the helicopter and froze. She considered popping her own door open and running for her life. But then she'd really be lost in the woods and her daughter would never find her. Instead, she gaped at the wild animal, praying to God she wouldn't have to watch it eat Johnson.

For its part, the bear's eyes seemed to glaze over as it began sniffing the air inside the cockpit. After a few moments it started to sniff the length of Johnson's body. The sniffing gradually concentrated on one of Johnson's jacket pockets. With its right paw, the bear held back the left jacket flap. Martha thought it was going to take a bite out of the man's chest but, instead, the bear slid a large Snickers bar out of the breast pocket of the jacket with its teeth. The bear pushed itself backward, forcing Johnson back into his seat, and ambled off into the night. The passenger side door swung shut and closed with a soft click. Johnson sagged back against the door, oblivious to anything that had just happened.

Before Geoffrey could catch her, Martha really did faint dead away.

Great. That's not going to help at all. Now she'll have more reason than ever to destroy the forest. I'd better think of something special to do for her when she wakes up. He would end up working half the night, confident that nothing too dramatic was going on back at camp.

****

At about that same time, a contented feeling flowed like warm honey through Sandra, almost unnoticed at first, percolating from the top of her head down to the soles of her feet and back again. She sighed and smiled at the glowing campfire. She put down her book and watched Austin as he gently stroked the peach fuzz on Little Jeffrey's head. Austin gave her a knowing smile and set the boy down carefully on a blanket. "He's asleep."

Sandra moved over to Austin's side of the fire and together they looked down at the baby. "He's such a beautiful child," she said.

"Like an angel."

"It's a shame his mother abandoned him."

"Yes, it is," he agreed. "But then I probably never would have known about him—or you—if she hadn't."

Sandra smiled just as knowingly back at Austin. Such a good man. Had he done something with his hair? He looked different somehow. So...so...good. Maybe it was the firelight.

As if responding to the same, silent command, they sat down next to each other on his sleeping bag.

"You know," Sandra said. "My mother doesn't consider it very ladylike, but I never get tired of camping out under the stars."

Austin put his arm around her waist. How cozy,

she thought. She gazed up at the full moon and snuggled into his shoulder. A small but urgent voice called to her from somewhere far away in the back of her head. The alarm it sounded was quickly and firmly silenced. What harm could it do to sit with Austin? He was so warm, so strong…and…she let her head rest against his chest.

"I meant to tell you earlier," he said. "I really admire a woman who can start a campfire with one match."

"Thank you." She leaned away from him to see his face. What she saw were two soft brown eyes, gazing into her own as earnestly as if he were confessing to a priest. How could she have ever doubted this man's sincerity?

"In fact," he said, "I admire everything about you."

"Oh, go on," she said playfully.

"Yes. Especially your hair."

She rolled her eyes and punched him lightly on the arm.

"It's more than that, of course. What you've done with your life. Getting your PhD. Coming to Alaska. Dedicating yourself to your research." He leaned toward her and slowly brushed a lock of hair away from her eyes.

"You're not so bad yourself," she said. She stroked his cheek with her fingertips.

"I know."

She chuckled. "Oh, you know, do you?" He held his index finger to her lips and she stopped talking. Then he leaned in slowly. She sighed as their lips brushed in a soft, caressing kiss. Their arms encircled each other, hands searching, marveling at the feel of each other's bodies.

"It's about time," he whispered.

"Oh, yes."

Slowly, luxuriously, Austin leaned her backward onto the sleeping bag. She couldn't tell if the sudden outburst of meteors in the sky overhead was real or just a reflection of how she felt at that moment. Bright streaks of light lit up the inky black Alaskan sky like Washington, D.C. on the Fourth of July. She could only muster a vague smile at the unusual cosmic pyrotechnics. She had other things on her mind.

"It's all so wonderful," she whispered. "So wonderful." She and Austin began tugging urgently at the buttons of each other's jeans.

****

As the moon dipped below the horizon, Geoffrey surveyed the scene and the helicopter and gave his handiwork one last look. Mentally, he dusted his hands where the butt of his white robe would have been, if he had been in that form.

That should do the trick. The old lady has a heart of stone if she doesn't appreciate this. He stood back to watch the show.

Without opening her eyes, Martha Coulton smacked her lips and yawned. Thank goodness that was over. What a nightmare. It had seemed so real. A light began flashing outside, and she squinted to see it. What kind of light would be flashing in the middle of the forest? Had the police found her? Her eyes batted open and her jaw dropped in disbelief as she gazed up through the helicopter's bubble windshield.

There, high in the Alaskan sky, hung an enormous shimmering curtain of light. Sheets of green, blue, and red that must have been tens, perhaps hundreds of miles high, weaved and darted across the sky. Sometimes they snapped and flapped like flags, fluttering like there was a breeze in outer space. Their colors shifted and changed, like God was trying to decide which set of cosmic drapes would look best over the North Pole.

As if this exhibition weren't enough, the whole scene was punctuated by meteor trails, dozens of them, blazing back and forth across the night sky and bursting in flashes of color and light, or burning out in silence.

Martha had no idea what was going on, but she scrunched down in her seat to get a better view of the spectacular display and giggled out loud.

"Would you look at that!" she said. In her excitement, she slapped Johnson on the arm. Then she remembered his condition and looked more closely at him to see if he was still alive. He snorted once and began to snore quietly. She waved him off.

"Just like all my dates these days." She snuggled into her seat to watch the astral fireworks alone, yearning for a big bag of popcorn. Then she remembered the candy bar the bear had taken from Johnson's pocket. Carefully, she prodded his jacket with her finger. He had another one! She removed it slowly, careful not to wake him up.

"You've been holding out on me," she told him. He grunted as if he had heard, but he didn't wake up. She peeled away the wrapper, softly humming "Hooray for the Red, White, and Blue." Quietly, she cheered each new change in the heavenly pageant until the first rays of the sun started to glow on the edge of the horizon, then her eyes drifted closed and she slept like a baby.

****

Humming one of his favorite Gregorian chants, Geoffrey floated back into camp shortly after sunrise. When he arrived, he saw only one large, lumpy form covered by a sleeping bag. *Oh, no. Had there been a fight? Had one of them fled the camp during the night?*

He looked more closely and realized with horror that Austin and Sandra were together in the same bag. He had given them a harmony blessing to lighten up their moods, but he had no idea they would go this far. Before he could think of what to do, the bodies in the sleeping bag began to stir.

"Oh my God!" Sandra screamed.

The bag came alive in a frenzy of flailing arms and legs.

"What on earth?" Austin said.

Together Sandra and Austin bolted from the bag in one big, flesh-colored flash, grasping for whatever they could find to cover themselves and running to opposite sides of the little camp. Austin held his shirt over his privates. Sandra had grabbed her blue jeans with one hand and the handle of a small cooking pot with the other. She held the blue jeans over her lap, but she could only cover one breast at a time with the pot. She switched hands, putting the pot down below and holding her jeans over her breasts.

"What have you done?" she demanded.

"What have *I* done?"

"Oh, my, what have I done?"

"This is unforgivable!" Sandra said. She would have run from camp or ridden away, if she hadn't been naked.

"I knew that Maximi should have been a Minimi!" Geoffrey quickly fired a low-grade sedative blessing

197

over the entire camp. Nothing too extreme, but enough to keep things from boiling over.

"When *did* you crawl into my sleeping bag?" Austin asked.

"*Your* sleeping bag?" But he was right. It was his sleeping bag. Some, but only some, of her anger dissipated into confusion. "You, you must have trapped me in there," she said.

"I don't remember doing any such thing." He was smiling now, but it was not an evil smile, which she would have expected. Instead, it was the smile of someone who was playing along with a joke at his expense. Trapping the jeans against her stomach with her elbow, Sandra ran her fingers through her hair. She couldn't remember anything that happened last night.

Geoffrey settled into his baby body and hoped the heavenly hosts were still at breakfast. He didn't want any witnesses, especially Gabriel.

"Are you sure you didn't spike my tea with something?" Sandra asked.

"You're the scientist. You tell me what it was, and I'll bottle and sell it."

He had a point there. She could hold her liquor as well as the next woman, but she didn't know of any drug that would have driven her to do what it looked like she had done and then not remember it in the morning.

"You must have been sleepwalking," he said.

She thought about this. Perhaps he was offering her a face-saving way out of the predicament.

"Maybe," she muttered. "You really don't remember anything…happening?"

"If we did anything like that I don't think I would

have forgotten." He was watching her closely now. Perhaps a little too closely.

"Please turn around," she said. "I'm going to get dressed. You see how Little Jeffrey is doing."

"Right." He took his time turning around, but eventually he did and he went immediately to check on the child. She snatched up the rest of her clothing and dashed behind the nearest tree. Her mind reeled as she slipped on her jeans. Had they really done what it looked like they'd done? She tried hard to remember any details from the night before, but the entire evening was just a warm, fuzzy blank.

She looked out from behind the tree at Austin, who now had his own blue jeans on. She watched the tattoos on his sinuous arms as he fed Little Jeffrey. Surely she would remember being in the embrace of such a man. Get a grip, she chided herself. So what if they had…well, "done it"? If neither of them could remember it, then maybe it really didn't matter. But if Austin really had done something tricky last night, how did she know he wouldn't try it again?

Sandra continued to keep an eye on him as she finished dressing. Austin set the baby down and scratched the scruff of his beard. Then he took a couple of steps toward her.

"You stay right where you are, mister."

He glanced up at the trees or down at the ground, anywhere but directly at her. "Look," he said. "I honestly don't know what happened last night, but whatever it was, I don't have any memory of it, so it's like it never happened."

"Something must have happened."

"Only if you insist on it. But what?"

"Well, it's obvious. You…took advantage of me."

"And how did I do that?"

"I don't know how you did it, but apparently you did. I'm sure I never agreed to anything." She buttoned the last button on her shirt and tucked in the tails.

"Do you see any signs of a struggle?" he asked. "How do I know you didn't take advantage of me?"

"Women don't take advantage of men."

Austin rubbed the stubble on his chin. "You don't know the women I know."

Sandra swiftly laced her boots, in case she needed to run, but then she heard radio static, crackling from inside her saddlebag.

"Sandra, dear? Sandra, are you there?" It was her mother. Sandra ran to the bag. If Austin tried anything again, at least she could tell her mother about it. She froze when he reached the radio first, but he held out the microphone for her.

She snatched it from his hands and spoke without taking her eyes off him.

"Mother, are you okay?"

"Oh, yes, dear. Wonderful. Simply wonderful."

Sandra swore she heard her mother giggling.

"You don't sound okay. What's going on?"

"The lights, honey. I stayed up all night watching the lights. Didn't you see them?"

"We've got to get going," Sandra said to Austin. "My mother's starting to hallucinate."

Chapter 13

After riding for two hours, Sandra reined her horse to a stop in the middle of a grassy meadow. She still hadn't figured out how Austin had gotten her into his sleeping bag, or what they had done there. All morning long she had been trying to understand it and trying to decide how she should treat the man. Her body didn't feel like anything had happened, which gave her some comfort. Austin claimed he was innocent and he sounded sincere, but she shivered involuntarily when he rode up by her side.

"How much farther do we have to go?" he asked.

That sounded a lot like, "Are we there yet," but his smile seemed sincere.

"I haven't given you permission to talk to me," she said, only half joking. "We're still a day away, but I'm not ready to make camp. I'm worried about my mother." She was also worried about Austin, of course, but she was glad to have her mother as an excuse for not spending another night alone with him.

"Your mother seemed okay to me. Just a little giddy."

"My mother has never been giddy in her life. As far as I know, giddy isn't in her repertoire. Anyway, I think we can shorten our trip and get to the helicopter early tomorrow, providing the Highline Trail is open."

That got Geoffrey's attention. It was about time

they took a shortcut. He was getting tired of riding in Sandra's backpack, but he knew that, as far as these two mortals were concerned, any deviation from the plan might be trouble.

"What's the Highline Trail?" Austin asked.

"It runs high along the eastern slope of the hills we've been skirting." Sandra pointed toward the low peak on their left as she handed her binoculars to Austin. He scanned a jagged, windswept ridge that ran below a broad, white snowfield.

"If it's open," she said, "we can bypass the trail in the lower drainage."

"That would be good."

"It's much more direct. But it's also more difficult."

"How's that?"

"It's not too bad in the summer, but it's a rocky trail and you can get some bad weather any time of year. In the winter it's impassable. Too much snow. In spring when the weather is changing it's anybody's guess. And there are some serious drop-offs."

"What's your guess?"

Sandra shaded her eyes with her hand and scanned the treeless ridge above them. "It's probably open." She hoped it was, anyway. "Do you feel up to it?"

"You're the boss." He handed back her binoculars.

"Thanks." *Now he says I'm the boss*. She reined her horse back onto the trail. Austin fell in behind.

All day long Austin had acted like things were as normal as they had ever been. Maybe he was just trying to put Sandra at ease, but she was still suspicious. The only thing that kept her from sending him back to the ranch alone was the fact that she couldn't think of any good explanation for her own behavior last night. That and the fact that Austin was still needed to pilot the helicopter.

But *something* had happened last night, and Sandra wouldn't be comfortable alone with Austin unless she figured out what. Until then, she wasn't sure she could trust him. She shook her head at the questions buzzing between her ears.

****

"Sheesh," Geoffrey said. *With any other couple, last night might have been the start of something beautiful. Is it my fault that people don't know their own desires?*

High above, on a slowly drifting cumulonimbus cloud, the Archangel Gabriel leaned over on one elbow, watching.

"Thinking of taking a shortcut, Geoffrey?"

"You stay out of this, Gabe. You've caused enough trouble."

"On the contrary. Things are going much too smoothly for you, Mr. Almaric." He stroked his chin thoughtfully. "Maybe we should do something else to make our bet a little more interesting."

"Don't you dare!" But the cloud had evaporated.

Thirty minutes later, the radio in Sandra's saddlebags crackled to life again.

"Robert Johnson to Sandra Coulton." Sandra scrambled to reach the transceiver.

"This is Sandra Coulton. Is that you, Mr. Johnson? Are you all right?"

"Yes, yes," came the response. "I don't understand it. The fever seems to come and go, but right now I feel great."

Sandra and Austin looked at each other.

"You tell my daughter I want her to get here anyway." Martha Coulton's voice sounded a little farther away than Johnson's. "We've got a lot to talk about."

"Yes, Ma'am," Sandra heard Johnson say.

"Mr. Johnson, can you fly the helicopter?" Sandra asked.

"Probably. If the fever stays away, I can."

Austin gave her a look of concern.

"How did that happen?" Sandra asked Johnson.

"I don't know," he said. "It just happened. One minute I was deep in a fever, the next minute it broke."

"Are you sure?"

"You get up here, dear," Sandra's mother said in the background.

"I'm feeling better every minute," Johnson said, "but I'm not so sure about your mother."

Johnson did sound stronger. Her mother, on the other hand, sounded…happy. Happiness was something Sandra hadn't seen or heard in her mother for a long time. She looked at Austin, who shrugged his shoulders.

"We're going to take a short cut," Sandra said to Johnson. "We can probably be there early tomorrow. Do you want to wait?"

"I think I can get us out of here now," he said.

Geoffrey's mind swirled. *How can this be?* "Gabe, have you been performing unauthorized miracles?" No answer, of course. Cases of spontaneous healing weren't uncommon, but often they were the result of divine intervention, either *sua sponte* by the Big Man, or in response to a prayer or something. Mr. Johnson didn't seem like the praying type. And anyway, a spontaneous healing would moot his whole mission, wouldn't it?

Undoubtedly Gabriel was behind this. Geoffrey sent Little Jeffrey into a nap and raced his angel consciousness ahead on the trail until he found the bright yellow helicopter again. Mentally, he put his hands on his hips as he surveyed the scene. There it was, the residue of an angel's aura, known in the trade as "angel dust." It was everywhere he looked. Johnson was covered with it. Such a sloppy job, too. No doubt Gabriel had been here, but Geoffrey wouldn't let him get away with it. He thought for a moment, letting his consciousness roam over the scene.

"Ah hah!" He had it. With a quick glance inside the helicopter he found the ignition keys dangling from the control panel. Slowly, they began to jiggle. *Careful now. We don't want to alarm anybody.* While Johnson was talking to Sandra, Geoffrey managed to slip the keys completely out of the ignition. They glided past Johnson's knee and floated gracefully out the door of the helicopter, where they hovered for a moment while Geoffrey tried to decide where to put them. They slid down and under the belly of the aircraft, across to the bottom, then up and in through the door on Martha's side.

Just as Martha reached across the seat to take the microphone out of Johnson's hands, the pilot saw the flap of her purse open, seemingly all on its own. The fever could be coming back, he thought.

Sandra heard scuffling on the helicopter end of the transmission. Then her mother's voice came over the radio more clearly.

"I've had the most marvelous experience," Martha said. "You should have seen it."

"Are you talking about the Northern Lights?"

"Is that what they're called?"

"Yes, and you can see them from the ranch."

"Well, I don't want to see them from that nasty old ranch. They're much more beautiful up here in the mountains."

"Suddenly my mother is a naturalist," she said to Austin. "All right, Mother. We'll have plenty of time later to talk about the lights. If Mr. Johnson is up to it, you should fly back to the ranch."

"Yes, dear." Martha actually sounded disappointed that she wouldn't be spending another night in the mountains.

They signed off and Sandra turned to Austin.

"Well," she said, "I guess our little horseback ride was all for nothing."

"I had fun. We should do it more often."

"Don't count on it. Your days at Misha Ranch are numbered."

Sadness fell over Austin's face like a shadow.

"Sorry," she said. "I thought you'd be glad to get out of here and back on the road."

"Somehow the road doesn't—"

"Johnson to Coulton." The radio interrupted Austin. Sandra still had the microphone in her hand.

"This is Sandra, go ahead."

"Looks like we've got another small problem," Johnson said.

"A fine pilot I hired," Martha said in the background. She sounded more like the mother Sandra had grown to know and despise over the last few years.

"What's the problem?" Sandra asked.

"We can't find the keys to this jalopy," Johnson said.

"What do you mean *we*?" Martha said.

"You mean you can't fly without the keys?"

Austin nudged Sandra's shoulder while Johnson confirmed that they were stranded.

"What?" Sandra said to Austin.

"I can start the helicopter."

"Don't tell me, you have a spare set of keys?"

"No. I just…know how to fix that, uh, particular problem, but I have to see the wiring set-up. If you cross the wrong wires, the whole system will short out and you'll never get the aircraft off the ground."

"Are you telling me you know how to *hot-wire* a helicopter?"

Austin looked away and nodded.

"Why am I not surprised?" Into the microphone she said, "Mr. Johnson, apparently Mr. Smith here has some experience stealing helicopters."

"Really?" Johnson sounded impressed.

Austin frowned.

"Really," Sandra said. "We might be able to hot-wire the helicopter's starter, but apparently it's a chancy procedure."

"I wouldn't want to try it if I didn't have to."

"Why don't you keep looking for the keys. We won't turn back until we hear that you've found them."

"Okay."

They signed off again and Sandra looked at Austin.

"I'm not going to ask where you learned that particular skill, or why," she said. "I'll just try to be glad that you have it. Maybe we should sit tight for a while. Johnson will probably find the keys, and we can save ourselves another two days of riding."

"Two?"

"One to get there from here, and one more to get back to this point. We can't all ride in the helicopter. Somebody has to ride back with the horses, and it's another two days to get back to the ranch from here.

"Right."

"So, this is as good a place to camp as any." She slid from her horse and started unpacking supplies before Austin could comment.

****

Once again, they went about setting up camp in relative silence. When Austin started helping Sandra with the tents, she turned away and went off to gather wood for a small fire, leaving him to put up the tents by himself.

Much later, as the sun dropped below the mountains, she stared into the flames and wondered what was going to happen that night. She could try to stay awake all night, if necessary, but that wasn't practical.

"Your mother seems to be taking all of this pretty well," Austin said.

Sandra knew he was trying to make innocent conversation. "She seemed happy enough on the radio." Too happy somehow, like she had stumbled upon something in the first aid kit. Ethyl alcohol, maybe. Was her mother having a party at the helicopter? "If we still need to go, we'll take the Highline Trail and reach them pretty early tomorrow."

Austin nodded agreement.

Sandra unrolled her sleeping bag and sat down on

it. "If it's okay with you, I don't feel much like cooking. When you get finished feeding Little Jeffrey, you can help yourself to the gorp." She gestured at one of the saddlebags. "And you can make yourself some tea, if you like."

"No problem," he said. "I like the Gwurp."

Sandra didn't bother to correct him. Instead, she stretched out, covered herself with the sleeping bag and hoped Austin would get the idea that she was retiring for the evening. She could have slept somewhere else, or in the tent, but she felt a little trapped in the tent, even though she couldn't get far enough away from camp to stop him from doing anything, if he wanted to. As she lay there, she watched Austin out of the corner of her eye. He was feeding Little Jeffrey from a jar of pureed peas, carefully scooping the overflow from around the baby's mouth. He didn't act like a man who was planning to force himself on her.

It wasn't impossible that she had taken the initiative the night before, rather than the other way around, if she had been in some kind of sleepwalking state. The idea seemed preposterous but, whether she liked it or not, her subconscious could have taken over in her sleep if her attraction to Austin was strong enough. She might have done something foolish in spite of her better judgment. Not likely, but scientifically possible.

Handsome as he was, Austin had not descended from Mount Olympus. He was just Austin Smith, poster child for Peter Pan, not the man of Sandra's dreams. But what if her pesky subconscious knew more about the man of her dreams than her conscious self? What if her subconscious had fallen in love with a man who may never have spent more than one night with any single woman? She watched Austin and realized that, given half a chance, a lot of women would happily fall into bed with the man. Sandra could have acted out an erotic dream in her sleep. If Austin had been a gentleman, he wouldn't have let her do that. On the other hand, if Austin wasn't a gentleman, he would simply blame her for her own bad behavior, and he still claimed he had no idea what they had done, if anything. It was all so crazy.

Sex was something Sandra didn't take lightly. It was much too important to engage in on a whim. She hadn't completely saved herself for marriage, exactly, but she thought it would take more than the body of Greek god to make her lose control, if that's what she had done.

She watched the fire-breathing dragon and arrow as they flexed on Austin's forearms while he fed the baby. His body art waved like a red flag, warning Sandra away from the rocky shoals of love. Run away, it said. If you don't, he will. Obviously, she needed to have a long talk with her subconscious.

"That's right," Geoffrey said quietly to his temporary parents. *"Stay calm. Don't do anything rash until I can save your mother."*

Sandra's admiration for Austin had grown, grudgingly, in spite of her better judgment. How could he devote himself to a child he didn't even know was his? Yet there he was, teaching himself the fine art of scooping drool from a baby's cheek with a spoon. His commitment to the child was as much a mystery to her as the appearance of the child himself. And where had that bundle of joy really come from, anyway? Sandra simply couldn't believe that the stork had stolen the baby from Austin and delivered him to the ranch. She wanted to explore that topic a little further, and now was as good a time as any.

She sat up, and Austin looked at her, spoon full of green pea goop poised in mid-air.

"Can you be honest with me for a minute?" she asked.

"Of course."

"Are you sure you have no idea who Little Jeffrey's mother is?"

A wan smile crossed Austin's lips. He gave Little Jeffrey one last spoonful, wiped the baby's mouth, and set the jar down. "To tell you the truth, I don't want to know anymore." He gently lay the baby in the makeshift crib and plopped down across the fire from Sandra. "Whether you believe it or not, I don't remember sleeping with anyone on my first visit to Prudhomme Bay. In fact, I haven't slept with anyone in quite some time—as far as I remember, that is." He said this last statement with a bit of an eye roll, acknowledging what may have happened the night before.

He still sounded sincere, but she pressed on. "Prudhomme Bay has a lot of seasonal workers," she said. "But, if Little Jeffrey's mother was in town for a whole year before he was born, she may live there full time."

Austin gave her a wary look and arched an eyebrow. Perhaps he really didn't want to find the baby's mother.

"Why don't you describe the woman who gave you Little Jeffrey? Maybe I'll recognize her."

"I don't know. She was a brunette."

"A brunette. That's not much to go on. Did she have any distinguishing features? You know, like a mole on her cheek, a big scar or something?"

Austin scrunched up his face, showing his discomfort. "I swear, I didn't know the woman." His head drooped into his hands.

"Well, you must have known her in the biblical sense." Sandra said this before she could stop herself.

Austin's head shot up and he snapped his fingers. "That's it! She had a Bible. A blue one with yellow lettering."

That would be Brother Billy Joe Gospel's Gold Letter Edition. Geoffrey, like most angels, was familiar with all of the versions of the Bible, Koran, Torah and other religious texts that had ever been printed. It was a requirement in his line of work. Brother Billy's "Ministry of the Airwaves" printed that particular edition of the Bible for $1.95 and sold it to the faithful for $69.95, plus shipping and handling. *Maybe I should ask Alphonse and Dimitri to pay the Reverend Billy a brief, faith-renewing visit.*

"A Bible," Sandra said. "No wonder you didn't know the woman. She didn't give you the Bible along with the baby, I suppose."

"No. She had it stuck in her belt, like you would a pair of work gloves. All I could do was stare at it when she handed me Little Jeffrey. I guess that's why she was able to get out of the bar before I got a good look at her."

"Not to mention the shock of realizing you had just become a father."

"Yeah." Austin looked at her, apparently waiting

for more criticism which, Sandra might have delivered if she hadn't realized at that moment who Little Jeffrey's mother was. She had seen that Bible many times. The woman had to be the missing Sarah Mockingbird, and Austin wasn't Little Jeffrey's father after all.

She looked down and stared at the glowing hot coals in the fire. Why hadn't she thought of it before? Sandra had heard that Sarah was pregnant. Mockingbird was probably not her real name, but a lot of people changed their names when they migrated to Alaska—it was all part of starting a new life. Sarah had arrived in Prudhomme Bay three years earlier, passing through on her way to the northern oil fields. Her single-minded goal had been to pluck a husband from the rigs. But, when the men of Prudhomme Bay discovered she had a talent for massage, they set up a shop for her and convinced her not to leave.

Unknown to the men, Sarah also had a talent for preaching and with no brighter prospects on the horizon, she set about stroking cash out of the sore backs of the local workers while she ministered to their souls. It was like getting a massage in church, and it was a testament to her skill as a physical therapist that her one-on-one ministry was a roaring success.

Eventually she struck up a relationship with a young man named Joel Yellerman, who was out to make his fortune in the world. He had no intention of staying in Prudhomme Bay for long, either, but Sarah's strong fingers converted him into her sweetheart overnight.

As far as anyone knew, Sarah and Joel's relationship was as pure as the snow that enveloped

Alaska each winter. The following spring, Joel left for the oil fields, saying he would call for Sarah when he found a job that could support them both. Apparently, he left before he knew Sarah was pregnant and, just as apparently, she must not have been sure whether to tell Joel.

In any case, Little Jeffrey had to be Sarah and Joel's baby, not Austin Smith's. Austin wouldn't get the chance to raise his child on some tropical island or in a South American barrio, but this revelation gave Sandra little comfort. She knew Austin would be crushed. She wouldn't tell him immediately. She simply couldn't.

And, if Austin couldn't raise Little Jeffrey, neither could she. That thought left her profoundly disappointed. In her idle daydreams, Sandra had envisioned herself as a mother *and* biologist, bouncing Little Jeffrey on her knee as she ran statistical data through the computer, going about her day caring for the baby without giving up her orderly, secure life as a research scientist. That had been a foolish dream, after all.

Little Jeffrey's last name was Mockingbird, or Yellerman, and his parents could easily be found. Sandra's love for the child had all been for naught. She was only a practicing mother, and even that would end very soon.

Austin pulled his giant knife from its sheath and started whittling on a piece of wood.

"I don't care who Little Jeffrey's mother is," he said. "I'm not going to let him grow up with parents who would desert him."

"I don't blame you," Sandra said. But she knew the

law didn't work that way. How could she tell him about Sarah Mockingbird?

Austin looked at her sideways. "Speaking of mothers, what *was* your mother talking about back at the ranch house? She said I should get you to tell me your story."

"It's better if you don't listen to my mother."

"You mean she was lying?"

"No," she sighed. "Never mind."

"Well, I was just curious. I've told you a lot about myself, including my warts."

Sandra took a deep breath. "There's not that much to tell."

"Try me."

"Okay, fine. You want the full story?" She sat up. "I was going to get married once."

"And you ran away?" A mischievous smile crossed his lips.

"Not exactly." She looked down at the fire again, remembering details of that awful day. "At the critical moment, I fainted."

"At the altar? Really." He almost laughed but checked himself.

"Yes."

"I'm sorry." His smile had almost vanished.

"What was the poor sucker's name?"

"Todd."

"What did you do then?" he said.

"Nothing. I fainted, remember? I—"

"No, I mean, why didn't you finish the ceremony later?"

"I don't really know," she said. But from Austin's silent, steady gaze she knew that explanation wasn't going to satisfy him. "I guess he simply wasn't the right guy."

"Seems like a good excuse to me. How did you know?"

"Because I fainted?"

"Hmpf," he snorted.

"What? Fainting isn't enough for a woman to tell?"

"No, it's not that. It's just that all this time you've been accusing me of not facing up to my responsibilities. And you, well…"

Sandra felt her face flush red. "That's not the same," she said, but she couldn't tell him why.

"No, I guess not."

"Really?" she asked. "It's not?"

"No," he said. "You didn't love him. It wasn't exactly the easy way out, but you're allowed to faint if you're about to marry someone you don't love."

Oddly, his statement came as a relief. She had loved Todd, or at least she thought she did at the time. No one had ever given Sandra a satisfactory explanation for fainting at the altar, and no one had ever truly forgiven her for hurting her fiancé, not to mention offending his family.

"But," Austin continued. "Do everyone a favor. Don't use that one incident as an excuse to run away from every guy you meet."

"Oh, come on." Her defenses went back up. "That's not fair. Did you flunk psychology in medical school?"

"Yeah, well, that brings us around to me."

"What about you?"

"I don't know. Maybe you were right when you said that people can't change overnight. What's the old saying? A tiger can't change its stripes?"

"What do you mean?"

"Nothing. It's just talk, I guess." He glanced over at Little Jeffrey, then lay down and flung the sleeping bag over himself.

"Well, good night to you, too," she said. She sat there a moment and looked at his still form. It sounded like he had come to some unspoken decision, and she felt an empty, hollow feeling spread through her chest. How could Austin Smith, of all the men on earth, cause her to feel such things? She opened her mouth to say something else. Instead, she exhaled a long, slow breath. They would go their separate ways soon enough, so why push the matter? She dropped down onto her own sleeping bag and rolled around, but she couldn't get comfortable. And it wasn't just the pine cones and roots underneath her.

Yes, she had left poor Todd at the altar. He hadn't been the right man for her. She knew that at the time, even if she couldn't face the truth without fainting. Even so, she wasn't about to fall into Austin's arms, just to show him she wasn't afraid of commitment. And what if she was? Maybe she had good reason to be afraid. She thought of her father again. He hadn't left her on purpose, of course, but she had loved him and he was gone forever just the same. She never wanted to experience that kind of loss again. If that was fear of commitment, so be it.

As the psychologists said, knowing the problem was half the solution. But how could Austin Smith be the rest? That idea scared her to death, too.

Unable to sleep, she lay on her back and gazed up again at the swath of Milky Way stars shining through the trees. She wished she could tell the future by gazing at the heavens like Inuit shamans. What was God doing up there, anyway? Was he even on the job? If He wasn't, then Sandra was on her own.

Austin and the baby started softly snoring in unison, and Sandra longed for the days when her life was simple and she, too, could sleep like a baby.

A few minutes later, she thought of a plan.

Chapter 14

Sandra gazed down at Austin's face, bathed in soft moonlight as he slept in the old army bag that was big enough to hold both of them. His expression was as calm as Little Jeffrey's, as though his world travels had unburdened him of any earthly responsibilities. She resisted the urge to slip into the bag again, if indeed she had done that a first time. Instead, she reached out to stroke his cheek, but stopped short.

She turned away and quietly led her horse and one of the pack horses a short distance away from the camp before she saddled them. Then she gathered up the few provisions she had unpacked the night before and stuffed them into a saddlebag. She lifted Little Jeffrey, still asleep in his pack, and slipped him onto her back.

The note pinned to Austin's shirt, hanging from a nearby tree, explained everything. She had no doubt that Johnson would find the keys to the helicopter, and if he didn't, the three of them could ride back to the ranch on two horses. Someone would rescue the helicopter later. Austin could easily find his way back down the trail to the ranch, and she'd left him a map. Then, just as quickly as he had arrived, he could ride out of her life forever. It was the easiest solution she could think of, and the best thing for everyone.

Two hours later, the sun was rising as she crested the most dangerous part of the Highline Trail. There wasn't much snow, but the slope on her right dropped off dramatically, sometimes as a cliff. The view held no interest for her. She was thinking about Austin and how people made important decisions in their lives.

She repeatedly assured herself she had done the right thing. The note she left Austin released him from any obligation as a father, and the whole episode was over.

But who was she trying to kid? There was no sensible reason for her pulse to race whenever she thought of Austin. It wasn't logical. Logically, she and Austin were a hopeless mismatch. Logic may have let her down, but it was better that Mr. Smith should ride out of her life now, before things got out of control. Before she lost her head and did something foolish. Again.

"What a world," she mumbled to her horse.

"Eh? What?" Geoffrey awoke from his slumber long enough to sense Sandra's pain. *"You've simply made the wrong decision, dear. It's what you mortals do best, I'm afraid."* He drifted back to sleep with the gentle rocking of the horse, satisfied that his mission to save the congresswoman was still on track, even if his temporary parents were not.

Lost in her thoughts, Sandra barely noticed when the horse shuddered and stumbled slightly on the rocky trail. It righted itself and kept walking while Sandra tried to imagine what a life with Austin would be like. Yes, it would be all love and attention for the first few months. All sweetness and light, and things would be perfect. But reality would slowly, inevitably creep in. The numbing sameness of Austin's day-to-day job, whatever it was, and the unceasing familiarity of whatever city they lived in would take their toll. She could imagine him sitting in front of the television for hours on end watching the travel channel. Eventually he would suggest, just in passing, that another town, another state, or another country might be a more interesting place to live. And she might agree, just to keep him happy. But in the end, she knew it wouldn't be enough. He would leave, and she would be alone again.

"Men," she growled. If they weren't getting themselves killed, like her father, they were walking out the door to look for greener pastures on the other side of the world. Why go through all that, just to end up where she already was? Alone.

Then it happened. From the corner of her eye, she noticed a faint shadow flashing through the air on her left. It swooped toward her so quickly she didn't have time to turn and see it clearly. It swooped under her horse's nose and swept away to her right. She tried to follow its path, but her horse whinnied and slipped again over a rock. Its hoof came down hard, dropping the horse to its knees and throwing Sandra forward. Her feet slipped out of the stirrups and, before she knew what was happening, she started tumbling forward and rolling sideways out of the saddle.

"Hey," she yelled. She clutched the reins but twisted awkwardly and pitched over the side of the horse's neck. Automatically she reached for the pommel of the saddle and almost, but not quite, got a grip. Her fingertips couldn't hold her weight and they slipped off the smooth leather. Knowing she was falling off the horse, she twisted her body even further to keep from landing on her back and the baby. At the same time, she tried to tuck her free arm under the strap of the baby's backpack, to remove it and throw it free. She got it half off before she hit the ground on her stomach. Her chin smacked the ground hard, causing her to see stars. Semi-conscious, she rolled toward the lip of a drop-off. The last thing she remembered was pushing the baby away from her body.

Geoffrey was snuggled down in his backpack, dreaming that he had retired from active service and was teaching at Elysian University, whose regents had unanimously offered him a senior faculty position in the Department of Human Idiosyncrasies and Italian Cooking. He stood at the front of an auditorium full of students, where he graciously acknowledged a standing ovation and was about to accept a lifetime achievement award from a particularly cute faculty cherub, when her freckled, angelic face morphed suddenly into a laughing, screeching flamingo with Gabriel's nose.

"Yikes!" His arms and legs flailed as he tried to escape the auditorium stage where the hideous creature laughed at him. "Oomph." It felt as though he slammed headfirst into a wall, even though he was fleeing backward. Disoriented, he started to spiral out of his dream. The golden plaque symbolizing his award slipped out of his grasp and melted away, leaving behind a lump of disappointment when he realized he was only dreaming.

He opened his eyes and saw Sandra as she tumbled over a cliff.

****

Austin opened his eyes and immediately knew that something was wrong. The sun was up and he hadn't heard any of Sandra's morning hustle and bustle. He sat bolt upright in his sleeping bag and saw that she and Little Jeffrey were gone. Then he found the scribbled note she'd left him.

Dear Austin,

Thank you for all your kindness, but your help is no longer needed. I can give Mr. Johnson the antibiotics if he still needs any, and I'm sure he will find the helicopter keys. They couldn't have gotten far. We'll all be fine.

More importantly, I know now that you are not Little Jeffrey's father. He's the son of a local woman you could never have had anything to do with. She is a good person who undoubtedly regrets making a bad decision. I will see that she gets her baby back and whatever other help she needs.

Please don't follow me or you'll get lost. When you return to the ranch, Doc Murray can give you transportation back to Prudhomme Bay.

It's been very interesting knowing you, to say the least. Perhaps our paths will cross again someday.

Sandra

"Oh, for God's sake," Austin said. "Doesn't she understand? I'm already lost." He crumpled the note in one hand and scrambled for his clothes. In less than ten minutes, with his jaw clenched, he had saddled his two horses and ridden out of camp at a gallop.

****

"Phew," Geoffrey said. *"That was close."* He had managed to wake up and change the direction of Sandra's fall at the last second, but he was not quite as successful at slowing their descent. She landed heavily

on a narrow rock shelf, no more than six feet wide at its widest, and about fifteen feet below the top of the cliff. She came to rest on her shoulder and had the wind knocked out of her. She spent a few anxious minutes unconscious. Still in his pack, Geoffrey settled on the ledge next to her and gently he caressed her aura.

"C'mon lady, stay with me. I know you can. You're one of the strongest women I've ever met. Foolish, yes, but very strong."

Sandra groaned and began to roll over onto her back, and unknowingly on top of Geoffrey.

"Whoa there." He gently applied the brakes and watched in fascination as some pebbles skittered off the cliff and into the abyss that opened up only inches from his chubby arms.

"Wake up, lady. I've done what I can. Now you've got to get us out of here."

Sandra moaned as he gently nudged her back to consciousness. Even as he did so, he knew their situation wasn't good. Escaping the ledge would challenge a skilled climber with ropes, and their equipment was still on the horses, wherever they were. Mentally he searched above his head and found both animals grazing unhurt beside the trail.

"It's okay," he assured the horse Sandra had been riding. "It's not your fault. You stay right there." The horse snorted in response.

Gabriel must be desperate to try something this stupid, but this is just a temporary setback. Austin would follow them and find the horses. Love did that to men like him.

Geoffrey was barely able to restrain Sandra when she jerked awake and realized what had happened.

"Oh, Lord, what have I done now?" Still dazed, she slid Little Jeffrey out of the pack and inspected him for injuries. Geoffrey put on his most reassuring smile and waggled his fingers at her.

"I'm a-okay, Mom."

"It's a miracle," she said. She stroked the few strands of hair on his forehead. Then she put the baby back in his pack and lay him down as far away from the edge of their narrow shelf as she could. What now? The radio was still in her saddlebags. She looked down over the edge of the shelf and saw that climbing down was clearly not an option. And, thankfully, neither of the horses had fallen to its doom. Fighting her grogginess, she rose to her knees and inspected the relatively smooth wall of stone behind her. It would be difficult, if not impossible, to climb back up to the trail and, if she fell again, the narrow ledge might not be wide enough to stop her from falling farther. She wasn't ready to face the climb in her current condition, but when she got hungry enough, she knew she'd have to try it.

She sat back down next to the baby. "I've really messed things up this time, haven't I?"

"I can't say I disagree. I hope your soul mate hasn't given up on you. Otherwise I'm going to have to think of something really clever to get us off this ledge."

"At least you're still happy with me, even if I have no idea what you're saying." She gathered up Little Jeffrey's pack into her arms and stared numbly out into space. Her eyes softly glazed over and she slipped into a slow series of unbidden thoughts and daydreams, mostly about her major life decisions, and all of the things she might have done but hadn't. She wondered vaguely if she was going into shock, or had suffered a concussion.

"Hey, that's not real helpful, right now," Geoffrey said. He rolled his eyes, but he recognized the peculiar human idiosyncrasy of comparing their current circumstance to whatever other choices they might have made, but didn't. Mortals often had to review their mistakes before they could forgive themselves for things they thought they'd done wrong. It was like self-confession. With nothing else to do, he sat back and watched in fascination as the swirling scenes of Sandra's life played out in her head. One episode in particular caught his attention.

He saw Sandra in the bride's waiting room at a church, smiling like a trouper as her mother and friends attended to her every need. Sandra in blinding white, so young and beautiful, escorted up the aisle by the head of her university's biology department. Sandra at the altar, standing next to some poor sap named Todd. The world seeming to collapse in on itself until nothing existed but that place and that time. The minister. I do? To this man? Sandra blinking at Todd as though she had never seen him before. A perfect stranger. Sandra turning slightly to see the blurred, expectant faces of her friends and relatives, seated in the pews. And there were the in-laws, with their slightly disapproving looks.

Cameras clicked away, click, click, click, almost the only sound registering in Sandra's mind. That and the minister, droning on, speaking so earnestly. Why can't she hear him? Sandra feeling the sudden surge of adrenalin pumping into her veins, fight or flight, but her leaden feet are fixed on the dais. I do? Forever? Mercifully, her narrow-tunneled focus on the world collapsed entirely, falling into a soft, forgiving darkness. Far, far way, a woman screamed.

"Good Lord—oops! Sorry." But this time no thunder broke. Heaven understood. The poor girl should never have been there. It simply wasn't her time to get married, but how could she have known?

Sandra tried to tell herself that what happened on that day had no bearing on the rest of her life except, of course, what it had done to her hair color. Certainly it hadn't changed the way she felt about love and marriage. Todd simply hadn't been the right man, but somehow that experience had warned her away from looking too hard for Mr. Right. From that time on she had immersed herself in her studies, and then exiled herself to Alaska.

And by now Austin Smith was probably halfway back to Fiji.

Geoffrey eyed Sandra with frustration.

"Listen, lady, I don't know about you, but I'm at my wits' end. I've got a congresswoman to save, so I'll make you a deal. I don't know how I'm going to do it, but I'll get you together with Mr. Right if you'll promise me you'll accept the arrangement. You may not know the rules, but I do, and I can't give you what you want unless you accept it in your heart, which I can't make you do. If you'll do your part, I'll do mine, and we'll both get out of here. Deal?"

Somewhere in the back of her mind, an odd sense of contentment settled over Sandra. She assumed it was the same calm acceptance that falling mountain climbers and parachutists feel when they realize their lives are about to be cut short, and there is nothing more they can do to save themselves. She sighed.

Then she heard a slapping sound and slithering on the rock next to her. She turned to see what it was and nearly jumped off the ledge. At first she thought a colorful snake had landed next to her, coiled up and ready to strike. It was only after two frantic heart beats that she realized the snake was actually a small pile of climbing rope, one end of which stretched up and over her head.

"Well," Austin called down, "are you going to take it? Or do you insist on getting out of this fix on your own, too?"

****

They pulled Little Jeffrey to safety first, but once Sandra was standing on the trail again she threw her arms around Austin and hugged him like she might never get a second chance. It felt as good as she imagined it would. She stopped when she realized Austin's own hug wasn't as enthusiastic as hers. She released him and took a step back.

"What's the matter?" she asked.

"What's the matter? Let's see. I woke up this morning and found that you had fled camp with my son. Oh, but there was this nice little note, letting me know that my son isn't really my son, and inviting me to take a hike. But I didn't want to do that, and lucky for you, since apparently you had a little trouble on the trail—"

She put her fingertips softly over his lips, silencing him.

"I'm sorry," she said. "I shouldn't have done any of that."

"Now we're starting to understand each other."

"But why didn't you go back to the ranch like I

told you to?"

"Right. You go back down the rope. I'll leave, and we'll pretend I was never here."

"No, no. I'm glad you're here." She hugged him again, which he half-heartedly returned, but she could tell that his attitude hadn't changed much from the night before. When she stepped back again, he held her gaze with his dark, searching eyes.

"He really isn't my son, is he?"

"No."

He was silent for a moment, looking out at the horizon, as if all the wild, exotic places he had ever visited were beckoning to him, calling him back to the road and to his life of adventure. Then he looked deep into her eyes, as if the answers to all his questions might be there. Once again under his gaze, she felt like butter in the hot sun. Melting, melting.

She wanted to reach out to him, but how could she fall into his arms now? He'd think it was only because he'd rescued her. She had abandoned him just that morning. It was unforgivable, but she had done it anyway, and she never felt so low. She looked down at her dusty boots.

"I really am glad you didn't go back," was all she could say. Austin seemed to ignore her feeble overture and turned his attention to the horses.

"Are you sure Little Jeffrey is okay?" he asked over his shoulder. He was just going through the motions now. He had bonded with a baby that wasn't his and never would be. Along the way, he had tried to get Sandra's interest, but that hadn't worked either. Now he was giving up.

"Yes," she said. "Through yet another miracle, the

baby is fine. He seems blessed." She skipped a beat and said, "You know we won't be able to call him Little Jeffrey much longer."

Austin paused in the middle of tying the coiled rope onto his saddlebag.

"He undoubtedly has a name," she said. "His mother is a good woman. A little odd, that's all."

Austin turned to face her, and the pain and sadness in his eyes struck an anvil blow at her heart.

"I know how you feel," she said.

"Do you? Do you really? Now that I've been a father, however briefly, do you think I can just get back on the road, living alone, as if none of this ever happened? As if I'd never met a child I thought was my son? Or you?"

Without thinking, Sandra stepped into his arms and hugged him again, harder, and this time he hugged her back. They stood that way for a moment before Sandra realized he must be looking down at her. She raised her chin from his chest and found herself gazing again into the deepest, darkest eyes she could imagine. The soft, wonderful image faded as she closed her own eyes, accepting, then fully welcoming his kiss.

"Yeah, now you're talking. The G-man always delivers." Geoffrey wriggled in his backpack while he watched their auras intertwine, exploding into a passionate shade of scarlet so intense he had to avert his eyes. But the cloud of colors faltered and shifted toward pink, then a neutral white. *"No! No!"* he shouted.

Sandra broke off the kiss. "I'm so sorry," she said breathlessly. She stepped away from him, running her fingers through her hair. "I mean I'm sorry about Little Jeffrey not being yours."

"Oh? You're sorry about Little Jeffrey. Not about the fact that we just…?"

"I know you've worked hard to be a good father, and finding out he's someone else's child must be a great disappointment to you."

"Yeah. A lot of things aren't turning out the way I hoped they would." The look in his eyes hardened again. "It was all too much to ask, really. I was kidding myself."

She cleared her throat. The awful, hollow feeling in her chest had returned. "I want you to know," she said. But then she paused. Was she going to make a stand? Tell him how she really felt? Change her life forever? Her head started spinning as she felt the blood draining away.

"Are you okay?" He reached out and grasped her arm.

Geoffrey, watching from his pack, sent Sandra a modest strengthening charm. He made sure it was a *minimi*. He didn't want a repeat of the incident two nights ago. Sandra covered her eyes with one hand and steadied herself.

"I want you to know…that I really care about you," she said.

"Okay. Great." He let go of her arm. "Thank you. That's one of the more polite brush-offs I've received."

"No, I mean it. You're a very…interesting… person." She felt in danger of swooning again, but she fought it.

"Interesting?"

"Yes. You could be the most interesting person I've ever known." Her vision blurred, but she shook it off.

"Thanks." He put his hands on his hips and looked away. "It's always nice to be well thought of." He picked up the baby in his pack and handed him to her. "Let's get going. We still need to find your mother." She took the baby from his hands and he mounted his horse.

Her shoulders sagged. How long had it been since she had opened her heart to a man, and "thanks" was all he had to say? Okay, so it hadn't exactly been a declaration of love. But she couldn't just blurt out an admission like that. Wasn't there something in between? Something just short of love that she could admit to first, to get used to the idea? She shook her head and slipped the baby's pack onto her back. Then she mounted her horse and rode ahead of Austin, more careful now on the rocky trail.

****

Austin kept his horses as far as he could from the steep drop-off, but he realized the trail could have been a metaphor for his life. He had always lived carelessly, too close to the edge, and too contemptuous of the safe road. It had taken a woman as strong-willed as Sandra and a baby to show him the error of his ways. Even so, he had no right to expect Sandra to love him, to try to bring her into his disheveled existence. That had been a bad idea. If he loved her, he shouldn't do that to her. And though he hated the idea, he had to step back, take a deep breath, and go on with life—without her.

He was still a changed man, a new Austin Smith. From that moment on he would live his life in a way that would earn the respect of the next Sandra Coulton who came along. Just in case lightening actually could strike twice. Sitting astride his horse, he could feel the road calling to him like a jilted lover, and he realized the idea of finding another Sandra was ridiculous. There was no other woman like her out there.

Geoffrey shook his baby head slowly. *Lord, give me a rescue mission any day. This love stuff is impossible.*

Chapter 15

The next few miles weren't as treacherous, but the trail was narrow enough that Sandra and Austin and the two spare mounts rode in single file. Sandra took the lead, and her spare horse put some space between her and Austin. If she hadn't heard the sound of horses' hooves clomping along behind her, she would never have known Austin was there. She hoped it was only the physical distance between them that caused his silence, but she couldn't be sure. She glanced at him each time she looked over her shoulder to see how her spare horse was doing, but he never said a word. She tried to start a conversation by pointing out a bald eagle, but Austin only grunted. He seemed to be lost in thought. Not unhappy, particularly, but lost in thought.

By mid-morning they hadn't heard from Martha or Mr. Johnson, so Sandra called them on the radio without getting off her horse. Johnson felt good, but they still hadn't found the helicopter keys. Martha was happy to learn that they were getting close, and Sandra decided to keep riding, rather than test Austin's silence by taking a break.

They descended from the Highline Trail and their path took them back into the forest. Sandra spied a low hill, not more than a twenty-minute ride away. Once they crossed it, they would ride into a meadow where she was certain they would find the helicopter. The physically challenging part of the trip was over, but she didn't know what to expect from her mother, or from Austin.

To Sandra, the slow rhythmic clomp of the horses' hooves eventually sounded like a march toward the gallows. The forest stretched away from her on all sides but felt empty. Even the breeze whispering gently through the pine trees sounded lonely. Her life felt empty, too, and she idly searched for memories of a time when she was happy. She quickly moved past her earlier life, and the day she threw rocks at Stanley Jaworski on the elementary school playground. That episode of puppy love ended with a few stitches and an afternoon in detention. Later on, she remembered saying goodbye to a stoic but crestfallen Arnold Baker, the only boy who truly had a crush on her in high school. But Arnold had done all right without her. He married Cynthia Cravats and made his fortune by opening a chain of computer stores.

Then there was Todd. Sandra truly believed she and Todd would be a good match, if she only could have stayed awake for the entire wedding ceremony. All she remembered was standing on the steps of the church with him later, as paramedics kept a respectful distance. She picked imaginary lint off the lapel of Todd's tuxedo while she tried her best to explain why they weren't going to spend the rest of their lives together. Todd had gone on to win a Pulitzer prize in journalism and was living in Paris. Just why Todd hadn't been the right man for her Sandra couldn't remember at that moment. But if Stanley, Arnold, and Todd hadn't been the right ones, how could Austin be?

If only her dad were here. What would he think of

Austin? Would he admire Austin's no-holds-barred approach to life, or would he say Austin was an aimless vagabond who would never amount to anything? She sighed. Her dad wasn't there, and he couldn't help her. Unless she got some kind of sign from God, she was on her own.

Just then Austin reached out and squeezed Sandra's hand.

"It's okay," he said. "Really." He let go, and they rode along in silence.

Geoffrey had been listening and rolled his eyes. Mentally, he drummed his fingers in frustration, waiting for their conversation and any possibility of a future together to grind to its inevitable end. He wanted to resume his rescue mission, which remained naggingly unfinished.

****

Sandra and Austin hadn't said a word to each other in fifteen minutes. Austin's shirt sleeves were rolled up, and Sandra glanced more than once at the arrow tattooed along his arm. She considered tattoos a sign of immaturity, or of a reckless youth. Austin had undoubtedly suffered from both. She wanted to believe that both were behind him now.

"You know," she said to get his attention, "I thought coming to Alaska to do my research was pretty adventurous."

"Yeah, I suppose it was. What with the bears and all."

After that, silence.

"Okay, so why are you suddenly so agreeable?" she asked. "First you give me a hard time for wanting too much security in my life, and then you admit that

Alaska isn't exactly a neighborhood park. Do you enjoy giving me a hard time?"

Austin's eyes opened. He drew himself up in the saddle. "What exactly is it you want?" He asked. "Do you want *me*, the wandering unemployed bush pilot, to put the seal of approval on your life? The choices you've made?"

"No, I certainly don't need that. I just don't think I'm the psychological mess you made me out to be."

Austin reined his horse to a stop, and Sandra automatically stopped, too. He stood up a little in the saddle, flexing his thighs and squaring his shoulders. His dark eyes flashed in the shadow thrown over his face by the brim of his hat.

"As long as we're parting ways when this thing's over, let's get something straight," he said. "You remember all those things I said about partnering up with you. Trying to work it out so you and me could raise Little Jeffrey, either together or whatever? All that?"

"Yes, of course,' she said.

"I didn't say any of that because I like hearing myself talk."

"For what it's worth," she said, "I assumed you were sincere, even if a little misguided."

"Misguided? Misguided?" He took off his hat and smacked it against his thigh, then jammed it back on his head. "Lady, misguided ain't the half of it. I was in love. It doesn't get any more misguided than that."

Sandra laughed, not because she thought what he said was funny, but the idea that he was in love suddenly thrilled her and seemed to lift a weight from her chest that she had been carrying ever since she had met him. She felt giddy and dizzy at the same time, just like the schoolgirl she always tried not to be.

"You don't really mean that," she said, smiling. She shook her head, bouncing her hair back and forth. "How could you be in love with a woman you've only known for a few days?"

The schoolgirl inside her was simply asking for more. More words that sparked the electric thrill that she hadn't felt with any other man. More proof that he loved her.

"How could I love you?" he asked. "That's a darn good question. I can't deny that I was attracted to you—any man would be—from the first time I opened my eyes and thought I was waking up in heaven. I was a bit disappointed when I realized I wasn't in heaven, I admit." His dark eyes locked onto hers, causing her to shiver.

"I'm very flattered," she said. "But you're old enough to know that lust isn't love. It's—"

"It's more than that. Yes. But I won't deny it. It was lust that got me interested in you, at first." He pointed a gloved finger at her. "It interested me long enough to see some other things. Things a man might fall in love with. Or I would, anyway."

Sandra felt herself blush. "Well…thank you, but I—"

"But you couldn't peek over the top of your computer printouts and textbooks long enough to see there was a man showing interest in you."

"How could I not notice," she said. "But you—"

"Yes, you're intelligent, at least in a dry as saw-dust professorial way, even if you haven't developed much in the way of street smarts."

"Okay, so how—"

"But I had plenty of time to see some other things about you, too."

"Look, I'm sorry I asked," she said. "You don't have to—"

"Sorry or not, you did ask. Now you're going to let me finish."

He put one hand on his hip, which drew Sandra's eyes further down, until she saw the long knife he had sheathed above his boot.

"Yes, I think I will." she said.

"Thank you."

He continued with heat smoldering in his voice, as if his falling in love had been her fault and it made him angry.

"For starters, I see the way you look at Little Jeffrey." He pointed a thumb at the baby sleeping in her backpack. "The poor kid isn't yours, but you love him anyway. It's an unconditional love that any child needs, and a father would love."

"Any woman—"

"Stop." He held up on hand. "You said you would let me finish."

"Yes, I did. Please go on."

"Then there's your dedication to your work, work that I admit I questioned. You may be doing research on bears because of your father, but you're still dedicated to it. You're not doing anything half-assed, except maybe where I made you. A man's got to admire that."

By way of a thank you, she gave him a little scrunchy smile. She was enjoying this, in spite of the fact that Austin was clearly frustrated that she sparked such feelings in him.

"Hell," he said, "I could go on and on." He started ticking things off on the fingers of his gloved hand. "There's the way you sit a horse, your passion for this forest, your uncompromising bull-headishness whenever you think you're right about, well, everything. And, like me, you're still looking for something."

"What?" She couldn't help asking. "What am I looking for?"

"Only you can decide that. All I know is, most of the people in this world—and I've seen plenty of them—are shut down and half asleep. You're still awake and asking questions."

She shrugged, accepting the compliment even though she wasn't sure what it meant.

"But most of all," he said, pausing. He pinched the bridge of his nose as if he were getting a headache. Or was he fighting back tears?

"Most of all," he said again, more quietly this time. "I know how I feel when I look into your eyes." He took his hand away and put it over his heart. "When I look into your eyes, I start falling into a soft green meadow in springtime, where the sky is clear, the air is clean, and the wildflowers are just beginning to bloom through the melting snow. The sun shines all the time and I know that, wherever this special place is, it's in your eyes, and it's…it's my home."

Sandra's jaw dropped open in disbelief. No man had ever spoken to her like that. Tears were welling in her eyes and she didn't know what to say, but he wasn't asking for anything. Not even a response.

"So," he continued. "You'll have to forgive me if I

seem distracted or a little let down. For the first time in my life I thought I'd found a woman I didn't want to live without. Maybe start a family of my own with. Then it turns out I've got it all wrong. The baby isn't mine and I haven't known you long enough for me to feel this way." He chuckled sadly and rubbed the two-day growth of beard on his chin. "I guess that's the way life works, sometimes. I apologize for unloading on you like that, but I had to get those things off my chest. I feel better now."

He flicked his boot heels and his horse resumed a slow clip-clopping walk down the trail.

Sandra watched his square shoulders ride away. He looked like a cowboy riding off into the sunset alone at the end of a Saturday afternoon matinee. She shook herself out of her emotional daze and followed him.

All this time she assumed that Austin was simply hitting on her. Now, apparently, it was a bit more complicated than lust. More troubling still, Austin was no longer arguing for a relationship. They couldn't keep Little Jeffrey, and without that connection, there wasn't much for Austin to work with. He wasn't going to be a father and he didn't need her to help him complete a family unit. All he had was love. Admittedly, hearing herself compared to a clear mountain stream and a field of wildflowers caused her heart to skip a beat, but she had rejected him and his idea of love. And how many times?

It bothered her that the decision, foolish as it was, had been taken out of her hands. As long as Austin was buzzing around her like a bee trying to find his way into a tulip, she could take him or leave him. And she hadn't taken him seriously. Now, things were less certain. She didn't want to run off with Austin to some foreign country, but she liked being someone's wildflower meadow. But what did that mean? He hadn't pursued the topic. As he said, he was just getting some things off his chest. But now she felt her heart breaking, the pieces tumbling over each other, not knowing which way to go.

"Aaarrgh!" Geoffrey groaned. He had witnessed this scene a hundred times. Mortal souls, blessed by God with the potential for true happiness, passed by each other like ships in the night, flashing a few tentative signals, then slipping away into the safety of darkness, alone. Then they blame it on each other. *"Sheeesh."*

And this was a particularly bad case. Two nights ago, Geoffrey questioned whether he needed to use the harmony blessing, since it looked inevitable that Sandra and Austin would find each other. Now it looked like they were finished, once and for all. Austin had accepted her fearful reasons for rejecting him. She felt crushed but couldn't overcome her fear long enough to act on her own feelings.

Lord, why do we bother with these creatures? They are so hopeless. He shook his small head in disgust, vaguely unsatisfied that he hadn't been able to bring Sandra and Austin together. *But so it goes.*

He bobbed up and down on Sandra's back as her horse broke into a trot, following Austin.

"Whoa! Watch out little chipmunks. Finally, I get to be the cavalry to the rescue." He waved his arms, wishing he had a scimitar, or at least a short cutlass.

Sandra felt like dead weight, bouncing heavily in the saddle with each step of the horse. Part of her congratulated herself for avoiding a serious complication in her life. Another part of her just wanted to die. At least she hadn't fainted this time. Maybe that was progress. She could put Mr. Smith behind her and focus on the problem at hand, getting her mother safely back to the ranch. It's what she'd wanted all along. Great.

"Too bad, so sad," Geoffrey said. But most of the time the Boss insisted they find a way to work things out for themselves, if they could.

"They can't very well go around with labels on their foreheads saying "Soul Mate" now, can they?" He would say.

Geoffrey sighed. His mission had to be saving the congresswoman, and his work would be done soon. Then he could go home, back to the limitless comforts of heaven.

****

At last Sandra and Austin rode over the low hill and saw the helicopter a few hundred yards away. Resting peacefully at the edge of a meadow, its slick yellow and chrome skin shone incongruously among the muted green and brown colors of the forest. The craft had landed clear of the tall spruce and ponderosa pine, but near a rock wall. Miraculously, Johnson had landed safely in the smallest opening possible.

Sandra spurred her horse into a trot, moving in front of Austin. As she drew closer, she saw her mother waving to her from the cockpit. Sandra waved back briefly, but her mother kept waving, even more intensely than before. Sandra raised her hand up higher, to make sure her mother saw her waving back, but it did nothing to dampen the enthusiasm of her mother's greeting. Martha was waving both hands now as fast as she could.

"The wait must have been horrible for her," Sandra muttered.

Austin rode up beside Sandra as if he were going to pass. Instead, he reached forward and pulled back on the bridle of her horse. The two of them clattered to a stop.

"What are you doing?" Sandra asked.

"Can't you see? Something's wrong."

"What?" Sandra looked back at the helicopter. Her mother had stopped waving but continued to stare out of the plastic bubble at them.

The only problem I see is that we keep stopping. But Geoffrey hadn't really been looking.

"I don't see anything wrong," Sandra said.

"Then why doesn't your mother get out of the helicopter?"

"Well, knowing her, I'd say she's waiting for someone to open the door for her. She probably never learned how to do it on her own."

Austin laughed a quick laugh, but then said, "Just to be safe, why don't you stay here for a minute while I go check it out."

"Oh, come on. What are you afraid of?"

"I don't know, but my horse is acting skittish." He walked his horses slowly toward Martha Coulton and the helicopter. Sandra gave him a half-hearted scowl, but in truth she was glad he was with her, especially if there was some kind of trouble. Particularly so, because she had the baby on her back.

She gave him a head start of ten yards or so, then fell in behind, slowly walking her horses forward. The closer she got to the helicopter, the more skittish her own horse behaved. Martha began to point at something on the other side of the helicopter. Sandra waved back, briefly, but then realized her mother was trying to tell them something.

"Look," Austin said. He nodded in the opposite direction at some bushes in front of a rock face, twenty or thirty yards away from the aircraft. There, partially hidden, Sandra saw Walter's pasty face, squinting out from under his Smokey-the-Bear hat. He, too, waved at them, beckoning them with some urgency. Since Walter was closer than the helicopter, Austin and Sandra rode over to him. Sandra found Spinelli and the film crew huddled behind Walter in the mouth of a cave. Metal cases full of camera and sound equipment were strewn around the entrance, forming a kind of barricade. Behind the group Sandra could see that they had started a small campfire.

"Hey, Walter," Austin said. "How did you get here so fast?"

"Never mind how I got here," Walter whispered. He was dancing back and forth in agitation, like he had to go to the bathroom. "Get inside here. Now!"

"What's the matter with everybody?"

Walter jabbed a finger in the direction of the helicopter, and Austin looked over his shoulder. It took him a few seconds, but what he saw sent a chill up his spine. A large bear stalked back and forth at the edge of the trees, a short distance from the aircraft. It clutched a Forest Service backpack in its teeth and slowly ripped it to shreds with its claws.

"You get inside," Austin said to Sandra. "I'll get the horses out of sight."

Sandra handed her reins to Austin and dismounted at the entrance to the cave.

The formerly sick Mr. Johnson appeared next to Walter.

"What are you doing here?" Sandra asked him. "Why aren't you in the helicopter with my mother?"

"Couldn't," he said. "I was outside taking, uh, a break, when that beast showed up. Besides, your mother's probably okay, as long as she doesn't open the doors."

"Is it locked?"

"No, but how smart can a bear be?"

Sandra didn't answer. She knew how smart bears could be.

"Are you sure that's not one of your trained Hollywood bears?" she asked.

"No," Spinelli said. "That's not Gretchin."

"Then we can't stay here," Sandra said. "This cave is probably the bear's home."

The men all looked at Walter, who shrugged his shoulders. "She's the expert," he said.

"It's okay," Geoffrey said. *"I can protect you."* But, of course no one was listening to the baby.

Chapter 16

Finding nothing of interest in the tattered remnants of Walter's pack, the bear tossed it aside and stalked toward the helicopter. It sniffed at the door, just inches from where Martha Coulton sat. It pawed at the plastic, apparently hoping Martha might be lunch. The Congresswoman remained oddly calm, smiling softly at the bear. In fact, she waved at it as though it were a small child, but her cheerful greeting apparently sent the bear into a rage.

"Oh, God," Sandra whispered.

In spite of her own warning, she and Austin joined Walter and the film crew inside the cave opening. Sandra set Little Jeffrey on the flat top of one of the crew's equipment cases. Since he was still in his pack, he could squirm, but he couldn't crawl away.

"We've got to do something," she said to Austin.

"Apparently you're the only one here who knows about bears." Spinelli said to Sandra. He gave Walter a sour look. "What do you suggest?"

Sandra had no idea. She looked out at the helicopter, where each swipe of the bear's paw just missed dropping onto the lever that held the door closed. The bear growled. With each swipe it got more frustrated and pawed a little harder at the plastic bubble.

"Hopefully the bear will get tired and go away, to somewhere other than this cave."

"That doesn't sound like much of a plan," Austin said.

"I know what to do." At last the reason for Geoffrey's mission was obvious. He would save Martha from the bear and go home. *"Everybody stand back. It's show time!"* His angel consciousness swept forward, robes fully extended and trailing white-hot flames—an affectation he couldn't resist, even if the mortals couldn't see it. He rose up before the bear, arms out to his side, and commanded it to stop.

Nothing happened.

Geoffrey circled the bear, probing its sparkling aura from every side. There didn't seem to be any opening at all. It felt like the bear wore a suit of armor.

Something's wrong. I've been able to intervene with furry animals since I was a cherub. He encircled the beast completely with his angel sense and tried to impose a general sedative, but nothing worked. Something was interfering. *Something, or someone.*

"Gabriel, is it you? This is no time for games. People's lives are at stake." Geoffrey's rival appeared, hovering upright above a rock, a short distance from the helicopter.

"Having some trouble, Little Man?" Gabriel asked.

"Stop interfering," Geoffrey snapped. "Can't you see an important woman's life is in danger?" As he spoke, he kept trying to reach the bear. Armpits, behind the knees, nothing worked.

"I'm not doing anything to stop you."

"Then what's going on?"

"What's going on? You're failing at your mission, that's what's going on. How does it feel?"

"I don't understand."

"You remember what we said when you started this little adventure?"

"Gabe. Buddy. I really don't have time for this. In case you've suddenly gone blind, I've got a little bigger problem here."

"Then you really don't remember?"

"Remember what?" If an angel ever could feel cold, Geoffrey felt an icicle stab at his core like a knife.

"You don't remember how cocky you were, back at the feet of the Master?"

"Cut to the chase, Gabriel."

"'It's too easy—cherub's play,' you said. 'I can do this with one wing tied behind my back,' you said."

"Oh, no," Geoffrey mumbled. The memory came back to him in a cool rush. He *had* been cocky. So cocky he had *volunteered* to give up one of his powers, to make the mission a little harder. Apparently, the power he had given up was large, hairy mammal intervention, or any kind of animal intervention.

But wait. Hadn't he saved Austin from a bear once? It must have been that da—darned Hollywood bear and Austin's hand signals. But what about the tick? Hadn't Geoffrey coaxed that tick off the pilot Johnson's neck? It could have decided to move on all by itself. And besides, a tick wasn't a bear.

Geoffrey groaned. His consciousness snapped back into Little Jeffrey's body, and tears streaked down the baby's cheeks.

Gabriel's image faded away. "I'll be waiting for you on the pearly steps to collect my bet," he said, chuckling.

Martha Coulton was doomed. The film crew stood about helplessly, holding their hands over their ears, trying to block out the horrible sound of the bear, its claws now tearing wildly at the plastic bubble of the helicopter.

Sandra turned to Brisbane, who stood against the cave wall next to Walter, chewing on the stem of his pipe. The enormous gun leaned against him. "Do something," she said. "Shoot the bear!"

"I don't know," Walter said. "Technically you'd need a permit to do something like that."

Sandra wheeled, her glare silencing him instantly.

"Well?" she asked Brisbane.

"Sorry, love," he said. "I'm afraid they quit making ammunition for this cannon back in '67, I think. Or was it '69?" He tapped his pipe ashes onto a rock outcropping.

"What?"

"It's just a prop now. It is the movies, after all."

Sandra threw up her arms. "This isn't the movies; this is real life! Have you all lost your minds?"

From inside the helicopter cockpit, Martha's muffled cries for help could be heard between the bear's growls.

"That's my mother out there," Sandra said. "We have to do something."

"She's right," Austin said. "It's just a matter of time before that beast opens the door latch and he gets inside."

"How do we know it's not Gretchin?" Walter said. "Maybe she's just going a little feral."

"Even if that were Gretchin out there," Spinelli said, "do you think it would be any easier to stop her, in her present state of mind?"

"If that's Gretchin," Sandra sobbed, "do what you

did last time she attacked us."

"I can't see any star on the bear's forehead," Austin said, as he took Sandra into his arms.

"We've got to do something," she whispered into his chest.

"Yes," he said. "We do." He released her and stepped back. He looked around and saw the campfire. He stooped down and ran the first two fingers of his right hand along the side of a charred piece of wood. Then he drew his fingers across his forehead and across both cheeks. It was the best imitation of Cheyenne war paint he could muster. Sandra watched in bewilderment as Austin pulled off his plaid shirt, leaving his muscled chest bare and rippling.

"What on earth are you doing?" she asked.

"I told you," Austin said. "When I'm in the woods, my real name is Chief Running Bull. I am a Cheyenne-Sioux warrior, and I've been waiting all my life to save a fair young maiden from a ferocious bear."

"Oh, no, Austin. There isn't any time for games— are you crazy?"

"Feel better now than in few minutes," Austin said, imitating the broken English of a Saturday matinee Indian.

"You're not going out there, are you?" Brisbane asked.

"Can you think of some better plan?"

"But you know that's not Gretchin. You'll be killed."

"Will someone please tell me what's going on here?" Sandra asked.

"I'm going to fight myself a bear for you, honey," Austin said. With that, he put one arm around Sandra's waist and pulled her to him. Her eyes went wide as he bent down and kissed her fully on the mouth. When their lips parted, he gazed into her eyes, which were those of a deer caught in headlights.

"Thanks," he said. "I needed something of yours to take with me."

He let go of her, and with a flick of his wrist, drew the enormous gleaming knife from the sheath strapped to his leg.

"No!" Geoffrey cried.

"Austin, no."

Austin leaped over the barricade in one smooth motion, just like the Chief Running Bull he'd always pretended to be. Behind him the film crew broke into applause.

Sandra turned on them. "What's wrong with you people? Don't you know he'll be killed?" She watched in horror as Austin strode fearlessly toward the helicopter. The knife looked pitifully small in his hand. "He'll be torn to pieces," she whispered. "I can't let him do that. I'll lose him forever."

Time seemed to freeze. Panic fogged Sandra's mind, but she realized with shining clarity that Austin was willing to give up everything, including his life, to save her and her mother. How could she let go of a man she loved—yes, loved—especially if he left her the same way her father had. No, it couldn't happen again. She wouldn't let him go, and she wouldn't leave him, either, not like she'd left Arnold. Not like she'd left Todd. She would do everything in her power to save this man.

"Austin!" she cried. "I love you!" Without thinking twice about it, she leaped over the barricade, to more applause. If they were going to their doom, Sandra wanted Austin to know that much, at least. Apparently he couldn't hear her over the sound of the growling bear.

Behind the barricade, Spinelli threw up his hands. "I hope *somebody* is getting this on film!"

Still in his pack, resting on top of a camera case, a cold soulless dread consumed Geoffrey. Gabriel had vanished and no other help seemed to be on the way. As a baby, he could do nothing. As an angel, he had chosen to give up the one power that might save Austin and Sandra. For the first time since cherub-hood, he faced the prospect of failing a mission. And now people could die because of it. It had all seemed so easy, too easy for an angel as important as he. How had he gotten into this fix?

"This is all Gabriel's fault. Somebody cheated. Somebody...Damn it!" He heard no rumbling of thunder overhead. Still, he tried to shake his infant fist skyward. *"Damn it! Do you hear me?"* But the heavens remained ominously silent. *"Aren't You listening? How can You let these poor people die? Why did You let me...?"* The awful truth washed over him and he couldn't finish. He had no one to blame but himself.

A century's-old but oddly familiar sensation crept over him. It was something he hadn't felt in a long, long time. It was shame. Shame that he had let things get out of hand. Shame that he couldn't save the very people he had been sent to watch over. And most shameful of all, shame at having blamed Him. Only the sin of pride could have driven him to blame his failure on someone else, especially... *Awful. Simply awful.*

He couldn't even suspend time, as he had done

earlier, since he knew the scene unfolding before him was probably his reason for being there. Whatever happened, whatever Geoffrey chose to do, was what God had intended should happen. The outcome couldn't be delayed while he second-guessed the Boss.

With each passing moment, Geoffrey felt the distance between himself and Heaven grow wider. He began to weep. He began to panic.

What to do? What to do? Get a grip on yourself. This isn't geopolitics. It's pretty basic stuff.

He racked his brain for an answer, searching all the way back to his days as a Cherub-in-training. *Let's see. Mortals in danger. Special powers ineffective. Ah hah! Of course!*

He grew quiet as his chubby infant cheeks flushed scarlet with renewed shame. Again, the answer should have been obvious. Gabriel's giving him amnesia had nothing to do with forgetting this piece of information. He knew what he had to do.

He closed his bright baby-blue eyes—he really couldn't bow his head—and fervently prayed.

"Dear Lord, Lord of Heaven and earth and all of the creatures living therein, please hear the prayers of your...very humble servant. We—! I—! I need your help. There are people in trouble here. It's my fault and there isn't much time."

"Geoffrey." A sweet, familiar voice jarred Geoffrey out of his ardent prayer. "Geoffrey!" No, it wasn't the Lord. It was his old friend and mentor, Antonitis.

The image of the old saint appeared above Geoffrey on the cave ceiling in two dimensions, like an ancient cave painting. He wore a dark green visor, and a handful of playing cards stuck out of one vest pocket. Otherwise, the angel looked as though he hadn't aged a century in the last millennium. Geoffrey didn't have time to ask questions about the costume.

"Antonitis, you're alive!"

"Yes, Geoffrey, and doing quite well, assuming I get back before this hand is over. They've got all sorts of amenities up here, stuff you'd never imagine finding in regular old Heaven, don't you know."

"Antonitis. I'm so glad you're here."

"Yes, I heard you were in a little fix down there. Your pal Gabriel has been making things difficult for you?"

"Not Gabriel, not this time. Just me, and I need your help."

Antonitis glanced over his shoulder and waved at someone Geoffrey couldn't see. "The thing is," he said. "I think I've already done about as much as I'm allowed to, my boy. Yes, I believe I have."

"What? Just by showing up? What was that, moral support? What good is that going to do me?"

"Think about it, kid. Think about it." His image faded back into the stone cave ceiling. "I've got to go now, the boys are getting restless. And, before I forget, they all send you their love."

"You tell them I said 'thanks a lot'." Geoffrey made no effort to hide his sarcasm. He turned his attention back to the bear, just in time to see Austin Smith crouch in front of the beast, knife in hand.

Oh, God. I've got to think fast. Why on Earth did Antonitis show up after all these years without doing something? You wouldn't think an angel who had volunteered for Final Intervention would drop in just to gloat. Hey, that's it! Final Intervention. "Thank you, Antonitis," Geoffrey whispered.

Apparently Austin wasn't meant to be saved. The Lord must have decided to recall him, and the only way Geoffrey could help now was by taking the poor man's place as the bear ripped him to shreds. *"Yes! Oh, No!"*

Geoffrey ignored the fear knifing through him as he realized what he had to do. He, too, leaped over the barricade, or at least his angel essence did.

The bear was apparently getting more and more enraged by the clear plastic barrier that kept it from reaching Martha Coulton. It hadn't noticed Austin yet, but when it did…

Austin shifted the knife from one hand to the other, looking for an opening to attack. What he would do when the bear finally turned his way, he didn't know. He just knew that he had to do something to save Ms. Coulton, Sandra, and the baby.

He stood no more than ten feet from the raging bruin, but it still ignored him, which did nothing to help the Cheyenne-Sioux Chief's pride.

"Hey, *nahkohe!* Why are you so angry? If you're hungry, you can eat me, but not without a fight." Austin smacked his chest with the palm of his hand. "You'd love a good fight, wouldn't you? Leave that old broad alone." He shifted the knife back to the other hand, searching the bear for some weakness, some possible advantage he could gain, but all he saw were rippling muscles protected by thick brown fur. Long vicious claws tore unrelentingly at aviation plastic. He raised the knife, then lowered it. He wondered exactly how one went about attacking a bear.

Since he could think of nothing else to do, he

picked up a large rock and chunked it at the bear, hitting him squarely on the side of the head. The bear glanced up at the sky, as if the stone had come from above. Then it looked at Austin, but it turned its murderous attention back to the helicopter.

While its head was turned, Austin got just enough of a look at the beast to confirm what he already knew. It wasn't Gretchin. Summoning all the courage of his ancestors, he charged the bear. With his knife raised overhead, he lifted his chin and let loose the Cheyenne war cry his grandfather had taught him.

****

Geoffrey's consciousness swept past Sandra, flicking a small rock into her path, which tripped her into the dust.

"Sorry, lady, there's nothing you can do for him, and I can only intervene for one of you." He kicked it into high gear, flying toward Austin, who had finally gotten the bear's attention.

The bear's first backhanded swipe knocked Austin over, rendering him unconscious, but Geoffrey saw the familiar flash of light. A tiny portion of Austin's aura slipped into the angel realm. It was his first step toward eternity, and if Geoffrey timed it right, he could change places with Austin before the end came.

Seeing Antonitis had given Geoffrey a measure of comfort that Final Intervention wouldn't lead to his own ultimate demise, but it still raised more questions than it answered. What did it all mean? Had he been chosen to go into some kind of retirement? After all these millennia, was the Lord through with him? Was he being discarded, replaced by an up-and-coming cherub? Or was this his punishment for failing in his mission?

None of that mattered. He was born for unquestioning service and, yes, he had backslid a little, but if the Lord wanted this of him now, he was on his way. *Can do. Tell the boys I'll miss them, but I've gotta job to do.* He mentally blew air into his clutched fists and rubbed his palms together.

"Here we go!" His ancient training kicked in as though he had waited all his life to perform this single duty. Hovering near Austin's still form, he purged all conscious thought from his mind. He transformed himself into a being of pure light and love, filling all the nooks and crannies of Austin's space and time, gently nudging the man's soul over the line between living and the hereafter, shielding him from the horror of his own death. Some other angel would be called to guide Austin toward the light, and home. As for Geoffrey, what happened to him no longer mattered. So it went in the service of the Lord. Service…service…his thoughts began to fade.

Then he felt the firm and gentle hand of Divine Grace on his shoulder.

"Stop, Geoffrey. You've done enough."

Geoffrey hesitated. "But, Lord—"

"Geoffrey!"

The archangel withdrew from Austin. There was nothing more he could do.

****

Sandra wasn't sure if she expected to save Austin or die with him. She only knew she had to reach him before he got himself killed, and she charged at the bear right behind Austin. Then she found herself face down in the dirt, but she leapt up and sprinted even faster.

"Wait!" she yelled. At the sound of her voice, Austin half-turned, and while he was glancing at Sandra, the bear smacked him with a paw, tossing him aside like a rag doll. That left Sandra facing the junk-yard-dog grin of the raging bruin alone. But for reasons Sandra couldn't see, the bear spun around abruptly and backed into her, pushing her face into a wall of rippling, growling fur and threatening to trample her underfoot.

She staggered backward and fell, hitting the ground hard enough to knock the wind out of her. The heel of the bear's hind paw kicked her in the back of the head and she saw stars. She was knocked about like so much flotsam. It seemed like the bear wanted to stomp her to death.

Get away! She had to get away! In spite of her dizziness, she managed to roll over, away from the bear. She gazed up through her mental fog and saw two bears, not one, looming over her. Had the blow to her head given her double vision? Both bears growled malevolently and circled each other, a few feet apart. Sandra watched in fascination with ringing ears.

"Wow," she said, but she couldn't hear the sound of her own voice. Her fear had fled, or perhaps it had been knocked out of her. Either way, she no longer had the strength to escape. Sitting in the dust, it looked to her like the two hairy brutes couldn't make up their minds whether to fight or dance. She heard music coming from somewhere. Or was someone ringing a bell?

She lolled her head over and saw Austin's motionless body, as he lay on his side. He appeared to be sleeping. Through her fog it slowly dawned on Sandra that something had gone horribly wrong. She looked back at the bears.

"Stop ringing that bell," she said. "They're already boxing." Indeed, the two bears were on their hind legs, waving their front paws at each other like they were throwing punches.

"No hitting below the belt!" she said. But deep inside her a fuzzy, disturbing thought formed and wouldn't go away. Something really was wrong. She looked again at Austin's still form.

"Austin!" She crawled over to him on her hands and knees, and with considerable effort, rolled him onto his back. He had a bad cut over his left eye and some abrasions on his forehead and cheek. A wave of fear washed over her. This did not look good. Behind her, the ugly noise of the bears grew louder. She bent down and held her cheek near Austin's nose. He was breathing. She laughed out loud. He was breathing!

She looked up, ready to tell anyone who was nearby that everything was okay. But all she saw was a writhing mass of golden brown fur. The bears were staggering toward her. Oh, Lord. She suddenly realized that she and Austin were right in the middle of two battling grizzlies. As the shadow of the bears fell over her, she lowered her head and covered Austin's body with her own, hugging him tightly.

"I love you," she whispered. "I do." Then she held her breath. Thinking she had said the last words she would ever say, she once again felt strangely calm, relieved that she had finally told Austin of her love, even if he would never hear.

The growling stopped. No ripping flesh. No pain. No darkness descending. She held Austin even more tightly, but still nothing happened. Everything had gone quiet. She looked up. The two bears were down on all fours, standing quietly beside each other. One of them, the male, was contentedly licking the other one's face. Sandra looked more closely. If it were possible for a bear to smile, Sandra was sure she saw a wide grin on the female's face. And there was a black star in the middle of her forehead. Gretchin.

Chapter 17

Austin sat in the open door of the helicopter and let Sandra dab at the cuts and abrasions on his face—in between her soft kisses. If he felt any pain, he wasn't letting on. His lips were as welcoming and tender as her own.

Geoffrey lay in his pack on one of the helicopter seats and tried to make sense of what had just happened. Yes, the congresswoman had been saved, but he hadn't done much to accomplish that. The Lord Himself had stopped Geoffrey at the last second, like Geoffrey was about to screw things up. So, did he lose his bet with Gabriel? Was he still employed as an angel? He wasn't sure what to think, but Gabriel wasn't lording over him the fact that he'd lost the bet, so he, Geoffrey, must have done something right. He let out a cautious sigh of relief and waited for a sign that his mission was over and he could go home.

The bears had wandered off, apparently happy together, and Spinelli wasn't inclined to stop them. After all, he'd said, they had plenty of film in the can, and Gretchin had earned her freedom. In any case, trying to capture one bear had almost proved fatal. He wasn't about to try capturing two.

Martha pulled herself away from Mr. Johnson and came over to stand by her daughter.

"Sandra dear," she said quietly.

Sandra stood up. "Yes, Mother." Apparently her mother had recovered from the bear attack. Indeed, her mother was remarkably calm. But Sandra was sure the incident must have solidified her desire to destroy the forest.

"I know what you're thinking," Sandra said.

"No, you don't."

"You can't use this incident as an excuse to—"

"I'm not," Martha said.

"These kinds of attacks don't happen very often, and—"

"Sandra, will you be quiet for a moment?"

"Yes, Mother." She crossed her arms.

"That's better. "I've made up my mind about a few things, and—"

"I won't let you destroy my forest," Sandra said.

"I'm not going to," Martha said. "At least not now."

"I simply won't let you—what?"

"I said, I'm not going to." Martha held her palm up, to stifle Sandra's questions. "There's been enough destruction around here, and I'm not talking about forests. I want you back in my life. And I want to be invited to the wedding."

Sandra gaped. Austin was all smiles.

"We've been enemies far too long," Martha continued. "I've blamed Harvey Coulton all these years, but I know that, as poor a father as he may—or may not—have been, our problems are not his fault. They're mine."

"Mother." Sandra felt the sting of tears in her eyes. They hugged, tentatively at first, but then tightly, making up for lost time. Martha stepped back and dabbed at her eyes.

"Let's not get too sentimental, dear. I'm still a congresswoman, after all. I never again want to need a boondoggle to come to Alaska and visit my daughter. I am getting to like this place. It's beautiful…and exciting. *Very* exciting."

"Oh, Mother."

"I haven't heard you say "mother" that way in so long, so very long." She smiled at her daughter and they hugged again, letting the tears flow.

****

Geoffrey felt an official, interplasmal tug on his aura. Time to go home. Time to find out what had really happened. Still feeling chastened, he soared away, surrounded by a heavenly glow that lit his way upward. The snow-capped Alaskan mountains beneath him dwindled to mere bumps. The blue-green ocean spread away, so far below that its flat surface was indistinguishable from the feathered clouds floating above it.

Somewhere near the sparkling interface between heaven and earth Geoffrey passed the baby-blue glow of Little Jeffrey's soul as it traveled down to earth to take up his life and body.

"Thanks for the loan," Geoffrey said. He got back a flash, the heavenly equivalent of a wave, from the real Little Jeffrey as he arched downward.

A warm breeze trembled past Geoffrey's cheeks and he heard the familiar rumbling Voice surround him.

"Geoffrey…"

He sighed. It was the Big Man. El Jéfe. The Boss. Perhaps it hadn't been enough that he renounced the sin of pride and asked for forgiveness. He fully expected to be assigned to some menial task for a millennium or two as penance.

"Yes, Lord?"

"Well done, Geoffrey. Well done. That was a nice touch, using the Northern Lights to set the mood."

"Thanks." But was He talking about the congresswoman, or…? At that point it probably didn't matter. Geoffrey smiled an impish smile and put a little extra flick in his wings.

"And Geoffrey…"

"Yes, Lord?"

"Next time, watch it!"

Epilogue

As he had done so often in the last few days, the Archangel Geoffrey Almaric Behir de Giverny reclined lazily on the edge of a soft cumulus cloud, watching the earth pass by below him. He took another satisfying sip of frozen strawberry-caramel-mocha latté, knowing he hadn't put a dent in the century's worth of Nova-buck coffee shop credits he had won from Gabriel. Idly, he drew rings in the fluffy white stuff and kept one eye on the rain-washed streets of Hong Kong, where the hapless Gabriel toiled twelve hours a day as a rickshaw cabby. Another result of the bet. With much gnashing of teeth, his rival had taken the job for the required six months.

Sweet success, Geoffrey thought. There's nothing like it. But his own visit to earth had been a teaching moment, and he knew the Old Man was watching to see if he'd really learned anything. Geoffrey would relent soon and forgive Gabriel the rest of his obligation. That would show Management his heart was in the right place again. Even so, he unleashed one more unseasonable downpour, so he could watch Gabriel splash barefoot through the puddles.

Entertaining as that was, Geoffrey was curious to know how Sandra and Austin were doing after their adventure. They were, after all, the real reason for his mission, even if he hadn't known it at the time. And he'd grown quite fond of them during his stay on earth. He let the monsoon shower drift away from Hong Kong and guided his cloud over the North Pole until he saw the familiar shape of Alaska. Listening carefully, he eavesdropped on the folks at Misha Ranch. Some of the cowboys were standing around the corral talking.

"I tell you I seen it again," Leonard said. "It's got a wing span this wide." Geoffrey could imagine the lanky cowboy holding his arms far apart. "It's been swooping around here all morning."

"You mean it's going to drop another baby on the roof?" somebody asked.

"I dunno, but something's up fer sure."

"Aw, that's the silliest thing I ever heard," Jake said.

"You're just missing Little Jeffrey, like the rest of us."

"It weren't very fair, that other woman coming back for him, after Miss Sandra went through so much for that boy, taking care of him like she did."

"Well, she *was* his real mother, and she still loved Little Jeffrey, after all."

"Yeah, yeah, I suppose." They all mumbled in reluctant agreement.

"And the real father did find himself a good job, so's he's take'n care of the two of them."

"Yeah, but that still don't make it fair, somehow. Not to Sandra and Austin, anyway."

"No, I guess it don't."

In the silence that followed, Geoffrey peeked over the edge of the cloud and saw the quiet group of cowboys, shaking their heads sadly.

Good grief. You mean after all they did for that

child, Sandra and Austin didn't even get to keep him? That couldn't be right. Geoffrey must have quit his assignment a little early. He shuddered to think what penalty he'd have to pay if he hadn't won his bet with Gabriel after all.

And besides, Sandra and Austin must be devastated. With great trepidation, he shifted his angel consciousness to the ranch house where he was pleased to see the room filled from floor to the ceiling with colorful, loving auras.

Now that's the way every home should look.

When he peered more closely, he saw that the shining rainbow colors of love were darkened here and there by just a touch of sadness and despair. *Okay, that's not so good.*

When he found the couple, they were not together. Austin stood at the window, gazing out at the distant mountains. A gentle, preliminary probe of the man's thoughts showed a clear, bright light where his feelings for Sandra resided, but where Austin thought of Little Jeffrey, the angel found only darkness.

Oh, dear. That's so sad. I don't want to look at that too much unless I have to.

Instead he looked for Sandra. He found her in a lab coat, standing at a work bench, watching a blue liquid turn pink in a test-tube. Next to her on the bench Geoffrey saw two letters, one of which invited her to join the faculty of the University of Washington. The other accepted Austin's request that he be readmitted to the university's medical school.

Geoffrey smiled, but Sandra's aura also displayed a discomforting mixture of joy and caution. As he watched, Sandra started to show something else. An intense curiosity. Then wonderment. And hope. And joy. *What's going on here?*

A wry smile broke out on Sandra's face. She shed her lab coat, snatched up the test-tube and walked into the living room. Austin still gazed out the window, seeming not to hear her when she entered. She stood behind him and placed one hand gently on his shoulder.

"Dear," she said softly.

Austin reached up a hand to cover hers. "Hmmm?" He smiled, but his eyes still focused on the mountain peaks beyond.

"I've been working in the chemistry lab."

"That's nice. All this time I thought you were a biologist."

"Even biologists have to know some chemistry." She tugged gently at his sleeve. Austin's face scrunched a bit, but he still gazed out at the mountains.

Sandra moved in front, between him and the window. Smiling, she said proudly, "I've been able to create a home pregnancy test." She shook the pink test-tube lightly in front of his face.

He looked from the tube to her, and his expression said he thought she had finally gone crazy.

Whoa, Geoffrey thought. A shaft of genuine fear shot through him. He remembered the night he visited Martha in the helicopter, when he left the two of them alone together. He had been so embarrassed he tried to forget the whole thing. But now...

"Oh, no! What have I done?" He hoped the Old Man wasn't listening.

Sandra looked closely into Austin's eyes and realized he didn't understand what she was telling him.

"You'd better sit down," she said. She took his

hand and led him to the sofa. He followed mutely and dropped onto the cushions. She sat next to him and propped the test-tube up on the end table.

"I had a reason for making the test," she said. She took both his hands in hers. "I'm pregnant." She continued without waiting for his reaction. "I'm sure there's no mistake. The test is pretty simple, but I've had other clues, of course—"

He grabbed her wrist and she stopped. "What do you mean? It's too soon—"

"Yes, well, I've been thinking about that, and I'm just as confused as you are. But there hasn't been anyone else. At least, not for a very long time."

"But, but…it has to be wrong." He let go of her wrist and placed his hand gently on her shoulder.

She could see him struggling, caught somewhere between utter confusion and smoldering concern that she might have been with some other man before he arrived.

Oh, for crying out loud. I might as well fill in the blank spots. As long as they're going to be parents, they should know the truth. They deserve it, after all they've been through.

"I've been thinking," Sandra said. "Do you remember our second night on the trail to the helicopter?"

Austin scratched his head. "Well, sure. I mean, no. I don't know why, but can't say I do. I'm sorry, there's a big blank spot."

"I have one, too. That's my point. That one night something happened, but I just can't put my finger on— Oh!" A jolt of pure sensual ecstasy flared deep in the core of Sandra's being. A fragment of memory, like a few seconds of a movie, flashed before her eyes. She and Austin were back in the forest. In the dark. Together in the sleeping bag. Really together, as she knew they had never been before.

She glanced up at him on the couch, looking for an explanation, still wanting to know if he had drugged her with his knowledge of medicine, and then done something to her while she was asleep. In the fleeting image she had just witnessed, she certainly hadn't been asleep. She had been a willing and active participant.

Austin's wide-open eyes and the stunned look on his face told her he was just as confused as she. And he'd felt the same odd sensation, just as strongly as she. She opened her mouth to say something, but that warm, wonderful feeling came flooding back, threatening to overwhelm her.

She gasped.

Austin clutched her arm, as if he were trying to balance himself. "Oh, my," he whispered. "Do you remember now?" He let go, put his arm around her shoulder, and held her close.

"Yes, now I—" Suddenly Sandra wasn't sure what she remembered and what she didn't. Slowly, clear memories of a night neither of them should have forgotten began to unfold, apparently in both of their minds at the same time. Along with the memories, their physical senses came alive, as though they were not just remembering, but literally reliving those earlier moments.

"Oooh, yes," Sandra grinned. "I remember now." In her vision, Austin's weight loomed over her, she reached up for him, and in a moment of almost unbearable pleasure they became one. On the couch, the real Austin leaned toward her, his breath quick and husky. Their arms encircled each other, and together they slumped down onto the cushions. Their lips brushed in an incomplete kiss as they each slipped into a dreamlike semi-consciousness, reliving the passion they had shared so fully and completely on that earlier night in the forest.

All's well that ends well, Geoffrey mused. *No need to trouble the Old Man.* Everything will turn out just the way it's supposed to, when these two love birds wake up.

Tactfully, he averted his angel senses and withdrew from the scene. He leaned back on his cloud and put his hands behind his head. Gazing at a swath of stars overhead, he whistled a soft, romantic tune.

Outside the ranch house, the cowboys watched a shooting star streak across the noonday sky.

"You don't see too many of those in the daytime," Jake said.

The other cowboys nodded their agreement.

A word about the author...

Katie Grant is the romance pen name of Steven Betzer Moores. Steven is an attorney for the U.S Environmental Protection Agency in Denver, Colorado, with a background in journalism and wildlife biology. When he's not writing fiction, he enjoys skiing, hiking, playing jazz saxophone, and pestering a cat named Griz. *Cherub's Play* and Steven's other stories have won a number of national literary contests.

Steven's historical romance, *Love's Last Stand*, is scheduled for release in 2018 by Five Star/Cengage. http://stevenmoores.net and, soon to come, stevenmoores.com

www.ingramcontent.com/pod-product-compliance
Lightning Source LLC
Chambersburg PA
CBHW060527260626
47161CB00003B/793